The metal  with a hollow boom

Taking the stairs two at a time, Bolan and Mackenzie charged onto the roof. The three assassins were standing on a low stone parapet.

The Executioner raced past his companion, ducking behind a brick wall jutting out from the elevator shaft. "Hold it right there!" he shouted.

One of the gunners turned and triggered a burst from his machine pistol. Bolan's AutoMag barked once, and the man pitched backward to his death.

Suddenly a crane from a nearby construction site rotated toward the wall. A length of beam swung into view, and one of the killers reached out to grab it. Then he swept the machine pistol in a tight arc, first taking out his comrade, then slicing across the roof.

Bolan heard a groan behind him and turned to see Mackenzie crumple in a heap. He rushed to his old friend and gently turned him onto his back. Blood bubbled from the man's mouth and gushed from two wounds in his chest.

"Just like old times, eh, Sarge? It's good to see you again."

Then he died.

MACK BOLAN®

The Executioner

DON PENDLETON's EXECUTIONER

MACK BOLAN.

Vietnam Fallout

A GOLD EAGLE BOOK FROM

WORLDWIDE.

TORONTO · NEW YORK · LONDON · PARIS
AMSTERDAM · STOCKHOLM · HAMBURG
ATHENS · MILAN · TOKYO · SYDNEY

First edition May 1988

ISBN 0-373-61113-7

Special thanks and acknowledgment to
Charlie McDade for his contribution to this work.

Copyright © 1988 by Worldwide Library.
Philippine copyright 1988. Australian copyright 1988.

All rights reserved. Except for use in any review, the
reproduction or utilization of this work in whole or in part
in any form by any electronic, mechanical or other means,
now known or hereafter invented, including xerography,
photocopying and recording, or in any information storage
or retrieval system, is forbidden without the permission
of the publisher, Worldwide Library, 225 Duncan Mill Road,
Don Mills, Ontario, Canada M3B 3K9.

All the characters in this book have no existence outside the
imagination of the author and have no relation whatsoever to
anyone bearing the same name or names. They are not even
distantly inspired by any individual known or unknown to the
author, and all the incidents are pure invention.

® are Trademarks registered in the United States Patent and
Trademark Office and in other countries.

Printed in U.S.A.

When the will defies fear, when duty throws
the gauntlet down to fate, when honor scorns
to compromise with death—this is heroism.

—Robert G. Ingersoll, May 29, 1882

Each man has the right to choose his own destiny,
to stand up for what he believes in. I'm no hero.
I only do what I know has to be done.

—Mack Bolan

THE
MACK BOLAN®
LEGEND

Nothing less than a war could have fashioned the destiny of the man called Mack Bolan. Bolan earned the Executioner title in the jungle hell of Vietnam.

But this soldier also wore another name—Sergeant Mercy. He was so tagged because of the compassion he showed to wounded comrades-in-arms and Vietnamese civilians.

Mack Bolan's second tour of duty ended prematurely when he was given emergency leave to return home and bury his family, victims of the Mob. Then he declared a one-man war against the Mafia.

He confronted the Families head-on from coast to coast, and soon a hope of victory began to appear. But Bolan had broken society's every rule. That same society started gunning for this elusive warrior—to no avail.

So Bolan was offered amnesty to work within the system against terrorism. This time, as an employee of Uncle Sam, Bolan became Colonel John Phoenix. With a command center at Stony Man Farm in Virginia, he and his new allies—Able Team and Phoenix Force—waged relentless war on a new adversary: the KGB.

But when his one true love, April Rose, died at the hands of the Soviet terror machine, Bolan severed all ties with Establishment authority.

Now, after a lengthy lone-wolf struggle and much soul-searching, the Executioner has agreed to enter an ''arm's-length'' alliance with his government once more, reserving the right to pursue personal missions in his Everlasting War.

1

Tranh Van Bao looked at himself in the mirror. He was not used to everything being built on such a scale and stood on tiptoe to see as much of his image as he could manage. Still cut off at the waist by the bathroom counter, he was able to see only the top part of his new jacket. It was the pockets that most concerned him. Fascinated by the flaps covering them and by the softness of the fine cloth, he wondered if he cut as dashing a figure as he believed, or at least hoped.

Smoothing the lapels, as if his hands were tiny irons, he adjusted the knot in his tie, then snugged the collar in around the awkward knot before fastening the collar tab. Western clothing was such a pleasure after the rough cloth in which he had spent the past twenty years of his life. The suit, he knew, would be condemned as an example of Western decadence, but it was a risk well worth taking.

So far, the mission had been going well, and if he managed only half the items on his agenda, no one, not even the most virulent members of the party elite, would begrudge him this one thing. Even they, the young firebrands of twenty and thirty years ago, the ones who had been there long before Ho was called Uncle and now wore beards as long as their disappointed faces, knew that Ho had been less than perfect, even dead wrong in some

things. After all, wasn't the very existence of his mission
a tacit admission that there was considerable room for
improvement?

Or so he told himself, as he admired the cut of the
Brooks Brothers 36 short, which was a bit too snug over
an unpredictable waist. He had wanted it slightly small,
perhaps in anticipation of losing weight or, more likely,
he only half acknowledged, as an inducement. It had
been years since he'd worn anything other than the coarse
Russian knockoffs of French, Italian and American de-
signers. Tucking his hands under the pocket flaps, he
convinced himself that the wait might have been worth it.

About to admire his profile, he cursed softly as the
phone rang. He left the bathroom reluctantly, tossing one
long, lingering glance over his shoulder, and watched
himself until he disappeared from view. The phone
snarled again, its proximity creating the illusion of im-
patience.

Snatching the phone from its cradle, he identified
himself in English then, when the connection had been
made by the desk clerk, switched to a fluid, if somewhat
archaic, French. The language still felt stiff in his mouth,
after so many xenophobic years of reeducation and setting a good example for the people. He had come to
mistrust his command of linguistic nuance in anything
but Vietnamese and wondered whether such nuance
could survive translation into any other tongue. Fortunately there was no nuance to escape anyone in this particular conversation. His car was downstairs.

Tranh had one more meeting to go. Four days in
Washington, D.C., had been frustrating, but, ever the
optimist, he had seen a glimmer at the end of the tunnel.
The tunnel was long, and the light small, but after more
than ten years of shadowboxing with reality, it seemed

both the Americans and the Vietnamese were prepared to face facts. Neither country was likely to disappear in the near future. Once the irrefutability of that notion was accepted, the only logical course was transparently obvious.

What frightened Tranh, however, was a truth that twenty years in political wrangles had made equally inescapable—there was no law that politics must be logical. Personality intruded its illogical tentacles, often so ensnarling logic in its writhing impenetrability that the whole unintelligible mess sank out of sight like a small fish captured by a lead octopus.

But experience had bred resilience. When he had been unable to find cause for optimism, Tranh had always managed to sidestep despair, skirting it like a mine field with gingerly steps. This morning, the French ambassador to the United Nations had agreed to meet with him. Moral suasion was the great unknown in the quantum physics of geopolitics. Everyone talked about it as if it existed, but no bubble chamber or radiation detector had yet verified it. Still, when it was the only force available, you used it, whether you could prove it existed or just hoped it did.

His bags were already packed. As he crammed the last of his briefing papers into his battered briefcase, a knock at the door stopped him before he could close the clasps. Peering through the peephole, Tranh recognized the two men, who were standing back away from the door far enough to prevent their features from being distorted by the fish-eye lens.

He undid the chain lock and struggled with the sturdy brass dead bolt for several seconds before getting it open. He yanked the door wide, stepping back to let in the two men, who were his aide and his chauffeur. They stepped in quickly, the latter slamming the door closed and re-locking it.

Whispering, as if afraid of being overheard, they asked if he was ready. Conscious of his new suit, Tranh responded softly, Vietnamese feeling awkward on his tongue. He noticed, or thought he noticed, Ngo Dinh Trang, the chauffeur, scowl at the severe, nearly British, pinstripes of the suit. Ngo said nothing, but made little effort to conceal his distaste at the sartorial adventure undertaken by his superior.

Switching to English, Tranh said, "The car is downstairs. The desk just called."

"I should have gotten it myself," Ngo grumbled. "I don't like having it out of sight for so long. Anything is possible, a severed break line, tainted gasoline, even a bomb."

"You know too little of New York City and believe too much," Tranh said. "A hotel like this one is probably the safest place for us to be staying. Its garage is no less secure. I'd stake my life on it."

"Let's hope no one covers your bet, Comrade Tranh."

"Why don't you two stop it?" The third man, older than either, but intermediate in rank, had grown tired of the constant wrangling. "We have only forty-five minutes before the meeting. Are all the papers packed?"

"Yes, in the briefcase. All I have to do is lock it."

"Did you read them, especially the exchange of correspondence?"

"Of course I did. Minh, sometimes you mistake age for authority. It is a bad habit."

"I have had many years to cultivate it. Would you have me uproot it so easily?"

Tranh, aware of his own condescension, and embarrassed by it, laughed. "I'm sorry, Minh. I just have so much on my mind, I—"

"Never mind. Please, let's just get down to the car. If we miss this meeting, it might take years before we can arrange another. Momentum is difficult to establish and easily dissipated."

Instead of responding, Tranh walked back to the bed and snapped the briefcase shut, spinning the five-digit wheels of its combination locks. Attaching the stainless-steel chain that would bind the briefcase to his wrist, he felt the least bit silly. It was a charade, although rooted in good reason, which had long outlived its usefulness. In a decade when countless women and children met death at the hands of terrorists, who dispatched the innocent to the hereafter as casually as one put out the trash, the chain was a useless fiction. If he was captured, it would no more prevent access to the papers than it would removal of the briefcase from his person—that, after all was a simple matter when one could buy a hacksaw for several U.S. dollars. Nevertheless, the charade was all part of playing hardball in the major leagues. He did it grudgingly, but he did it all the same.

When the chain was securely locked, he nodded. Ngo and Minh each grabbed a suitcase and moved to the door. Ngo put his bag down, looked through the peephole and, satisfied, unlocked the door. He grabbed the heavy bag and pulled the door open. He stepped into the hall, checked both ends, then nodded. Tranh followed him out, the heavy steel chain clanking against itself as he moved. Minh brought up the rear, locking the door behind him.

Moving swiftly, with Tranh the apex of an inverted vee, the three men reached the elevator, held by another Vietnamese, and stepped in. Tranh moved to the rear of the car and turned just as the door closed. He watched the indicator lights flash from floor to floor as the car descended. It halted smoothly, and the fourth man planted himself directly in front of Tranh as the door hissed open.

The bodyguard stepped onto the polished marble floor of the lobby and, slipping one hand into his jacket, scanned the sparsely populated expanse with a practiced eye. The clustered furniture, overstuffed and immaculately clean, was inhabited by a few elderly hotel residents reading newspapers by themselves or talking softly in couples. Paying particular attention to the tall ferns and potted palms, which might conceal a man, using the abundant mirrors to check their far sides, he waved vaguely with his free hand, and the other three joined him in the lobby.

Tranh, now the focus of an equilateral triangle, was conscious of the hard slap of his leather soles on the marble floor. The rapping, which was arhythmic to compensate for the irregular stuttering step of the bodyguard, sounded awkward to him. He had never before realized how accustomed a man can become to the sound of his own steps. In a way, it echoed the rhythm of his life or, perhaps, even governed it in some transcendental way.

The huge bronze doors of the hotel, their thick glass distorting the pedestrian traffic on Madison Avenue, loomed ahead of him like the gates of another world. They looked something like he imagined the gates of heaven would. Always baffled by the concept, which seemed to dominate Western art and poetry, he had finally settled on glass and bronze as the most likely materials, ''Pearly Gates'' notwithstanding. Tranh, like so many Eastern politicians, understood what so few of his

Western peers had grasped—the extent to which culture can govern policy.

As the doors drew closer, the wavy light passing through them seemed to crystallize, as if some sediment were settling out of a clear fluid. Individual forms and faces emerged from the indiscriminate stream of humanity surging past the doors. The dark yellow blurs beyond now resolved themselves into taxicabs. His eye fell on a dark bulk waiting at the curb—his limousine.

The bodyguard was the first man through the doors, followed by Minh and Ngo, each carrying a bag. The bodyguard walked quickly to the car and opened the rear passenger-side door. Tranh saw the glint of morning sunlight on the polished chrome of the inner door handle. He could smell the luxurious leather of the car's interior. It all seemed too good to be true.

Stepping out onto the pavement, he looked up at the tall buildings towering above him, their faceless windows staring back like a thousand bloodred eyes. A thousand suns rose on his future, and he could not believe his good fortune. To be at the center of the universe, the place where things were made to happen, had been his dream. Years of scrambling through the mud, hiding in caves and living on a cup of rice every other day, wearing shoes made out of abandoned tires, all of it was behind him. And now, the morning air of the world's greatest city filling his lungs, there was no doubt in his mind that it had all been worth it.

He had it made.

He hefted the briefcase, taking satisfaction even in the clank of the gleaming chain around his wrist. He turned to look up the block and an impatient hand, planted gently but firmly in the small of his back, shoved him from behind. "You must not expose yourself unnecessarily, Tranh. Get in the car."

The man turned to argue, but thought better of it. He stepped forward reluctantly and bent to enter the car. Then, as if he had forgotten something, Tranh straightened up again. He turned back to the hotel doors, admiring their stately bulk.

It was for this reason the bullet struck him from behind, leaving a small hole just above his left ear. The remains of his ruined face splattered the thick glass of the hotel doors, clinging with the sticky tenacity of shattered tissue, only slowly sliding down the smooth surface under the irresistible pull of gravity.

He never heard the shot, or the others that followed.

2

Aloysius Mackenzie looked at the big man sitting next to him. Glancing at his own face in the mirror, he realized the years had been harder on him than on his old friend— much harder. The craggy features they'd once shared had, in his case, degenerated into sags and a jowly puffiness. His hair, unlike that of the man sitting next to him, had thinned and receded. Mackenzie hated to admit it, but he was getting old. Everybody was, of course, but he didn't want to be the only one to show it.

"Sarge," Mackenzie asked, tearing his eyes away from his reflection, "what brings you to the Apple after all these years? Christ, it's been so long, I thought you were dead. I asked around every once in a while, and every time I saw one of the guys from our old unit, I asked about you. Nobody knew where the hell you were."

"I try to keep a low profile, Al. You know how I used to be? Well, I haven't changed. Too much attention makes me edgy."

"Well, it's great to see you, anyhow."

"How much time you got in, Al? You should be about ready to call it quits."

"Hell, Sarge, it's been a long time, but not that long. I still got five years to go before I can retire."

"Then what?"

Mackenzie thought about the question as if it had never occurred to him before. When he finally responded, it was almost as if he were describing some dream, or a life planned for someone else. "Mary Margaret wants to open a small shop someplace out of the city. I don't know, though. We've both lived in the city all our lives. I don't know whether we could adjust. But I sure as hell will give it a shot. That woman has put up with a lot from me all these years. I at least owe her that. So..."

As the two men cruised down Madison Avenue, Mackenzie kept one eye on the street. He was on a special detail, and they were getting close to the Continental Hotel. All sorts of rumors had been floating around in recent weeks, but Al Mackenzie was used to that. Guarding bigwigs, arranging security for visiting dignitaries, however you phrased it, it was still a boring job watching somebody else's ass. He'd been in the Security Unit for six years, and there had been only two incidents in the entire time.

One had involved a case of mistaken identity when an old woman mistook the prime minister of France for the son of an old friend. Mackenzie had had to wrestle her to the pavement twice before he could convince himself that she was harmless and her that she had made a mistake. The extravagant photo coverage on the front pages of the *News* and the *Post* had earned him the nickname "Two Falls" around the station house.

The second was the genuine article, however, and he'd earned a commendation and promotion to lieutenant for nailing the would-be assassin of Sheikh Yamani, in town for a UN address.

But as boring as the work might be, he never let his guard down. Too much depended on it. And the one indisputable thing he had learned about protecting high-profile targets was that you took nothing for granted. Anything you saw from the corner of your eye, no matter how slight, you checked. A man in a crowd, his eyes darting a little too much—or not enough—a woman with a raincoat on a sunny day, an unfamiliar street vendor, all were grist for the mill. This particular mill was one he didn't particularly care for. Defending a Vietnamese honcho seemed like a slap in the face, and he took it personally.

"Sarge, you still have nightmares about Nam?"

The big man nodded. "Now and then. Sometimes I wonder what it was all about, but . . ."

Mack Bolan paused, seeming to lose his train of thought. His mouth opened to continue, but the radio crackled before he could do so.

"You there 2351? Two Falls?"

Mackenzie snatched the mike from its cradle. "Mackenzie here. What's up, Tony?"

"You better get over to the Continental Hotel PDQ."

"What's going down?"

"We're not sure. There's been shots fired, that's all I've got. The uniforms are already on the way."

"It wasn't my hen house, was it?"

"'Fraid so, Al."

"Shit!" Mackenzie looked at his watch. It was eight-thirty. A half hour ahead of time. "The son of a bitch wasn't supposed to leave for thirty minutes yet. What the hell is going on?"

"That's what the captain wants you to tell *him*."

"Roger. I'm on the way. ETA three minutes."

Mackenzie slammed the mike back into its cradle at the same time he leaned on the accelerator. The car shot forward, narrowly missing a taxi as it changed lanes. He hit the siren and slapped a suction-cupped flasher onto the roof of the unmarked car, reaching out through his open window.

"Sorry, Sarge, but I guess you'll have to come along. I can't afford to lose any time."

"Don't worry about it."

There was something odd in the big man's tone of voice, something Mackenzie did not remember ever hearing before. But, then, fifteen years was a long time. People changed. God knows, he sure had. Why should Bolan be any different?

Threading his way through the traffic, Mackenzie drove like a man possessed. His passenger leaned into the back seat and grabbed his briefcase. Yanking it forward, he propped it on his lap and snapped the latches open. Mackenzie glanced the contents.

"Nice piece, Sarge. What the hell is it?"

"A .44-caliber AutoMag, Al. Something tells me it might come in handy in a couple of minutes."

Mackenzie's Dodge swerved to the left as he ran a red light at Park and Fifty-third. He smiled at the squeal of brakes as a half dozen cars narrowly missed piling up. Staying in the outside lane, his tires nearly riding up on the dividing island, he glanced at the speedometer. The needle was sitting just under seventy. Ahead, cars were scrambling to get out of his way, squeezing together in that typical way of New York drivers, who yield as little as possible. Mackenzie smiled as he imagined the language being thrown his way.

Bolan shucked his jacket and slipped on a holster, then slammed the big .44 snugly into place. He put his jacket back on and sighed. "I guess if this was Dodge City, you could deputize me. But that doesn't go in this town."

"No, it doesn't, but if you want to come along, feel free. I don't even want to ask why you're packing that automatic. Something tells me I wouldn't get a straight answer, anyway."

Before Bolan could respond, the car spun right onto Forty-third, narrowly missing a double-parked van. "Bastard!" Mackenzie snarled. The car squealed as the van's bumper gouged a shallow scratch the length of the passenger side, then lurched as it tore itself free.

Mackenzie swerved around the corner, heading north on Madison. A block ahead, the street was jammed with blue-and-whites, their red flashers strobing in the early-morning sunlight.

"Hold on, Sarge, I'm going to squeeze in between those two cruisers on the left." Mackenzie drove with an icy calm, his intense expression making his face more familiar to his companion than at any time that morning.

He braked hard and left the car rocking on its springs. The front doors of the Dodge stood open like pathetic wings, Mackenzie dashing onto the sidewalk, his leather ID case flapping in his left hand.

"Over there, Lieutenant, right in front of the main door." Mackenzie followed the pointing arm of the uniformed officer, and his heart stopped for a second. Sprawled on the pavement, lying on his back, was Tranh Van Bao, the man he was supposed to protect. A pool of bright blood glistened around what was left of the man's head, seeping back toward the marble threshold of the revolving door.

Mackenzie grabbed a uniform sporting sergeant's stripes. "What have you got?"

"Not much, Lieutenant. The shots came from across the street, not more than five minutes ago. Two witnesses saw an open window in the office building. We sealed the building and started a floor by floor. That's about it.''

"All right, Sergeant, thanks."

"Come on, Mack. I think you might as well follow me." Mackenzie dashed across the street. In the distance, an ambulance siren warbled in the stony canyons of midtown New York. If it was for Tranh, it was far too late. Mackenzie sprinted to the yellow cordon and jumped it like a hurdler, flashing his ID as he cleared the taut plastic. "He's with me," he tossed over his shoulder at the two startled police officers.

Heading across the lobby, the lieutenant disdained the elevators. He dashed to the fire stairwell and banged the metal door open with a hollow boom. Taking the stairs two at a time, he heard footsteps right behind him and smiled. It was just like old times. A new jungle, but the same old war. With an instinct that spanned a decade and a half, the two men alternated leading up each flight, switching places at every landing.

Mackenzie puffed a little, but otherwise, the intervening years seemed to have had little effect on him. At the fourteenth floor, where the sergeant had indicated the open window, Mackenzie stopped for a second. He opened the fire door, but the long hallway was empty. A police officer stood at the far end, his back to Mackenzie, and he let the door close, continuing on to the next floor.

"I think we might as well go on up to the roof and work our way down," he grunted. "The others will be working their way up from below. If he's still in the building, I think we've got a good chance of nailing him."

At the door to the roof, Mackenzie paused. "Okay, this is it. I don't have anything to teach you about this sort of thing. Just be careful out there. Let's go."

He shoved the roof door, but it opened only part way. Putting his shoulder into it, it groaned, then gave with a suddenness that sent him sprawling.

Across the roof, framed through the open door, three men—two short and apparently Oriental, and one tall, slender white man—were standing on the low stone parapet, gesticulating with both hands.

Mackenzie got to his feet as his companion dashed past him. Ducking behind a brick wall that jutted out from the elevator shafts, Mackenzie saw him drop to one knee, the AutoMag in one fist. "Hold it right there," Bolan shouted. "You aren't going anywhere."

The Caucasian, bracketed by the other two men, turned and fired a short burst from a machine pistol. Bolan brought up the AutoMag, aiming coolly. The big gun barked once, and the Oriental on the left pitched backward off the stone wall and disappeared. Behind the two assassins, a dark red gridwork, like a child's erector set, towered over them. The building under construction next to the office building was no more than a shell. But Mackenzie noticed the crane moving, its long arm swinging slowly toward the wall as its pulleys creaked and its cable thrummed.

A length of beam, cabled at either end, swung into view, and the Caucasian reached out to grab it. As his companion reached for the other cable, the white man delivered a vicious kick into his groin, sending the smaller man sprawling backward onto the graveled roof. He swept the machine pistol in a tight arc, starting at the fallen Oriental and slicing across the roof.

Bolan heard a groan behind him and turned to see Mackenzie crumpled in a heap. He turned back and fired three quick shots at the remaining assassin, now nearly out of sight below the rim of the roof.

One of the big .44-caliber slugs twanged on the cable, sending a shower of sparks down and out of sight. Bolan rushed to the edge of the roof, but the beam was moving rapidly out and away. Beyond the assassin, little more than a slender profile among the tangled beams, people milled in the street below. The big man didn't dare chance a shot. He knelt by the fallen Oriental, checked his pulse and, detecting a faint throb, grunted in satisfaction.

Racing back to Mackenzie, he turned the fallen man over onto his back. Blood bubbled from his mouth and gushed in small fountains from a pair of wounds in the chest. One of them, at least, had severed an artery.

Mackenzie struggled to speak, but Bolan pressed a pair of fingers against his friend's bloody lips. Mackenzie shook them off, and the warrior bent low, pressing his ear close to the wounded man's mouth.

"Just like old times, eh, Sarge? God, but it's good to see you again." He coughed, spewing a bloody froth over the big man's cheek.

Then he died.

Bolan looked up at the sky, its morning sun an angry white-orange ball.

Old times indeed.

3

Mack Bolan sat helplessly on the roof, Al Mackenzie's head cradled in his lap. The warrior rocked gently back and forth, like a man at prayer. His eyes avoided the face of the dead man in his arms, seeking instead the white-hot sky.

Behind him, he heard the groans of the wounded Vietnamese, but he ignored them. The door through which he and Mackenzie had burst only moments before yawned open, its mouth full of shadows. He tore his eyes away from the sky and stared into the gaping blackness, a bright ball still lingering on his retinas where the sun had been. Shadows erupted beyond the fading image of the sun, then took shape. Two uniformed policemen plunged through into the harsh sunlight, guns drawn.

Cautiously, keeping their guns trained on Bolan, they crossed the graveled tar to the sitting man. The lead cop dropped to one knee as he reached the pair, conscious that Bolan posed no threat.

"What happened?"

Bolan nodded toward the wall behind him, half turning as he did so. "They had it all set up."

"Lieutenant Mackenzie got one. I saw the guy land in the street. Splattered all over like a watermelon."

Bolan chose not to contradict him. There was nothing more he could do for Mackenzie, at least not here and not officially.

The second cop had paused just long enough to listen to the first part of the exchange, then continued on toward the wall. "This one's still alive," he hollered. Bolan turned to see the second cop kneeling alongside the fallen Vietnamese.

The young cop jerked his radio from its leather sling and called for a medical team. The howling sirens—ambulances and additional police—echoed up through the concrete canyons, turning brittle on the smooth glass of the city, grating on the nerves like a dull saw.

The familiar *whomp-whomp* of a chopper suddenly flooded the sky, and Bolan looked up to see a police helicopter swoop toward the roof then veer off and back out over the street. He cursed the pilot for a curiosity seeker, then almost instantly, regretted his harshness. His lap was sticky, and the sun was making him sweat.

White uniforms exploded through the doorway, and a medical team sprinted toward them, instinctively ducking under the sound of the chopper's rotor as if mimicking the opening footage of a *M*A*S*H* rerun. The lead EMS paramedic took a quick look at Mackenzie, shook his head and continued on to the fallen assassin.

Daring to look down at his dead friend for the first time since cradling him in his arms, Bolan saw another face in another time. The last time he'd seen Mackenzie had been much like this, only it had been Mackenzie himself who sat stunned into silence, a stone of a man, too emotionally overwrought to cry and too angry to express himself in intelligible speech.

In his lap had been a young man, a boy, really, no more than eighteen or nineteen. All around them was the jungle, as hard and unforgiving as the stones of Manhattan, and just as impenetrable. The birds had been struck dumb, and all Bolan could hear was the distant fire and, closer and infinitely louder, the buzz-saw whirring of insects. It had been the dominant sound of Vietnam, more constant than the seemingly endless detonation of claymores and artillery, more incisive than the high-speed whine of automatic weapons from half the countries on Earth.

The kid had been new, with them less than two weeks. Mackenzie, a short-timer by then, had taken a special interest in the kid, tried to pass along the wisdom accumulated during his own two tours. Late one night, when huddled under a heavy rain on an ambush, Mackenzie had confessed his strange fascination with the kid, almost an identification. He had told Bolan he thought the kid was himself, returned to the jungle in some macabre, Dantesque purgatory, doing time for sins forgotten or misunderstood.

Bolan knew the feeling. His response then had not been so different from the silence with which he now contemplated the immutable fact of Aloysius Mackenzie's death. Some things were too cruel to accept and too arcane to be understood.

Bolan, wrapped in an impenetrable shroud of silent rage, seemed to be invisible. He was ignored, as if he had never been on the roof. Even when the stretcher team passed by, bearing the writhing form of the wounded assassin, no one said a word. A moment later a second team of paramedics climbed through the doorway onto the roof.

They stood to one side, already informed that Mackenzie was long past needing their attention. Silently Bolan eased out from under Mackenzie, sliding to his knees, still cradling the bloody head in his hands. Gently, like a new father placing his firstborn in bed for the first time, he lowered Mackenzie's head to the tar, swept his hands over the staring eyes to close their now useless lids and got to his feet.

Like a man in a dream, Bolan looked at his lap, brushed idly, almost casually at the bloody cloth. His hands felt sticky, and the pants clung to his thighs. He looked at his hands then bent to pick up the AutoMag, almost as an afterthought. When Big Thunder was snugly in its sling, he started walking toward the door, stepping through into the cool darkness and realized that the war was far from over. Whatever had happened out there, down in the street and up on the roof, had something to do with a war he'd been trying to put behind him for more years than he could count.

Not yet.

And now there was one more score to settle. And this one was the most personal of all. Not that he felt responsible for Mackenzie's death. He knew better than that. Hell, they were, after all, in the same business. But it was personal, nonetheless.

And he would get even. No matter what the cost. He could not forget the sarcastic grin on the features of the assassin as he swung down and away on the dark red iron, swinging off like a child's toy. No, he wouldn't forget that face.

Not until its eyes were as glazed and still as Al Mackenzie's.

BOLAN THREADED HIS WAY through the crowd of officials and police. They were too busy trying to control the crowd of reporters and other ghouls to pay much attention to him. He slipped under the hastily assembled barricade, then walked toward Mackenzie's Dodge. He reached in through the open window, grabbed his brief-case and hailed a cab. If anybody even noticed him, they chalked it up as one more score for the buzzards and other scavengers that seemed to gather at the first hint of blood in the New York air.

By the time the first cops on the roof realized he was gone, Bolan was forty blocks away. His pants, still sticking to his thighs, were bound to attract notice, but there wasn't much he could do about that. When he reached his hotel, Bolan left the cab and went straight to the elevators. The dim light of the lobby, that low-wattage illumination fashionable hotels call intimate and more honest establishments call economical, was a small blessing.

He had the elevator to himself, and the seventh-floor hall was empty. Once in his room, Bolan turned on the shower full blast and peeled off his clothes. Stepping under the stiff spray, he backed the cold off until he could barely stand the temperature of the water. Even then, he wondered if he'd ever feel free again, ever be able to wash away the blood.

His mind kept flashing on the Caucasian assassin. The man's face had seemed somehow familiar. Under oath, he would swear he'd never seen the man before, and yet . . .

As he rubbed away with the scented hotel soap, the shower filled with the artificial smell of flowers, and he came close to gagging. It had been a long time since he'd seen a friend die, held him close while the last breath rattled and the eyes glazed over. Like a history of modern America, their faces, one by one, flashed before his eyes, as if projected on the off-white tile of the shower stall.

Each was as vivid as the day it happened, each as indelible as a mark branded into his soul.

It was the worst thing about watching someone you cared about die—having it happen was hurtful, and the pain stayed with you, slowly fading, for sure, but never quite leaving. But actually to see it, and to bear the awful burden of the ultimate helplessness. Maybe, he thought, it was the only thing separating us from animals. They forgot. And we, whether we want to or not, remember.

After what seemed like an eternity, Bolan shut off the water and listened to it drip slowly from his body for a couple of seconds before stepping out onto the bath mat.

He dried himself cursorily, dressed quickly, then sat on the bed. He stared at his hands, lying lifelessly in his lap. Slowly, as if frightened of what he might see, he raised his eyes to the mirror on the wall across from him. What he saw was just what he feared...and no less than he expected.

The warrior took a deep breath, holding on to it as if it were his last. Expelling the air slowly, he stood, ran a comb through his hair and grabbed a jacket. He wrapped his bloody clothes in a plastic bag he found in the closet and walked down the hall to the incinerator shaft. He wadded the ball still more tightly, then stuffed it in. The flimsy plastic whispered faintly as it caressed the shaft on the way down, ending in a dull thud as it hit bottom.

Back in his room, he debated whether to wear his weapons, and decided against it. His first visit would have to be to the police. It was the only way to defuse their curiosity, which, unsatisfied, would fester into a suspicious hostility. If he told them a selectively truthful version of what had happened, they would turn their attention elsewhere, where it belonged, on the assassin himself.

Bolan was also curious about the killer's initial victim. The garbled scraps of conversation he'd overheard and the hurried abstract Mackenzie had given him were less than complete, but he knew enough to realize this was no simple sniper attack. The killer was a real pro, and that meant two things—the victim's death was a matter of significance to the assassin's employer, and real money was available to get the job done. The police might have more information, but it was doubtful they'd be willing to share it with him. That would leave him in the rather porous and decidedly spastic hands of the New York papers for details.

But he was definite about one thing—this was personal. He might use his contacts and connections as a last resort, but whatever needed doing would get done his way.

Bolan passed through the hotel's revolving doors, stepped off the curb and hailed a cab. An uneventful twenty minutes later the vehicle screeched to a halt in front of the Thirty-first Precinct, where Mackenzie had been assigned.

Bolan paid the cabbie and stepped onto the curb. The building had seen better days, as had the neighborhood. Nearly indistinguishable from the rest of the buildings on the block, it would no doubt one day be sold by the city to a friend of a former mayor and go co-op. For the time being, its rather seedy red-brick exterior did little either to beautify the block or to reassure its neighbors, the majority of whom were clinging to the very edge of legitimate society by their ragged fingernails. The concrete steps, concave in the middle from countless shoes of flatfoot and malefactor alike, were alternately slippery and sticky.

Bolan paused in front of the chipped paint of the tall double doors that separated the station house from reality. Once inside, he realized there was no difference. He looked for the desk and, finding it, came face-to-face with a living caricature. The desk sergeant, Cudahy by name, was a compendium of Irish cop clichés, the quintessential denizen of a world where Pat-and-Mike jokes were born, made the rounds and died without anyone batting an eye. Sergeant Cudahy was not in a good mood.

Bolan stood patiently, watching the ruddy man shuffle papers with more energy than system. Finally, satisfied that bureaucratic chaos had been rearranged into another, more palatable but not less chaotic version of reality, he looked up.

"And what might you be wantin'?" Cudahy barked.

"I want to speak to someone about the murder of Lieutenant Aloysius Mackenzie."

Cudahy's face froze for just an instant, then his chin rose slightly. He shouted, "Captain Flynn? Front and center!"

4

Captain Michael Flynn was Sergeant Cudahy in spades. Even behind the desk, his low center of gravity was evident. He waved Bolan around the desk and turned to waddle down a short hallway to his cluttered office.

Not given to ceremony, he immediately fell into his chair, which creaked threateningly as he leaned back. He pointed to a second chair, and Bolan sat easily.

"Why the hell were you on the roof?"

"Did I say I was on a roof?"

"Don't play games with me, boyo. You and I both know you were up on the roof of that building this morning when Al Mackenzie bought the farm. Tell me about it. Starting with your name."

"My name isn't important."

"Let me be the judge of that, why don't you? Listen, you keep jerking me around, and I'll toss you in the slammer so hard you might go through the back wall."

"On what grounds?"

"Obstruction of justice, interference with an officer in the performance of his duty, impersonating a police officer, suspicion of second-degree murder, hell, criminal trespass. Whatever'll stick long enough to cut you open and see what's inside."

"Al Mackenzie was a friend, Captain. Your hard-nosed attitude is getting old pretty quick. I came in here voluntarily. And you don't even give me a chance to open my mouth before you start some third-rate tough-cop routine."

Flynn passed a hairy-fingered hand wearily over his eyes. He ran the appendage, more like a bear's paw than a human hand, up over his forehead and back through shiny black hair, which was graying a bit, but still thick.

The captain got to his feet wearily and walked to a coffee machine in one corner of his office, nearly out of sight behind a stack of files piled precariously on a cabinet already bulging with too much paper. "Coffee?" he asked.

"Black."

While he made the coffee, Flynn did his best to wipe the slate clean and start over. "Look, I'm sorry if I came down on you too hard. It's just…shit…Al and I go way back. You know what I mean?"

Bolan nodded.

"There's no way to explain it to anybody who was never in the service or a cop. There's a kind of, I don't know, a bond, I guess. You're more like brothers than brothers usually are."

Flynn finished with the coffee and walked back to the desk with a cup in each hand. He set his own down, balanced on the edge of a stack of books, then leaned over to hand Bolan the other. "Why don't we start over? My name's Mike Flynn." He stuck a paw out, and Bolan took it, noting the thick wrist jutting out from a frayed shirt sleeve.

"My name's Mike Belasko," Bolan responded, using a favored alias.

"You knew Two Falls…Al?"

Bolan shook his head yes. "In Nam. A long time ago."

"Funny, he never mentioned you. I would think he would have. We were partners for three years, back in the early days, just after he got out of the service."

"Al and I were partners, too."

Flynn nodded gravely. He understood precisely what Bolan meant.

Partners were special. They had secrets, things they shared with no one else. Long after the plastic surgery had changed him beyond recognition, Bolan believed Mackenzie would know him instantly, from a block away. They had been that close. And he'd been right.

"Captain," Bolan asked, "do you have any idea what was behind the assassination?"

"I want to ask you a few questions, first, if you don't mind."

"Go ahead...."

"What were you doing on that roof?"

"Al was going to drop me off in midtown. When the call came in, there wasn't time. We went right to the Continental. The rest just happened."

"Did you see anything unusual while you were there?"

"No, not really."

"Nothing at all?"

"No, why?"

"Because we can't find the gun used to kill the sky diver. We don't have the slug, either, but the metal fragments we dug out of the dead guy don't make sense. We're not sure what kind of gun it was, but we do know one thing. It wasn't Al's. I don't suppose you had a gun?"

"I'm afraid I can't help you on that one, Captain."

"I didn't think so. And I'm sure you wouldn't withhold information or evidence."

"I want to see to it that whoever killed Al Mackenzie gets what he deserves."

"Uh-huh. Did you see him clearly?"

"Reasonably. He looks quite a lot like that artist's sketch on your desk."

"Anything you can add to that?"

"No."

Flynn looked openly skeptical, but he seemed to understand Bolan couldn't be pushed. He didn't try.

"Now," Bolan said, "what about my question? Do you have any idea who might have been behind the assassination?"

"Why do you want to know?"

"When someone you care about dies like that, you want to know why. It's hard enough accepting it, but if you can understand why, if it makes some kind of sense, no matter how crazy, it's a little easier to take."

Flynn didn't answer immediately. He fiddled with some papers on his desk, then snatched up a pencil to drum on the stiff cover of a book. The dull thud of the eraser was the only sound in the room for a long minute. Whether Flynn was exasperated or just trying to decide whether, and how, to answer his question, Bolan wasn't certain. Finally the captain spoke.

"Look, Mr. Belasko, the department has a pretty good idea who might want Tranh dead. That's easy. So easy it's hard. The list is as long as your arm. The Chinese are a strong possibility. The Russians, too. The Albanians do what the Chinese tell them, and sometimes they try to jump without asking how high, you know what I mean?"

Bolan nodded.

"The Iranians, the Lebanese, the Syrians, take your pick of the Middle East, they all have reason to want to embarrass the United States. What better way to do that than to nail an ambassador from a country making overtures? Then you have your organized crime possibilities."

"Where does that fit in?"

"Look, you know and I know that heroin is pouring in here from the Far East. Most of it gets distributed to the ultimate consumers, the street addicts, by one mob or another. There's a dozen I can think of might be involved. And that's without any digging at all. I grab a shovel, God knows what I might turn up."

"You're saying anybody could have done it. And because that's true, there's little likelihood we'll ever know."

"You said that, I didn't. Look, the truth of the matter is that Al got caught in the switches. He was an innocent bystander, really. It didn't matter that he was a cop and that he carried a badge and a gun. If he'd been a construction worker with a crowbar, he still would have been blown away, because he was interfering. The guy who shot Al was a pro. You know that. You also know the cardinal rule is don't get caught. No matter what it takes, don't get caught."

"You're not going to try to find the assassin, are you, Captain?"

"Where do you get off talking that kind of bullshit to me? You think you were Al's only friend? Listen, pal, there's two dozen guys in this precinct alone who'd give their left nut to get a piece of that shooter. You got no monopoly on caring. Hell, you haven't even seen him in years. I know you were buddies in the war. I also know how deep, how permanent, those ties are. But they're no deeper, no more permanent than the bond you develop riding a blue-and-white with a guy for three years. What I'm saying, Belasko, is we'll knock ourselves out to nail

the bastard, but I don't think it'll happen. The hit was too
smooth, there was too much money behind it. And that
kind of money buys a whole hell of a lot more than
marksmanship. You understand what I'm staying to
you?''

"Yeah, I understand.''

"But you don't like it. . . .''

"No, I don't.''

"That's all right. I don't like it, either. But it's life. You
better go back to wherever the hell you've been for the
past ten years or whatever. Go back to your life. Al's is
over. And if we can get the son of a bitch who put an end
to it, we will. But you got nothing to say about it. Go on
back to doing whatever you know how to do.''

"I intend to.'' Bolan stood quietly. Flynn offered his
hand, and Bolan took it, but the contact was brief. The
captain was already thinking about other matters.

So was the Executioner.

5

The Lower East Side of New York is the ultimate melting pot. If you can't find some commercial manifestation of a particular ethnic group within walking distance, then the group doesn't exist. Everything from grocery stores to import-export firms mingle cheek by jowl. You can buy anything you want, and for less than anyplace else in the country. The Vietnamese community is small, but growing.

Mack Bolan was no stranger to the seamier side of large American cities, and this part of the Big Apple had more than its share of worms. Parking his rented car in a vacant lot, he sat for a moment and wondered where to start. He'd tried Flynn at the station house one more time. The captain had been guarded but conciliatory. Bolan didn't want to speculate on the captain's motives, but he wasn't above using whatever information he could pry out of him. He'd learned that the wounded Vietnamese prisoner lived off Avenue D, in the part of town known as Alphabet City, because its broad north-south thoroughfares were lettered rather than numbered.

Before he could make up his mind what to do, he was startled by a rap on the driver's-side window. He reached for his gun and was about to pull the Beretta 93-R when he realized the surprise visitor was nothing more than a wino. The man, hiding behind a few days' growth of grizzled whiskers, gestured wildly with both hands for Bolan to roll the window down. Keeping one hand on the Beretta's butt, Bolan cracked the window a couple of inches.

The drunk leaned in to mumble through the narrow opening. "You got a dollar you can let me hold for a couple days, man? I pay it back soon's I get me a job."

Bolan shook his head, and the wino cursed him. Used to rejection, he didn't bother to put up an argument. He turned smartly, almost militarily, on his heel and strutted off through the cracked brick and shattered mortar littering the vacant lot. His back was as stiff as a ramrod, and his slight stagger could have been attributed to the uneven surface over which he dragged his injured pride. It wasn't until the drunk had returned to the pavement and leaned against a light pole that Bolan realized the man was wearing a single shoe.

Rolling the window back up, Bolan left the car and locked it, walking around to the passenger side to make certain all four doors were tight. Then, his shoes crunching on the broken remains of a long-gone building, he made his way to the sidewalk. The drunk was still leaning against the pole, but had slid halfway down, resting on his haunches. He looked, and for all Bolan could see might have been, asleep.

Avenue D looked like a moonscape. There were as many empty lots as there were buildings, and half of those that still stood were boarded up. All were in an advanced state of decay, an apt emblem of the social condition of their inhabitants. You lived here because you had to, not by choice. And, Bolan thought, if you did have a choice, you might have preferred the hard oak of a bench in Grand Central for your night's sleep. At least there you didn't have to worry about rats.

Three blocks to the south, the number of buildings began to increase. They showed at least some attempt to stave off further decay, and some had even been recently painted. Curtains hung in some windows, and the small shops on the ground floors seemed viable if not prosperous. It was a hot night, and people were scattered on street corners and gathered in small knots on a few brick stoops.

The sharp rap of heels behind him caught Bolan's attention, and he turned to find himself the object of pursuit. The young black woman, making little effort to conceal her physical endowments, wore a bright red skirt that stopped well above midthigh. The loose fitting halter top would have been too large on a woman twice her size. Her white boots were scuffed and ended just below her knees. Before Bolan could turn away, she waved. In such ungainly footwear, her cruising speed was little short of astonishing.

"Where you going, man? What's the hurry?"

Bolan ignored her, but she grabbed his arm before he could resume his walk. "You lookin' for a party, man?"

"No."

"Bulllll*shit*! You are, too. Ain't no other reason for a man like you to be down here this time of night."

The woman grabbed his left hand, lifting it toward her face. He thought for a second she was going to kiss it or bite it. Instead, she leaned forward. A moment later, she let it drop. "Either you not married or you don't wear no wedding ring. A tan like you got, it would show, otherwise."

"You're very observant," Bolan said. He meant it, and she was pleased.

"Got to be, you want to make a living, man. The way I do, I make a mistake, you don't even read about it in no paper. Know what I mean? So, come on, tell me. You want to party?''

"No, I don't.''

She stared at his eyes, as if trying to see to the bottom of a dark well. "I believe it. So, what *are* you lookin' for? You don't look like no cop.''

"Let's just say I'm looking for information. Vietnamese information.''

"Information or pussy? Some guys, they think Oriental stuff is different, you know? Better or something. But it ain't no different.''

"Information.''

"You are a cop, aren't you? Had me fooled, I got to admit that.'' She leaned forward, her loose top gaping open. Bolan glanced down in spite of himself, and she smiled.

"Can't you get your information later? You won't be sorry.''

Bolan sighed, then shook his head.

"You sure?'' She pressed forward, rubbing her breasts against his arm. "You change your mind, we can talk about price, all right?''

Bolan nodded. He was aware of a man lounging on the steps of an abandoned building across the street. The man watched intently without seeming to pay the least bit of attention. Bolan walked off, keeping an eye on the lounger. As he expected, the hooker lurched across the street and bent forward to whisper to the man. Bolan quickened his pace and was nearly a block away when he heard footsteps racing after him. "Yo, my man, wait up.''

Bolan ducked into a deserted alleyway, sprinted half a block, then pressed himself flat in a doorway. The pimp had seen him duck into the alley and was running full tilt when he passed the doorway. Bolan reached out of the darkened doorway, his stiff forearm catching the runner just above the collarbone and sliding hard and tight against the unsuspecting pimp's Adam's apple. The man gagged and pitched forward onto his face, struggling for air. He rolled onto his back and brought his knees up to protect his midsection.

Something flashed and Bolan wasted no time. He yanked the Beretta from its holster and pressed its cold steel eye against the fallen man's forehead. "I'm going to tell you what I told your girl. But I'm only going to tell you once. Stay out of my way. I have no business with nor interest in you or the girl. You got that?"

The pimp nodded as best he could, the gun's muzzle severely limiting his movement. "I got it. But Velma say you looking for information about Vietnamese."

"That's right. And you don't look Vietnamese to me. I'm going to let you up, and when I do, you're going to start running. If you're still in this alley when I get to five, I'm going to shoot you. Understand?" Bolan backed off with the Beretta, and the answering nod was more vigorous.

"But wait a minute. How you know I don't have no information? How you know I can't tell you what you want to know?"

"I don't, but I know you'll tell anybody what he wants to hear, if there's a buck in it for you. I am not paying for information, I'm collecting it."

The pimp nodded. "But dig, man. Them slopes is movin' in on my turf. You want to take them down, I'm all for it."

"That's not why I'm here. Get up and start running."

The pimp scrambled to his feet, paused to brush off his clothes—a failed attempt to preserve his self-esteem—

then broke into a fast trot. He turned the corner just as Bolan reached eight in his count.

The voice came echoing down the alleyway, almost mocking in its tone. "You change your mind, ask for Reggie. Everybody knows where to find me, man."

Bolan continued on through the alley, exiting onto Avenue C, then continuing south. After another block, he cut back to Avenue D. Turning right, he spotted a small sign jutting out at right angles: Minh Dong, Imports. The amateurishly hand-painted letters wavered and a few drips of paint trailed off from the last line and ran down to the bottom of the sign.

According to Captain Flynn, if you wanted to know something about Vietnamese affairs in New York, Minh Dong was the man to see. The block was neater, and the gutters and sidewalks had been swept clean. The buildings showed some signs of regeneration, but the businesses themselves were marginal, at best. They were the kind of small shops that gave more evidence of pride than profit. A few curious porch sitters watched the warrior's progress, but no one bothered to approach him. There were hardly enough Vietnamese to justify the neighborhood's name of Little Saigon but, to distinguish it from Little Italy and Chinatown, it would have to do.

The windows on Minh's shop were clean, but the display cases were dusty, and the few items in them were sun-bleached and had obviously been there a long time. Bolan glanced at his watch. It was nearly eleven-thirty. A small, handmade sign tucked in the lower left corner of the door window listed midnight as closing time Sunday through Thursday. Friday and Saturday, the shop closed at 1:00 a.m. It must have been a curious kind of clientele to conduct import business so late at night.

Bolan pushed open the door. A small bell tinkled, then again as the door closed behind him. The shop smelled vaguely familiar, but Bolan couldn't place the fragrance immediately.

He stepped to the counter and waited. When no one appeared, he called, ''Hello? Anyone here?'' His voice bounced back at him from the storeroom behind the counter. Off to the left, a small office, its door open, but light off, was tucked into one corner.

Bolan turned to examine the contents of the shop. There was the usual assortment of ethnic foods, bamboo mats and pseudo-Oriental decorative items. Rough baskets lined a tier of shelves, and he took a closer look: rice, rice cakes, a variety of dried vegetables and fruits, small carvings—probably imitation ivory—brass bells and, in one, a dozen heavy metal Buddhas.

As Bolan placed one of the statues back in its basket, he heard a muffled sound, which seemed to be coming from beneath his feet. He listened intently. Two voices were arguing, and Bolan realized they must be in a basement. He walked behind the counter and entered the storeroom. Ceiling-to-floor shelves, cluttered with the same kind of merchandise displayed out front, broke the room into a series of parallel corridors. Open at either end for access, they overwhelmed the big man, who had to turn nearly sideways to make his way among them.

At the back wall, he spotted a partially closed door in the left-hand corner. The voices were louder now, arguing in Vietnamese. Bolan's command of the language was rusty, but it was evident the subject was money. He drew his Beretta and walked softly toward the half-open door. As he reached for the knob to pull it open wider, he heard the unmistakable sound of something hard striking human flesh, followed immediately by footsteps on the stairway. Fighting the impulse to charge down the stairs, the warrior ducked into the last of the shelf-lined corridors, a brick wall to his back.

The door banged open, and Bolan caught a glimpse of a stocky man in a shiny suit, sporting a thin mustache. The man moved quickly without seeming to be in a hurry. Bolan crept along the wall and moved toward the door to the outer display room. As he neared the doorway, a cash register clanged, and the drawer banged open. The sounds of bills crumpling and the drawer slamming shut were followed almost at once by the tinkle of the entrance bell. The door banged shut, and the place was once again silent.

"What are you doing there?"

The voice took Bolan by surprise and he wheeled, drawing the Beretta into target acquisition. He found himself staring at an elderly man in a white shirt and rumpled gabardine pants. As slender as a reed, the old man seemed hardly able to stay on his feet. A small trickle of blood ran from one corner of his mouth, and a dark swelling on one cheek seemed to grow larger as Bolan watched.

"What are you doing there?" the old man repeated.

"Are you Minh Dong?"

The old man nodded. "Get out. I have had enough company for one night. I need to close the shop."

"I have to talk to you." Bolan put his gun away.

"Not now. Come back tomorrow."

"I'm afraid it can't wait."

The old man sighed, placed fingertips gingerly to the swollen cheeks. "It never can. You Americans can never wait for anything." He shook his head, more in resignation than bafflement. "Wait in my office, please."

"Are you all right? Do you want me to get a doctor?"

"No doctor can cure what is wrong here. Please wait in my office."

6

The chunky Vietnamese, whose name was Cao Dong Hua, was a model of efficiency. Bolan had been following him for two hours, and not a step had been wasted. Cao was driving a big Buick, knew his way around the neighborhood and parked with impunity wherever it suited him. That some grease was involved was beyond question. Three separate times, a blue-and-white had squeezed past the double-parked Riviera, and nothing happened. The cruisers kept right on moving.

Cao moved in and out of the crowd, stopping for a piece of fruit from a street vendor once, and once pausing at an open-windowed juice vendor for a drink. It wasn't hard keeping him in sight, and he seemed to care so little about whether or not anyone was watching him that he never once turned to look over his shoulder. Cao was behaving like a man who *knew* nobody would bother him.

Bolan had seen it all before. In the old days, going head to head with the Mafia, he had watched the hard men and the wise guys cruise through secure neighborhoods, cocks of the walk, like they owned the sidewalk and the earth beneath it. The police presence was cosmetic only. Everybody knew who really kept order in the neighborhood. And everybody knew how. From what

Minh Dong had told him the night before, this was just one more variation on a tired old theme.

Cao had made more than a dozen stops, each time drifting casually into a small store or a shop empty-handed, then drifting out a few minutes later, tucking a small bag or envelope into the inside pocket of his jacket. Despite the heat, Cao wore a business suit, the pants a little baggy, the seat shiny. The jacket fitted him snugly, and it hadn't taken Bolan long to spot the barely concealed weapon bulging under Cao's left arm.

So far, Bolan had been content to sit and watch. But not much longer. He wanted to send a message, and there was only one way to do it. Cao, although he didn't know it, had been chosen to be the messenger. Bolan remembered the ancient practice of kings and how they dealt with those unfortunate enough to be the bearers of bad tidings. The mob, too, had been reluctant to accept unhappy news. That Cao was in for a bad time later that day was probable. That it bothered Bolan not at all was beyond question.

Judging from the size of the envelopes, the payments were considerable. Minh had told him that he paid three hundred dollars a week, and that others paid even more. If Cao was making an average haul, he already had better than four grand in the car, and probably more like twice that. Some of the stops had been at fairly prosperous businesses, and they were moving out of Little Saigon toward midtown. The classier the neighborhood, the higher the tab. That was one rule that never seemed to change, whether you were just eating at a restaurant or the owner of one.

Leaving the Lower East Side behind, Cao headed up Third Avenue, drifting comfortably, timing the lights. He clipped off nearly twenty blocks between lights, and was

scrupulously observant of traffic regulations. Bolan
wondered whether that meant the grease only covered
Cao's home precinct. At this point, that was probable.
But as Cao's boss—whoever it might be—grew more
confident, he'd spread a little more around, widening his
sphere of influence. Eventually he would start branch-
ing out, taking on other "clients," and that would bring
trouble for everybody.

It had happened before, more than once. The twenties
had seen the Italian and Jewish mobs muscle in on their
Irish predecessors. Some of the Irish managed to coex-
ist, more or less peacefully, but not for long. The thing
about greed was how impossible it was to satisfy. And
when Owney Madden retired, it was all over for the Irish.

Again in Harlem, the black mobs had grown up under
the oppressive Sicilian thumb, and resentment was never
very far from the surface. Resentment turned to opposition, opposition to outright defiance, defiance to war.
And when the war was over the Harlem residents un-
lucky enough to be under the protection of the Mafia
found themselves dumping the same old tribute into a
new set of hands.

The recipients might have changed, but the hemor-
rhaging continued. Excess cash, instead of going into
neighborhood improvement or business expansion, kept
dribbling into mobster pockets, and as long as the money
kept flowing, there wasn't enough political clout in the
world to secure adequate police protection. Madden,
Lansky and Luciano all recognized that the nicest thing
about money was that it could buy anything—even cops.

The Riviera drifted slowly along Third Avenue, like a
shark letting the tide do its work. In Murray Hill, the
Buick slowed still further, and Bolan was forced to drop
back a block. When they drifted past a Vietnamese res-

taurant in the lower Thirties, it was apparent Cao was looking for a parking place. He hung a right on Thirty-fifth, but the few legal parking places were jammed bumper-to-bumper. Bolan smiled as he drifted down the block behind the slowly moving vehicle. There could be no doubt about it. So far, Cao's boss had influence only in the Vietnamese community, or the bag man would have double-parked.

Heading downtown on Second Avenue, Cao hung another right on Thirty-third. Bolan pulled over, waiting as Cao surrendered to the inevitability of New York traffic and pulled into a parking garage. When the chunky Oriental bounced up the ramp and out of the garage, Bolan shot forward and turned into it himself.

The attendant tore a ticket in two, tucked the long end under the windshield wiper, and, giving Bolan the stub, asked how long he expected to stay.

"I'll park it myself," Bolan said. "I'm just waiting for somebody."

"You see that sign, buddy?" The attendant pointed to a metal sign on the wall advising drivers to leave ignition keys only and not to park cars themselves.

"Yeah, I see it," Bolan answered.

The attendant glared at him just long enough to notice the hard blue eyes that stared fixedly back, then turned away.

"Just don't hit nothin'," he mumbled, moving back to his Plexiglas cubicle.

Bolan gunned the engine and coasted up the ramp to the next level. He grabbed a spot next to the Riviera, killed the engine and got out. He tried the front door of the Buick, and, as he expected, found that it was open. Slipping inside, he hid himself on the back seat floor under a knitted Afghan and waited. If things were running true to form, he wouldn't have to wait long.

A briefcase lay on the back seat, and Bolan tried the clasps, but it wouldn't open. It was one of the combination-lock variety. On a hunch, he thumbed the small wheels on each latch to read 0000. He pushed the release again and was rewarded by a sharp snap. The other lock opened easily, and Bolan lifted the lid of the briefcase. More than two dozen envelopes lay inside, bound in groups of four with rubber bands.

He slipped one envelope out of its stack and opened the flap, which was unsealed. Counting quickly, he tucked the crisp new bills back in place. There were twenty brand-new hundreds—two thousand dollars. This was heavier coin than he had expected. Whoever was pulling Cao's strings had plenty of muscle behind him. You don't extort that kind of money without considerable fear as an ally.

Bolan closed the case and pushed it back into place. He heard a heavy engine rumble up the ramp and dropped down out of sight under the knitted blanket. The attendant backed the new arrival into place next to Bolan's rented Olds. A moment later, he yanked open the driver's door of the Riviera and dropped into the seat.

He cranked the engine and peeled out, maneuvering the big car easily through the tight turn into the down ramp. So far, so good. The car squealed to a halt and the attendant got out. Cao handed him some money, told him to keep the change and dropped into the driver's seat. Bolan heard a shuffle and realized the briefcase was being hauled to the front. The locks snapped open, then the lid slammed shut. The briefcase bounced back onto the rear seat, and the car lurched forward.

Keeping track of the turns as best he could from his concealment, Bolan realized they were headed back downtown. He waited until any sounds of movement would be drowned by a heavy truck to the Riviera's left, and poked his head out from under the Afghan. They were in Tribeca, someplace on the West Side. The car pulled to the curb and Cao got out. Bolan waited a few seconds, then peered over the back of the seat. Cao was ducking through the front door of an art gallery, which advertised itself simply as Kwan Lee Gallerie, specializing in Orientalia.

Curious, Bolan slipped out of the vehicle and followed Cao inside. The place was a typical lower-New York gallery—high ceilings, paintings scattered over huge expanses of white wall, several free-standing sculptures, either on the floor, or mounted on stark white pedestals.

Cao made no pretense about the purpose of his visit. He strode past the artwork without a sideway glance. Bolan followed him to the rear of the gallery, where a large plate-glass window dominated half the rear wall. Through the glass, Bolan saw two Oriental women seated at facing desks, busily shuffling papers.

To the right of the window, a pair of ornately carved mahogany doors yawned open. Cao barged through, and Bolan, feigning interest in a piece of sculpture, slowly drifted after him. Poised outside the door, he could hear angry words being exchanged, first in Vietnamese, then in English.

"No, no more, I tell you." The words were uttered in a beautifully modulated Oxbridge accent. "I will not pay another penny."

Cao responded with something unintelligible, which was punctuated by the sharp, flat sound of an open palm slapping flesh. The blow brought a cry of pain from the woman who had been arguing with him.

"Ky will not like this. Not at all."

"The hell with Ky. You tell him for me that it is over, finished. I am through being bled to death by the likes of you. Now get out."

The woman shrieked again, and this time, Bolan was certain Cao had struck her with a fist. The dull, sickening thud was unmistakable. The warrior dashed to the wide window and leaned in through the sliding glass panel. The two women who had been seated at the desks cowered in one corner.

"What's going on in there?" Bolan shouted.

Cao struck the woman again, and she fell backward, the front of her blue silk dress ripping open before he let her go. He turned angrily and leaped toward the window.

"Mind your own business. Get out of here," Cao ordered. "This is private."

He leaned toward Bolan to make his point, and Bolan grabbed the chunky bag man by his coat and tie, yanking him through the open window.

As Cao reached into his jacket to find his gun, Bolan delivered a quick combination, finding the point of the shorter man's jaw with a left hook that knocked him back through the window.

Bolan dived through right behind him, landing heavily on the prostrate man. He ripped the jacket open and yanked the pistol free, tossing it to the far corner. Getting to his feet, he grabbed Cao by the throat and hauled him upright, twisting the man's left arm behind his back.

Prodding Cao with his knee, Bolan forced him through the office doors toward the front of the gallery. The smattering of patrons stared, uncertain whether to run or offer assistance. Their indecision made them just another handful of statues. Outside on the pavement, Bolan let go of Cao's arm and gave him a shove, sending him sprawling to the ground. His head slammed into the hubcap of a parked car, the hollow toll of the polished metal dying away slowly.

Cao struggled to get up, seeming more disoriented than he should have, and a second later Bolan knew why. A long slender blade glinted brightly in his hand as he charged forward. Bolan sidestepped him easily, then dropped him with a hard right to the back of the head.

He grabbed Cao by the collar and shoved him toward the Riviera. The bag man's left arm was pinned behind his back and bent up toward the shoulders. Bolan opened the car door and shoved Cao inside, giving the arm an upward jerk. The sharp snap of breaking bone sounded like a pistol shot. Bolan let go of the broken arm and yanked the briefcase from the back seat, setting it down alongside the car.

"Now, Mr. Cao, you tell your boss it's all over. You tell him he's out of business."

Cao groaned. "If I see you again, you're dead meat."

"Don't worry about that. You won't see me again. Because I'll see you first, and I'm out of patience. You can tell that to your boss, too. Now get out of here."

Cao struggled to sit upright, moaning as the broken arm moved despite his attempt to keep it stationary. He managed to get the car started, and drove off, the Buick moving unsteadily as he struggled to control both it and the agonizing pain shooting through his left arm.

When the car was out of sight, Bolan walked back to the gallery. Out of the heat, he noticed the patrons had left. He locked the front door and walked back toward the office. It was time to start getting some answers.

But first he had to figure out the questions.

7

As Bolan entered her office the young woman was struggling to pin her dress together. An angry bruise had begun to discolor her left cheek, a dark smear under the thin veneer of her makeup. The two other women in the office huddled around her, alternately trying to lend assistance and offering sympathy tinged with anger at the assailant.

When she noticed Bolan in the doorway, the woman brushed her comforters to one side. She stared angrily at the big man, clutching the tattered bodice of her dress over a slender torso.

"Why did you interfere?" she demanded. "You had no business getting involved."

"Maybe not," Bolan conceded. "But I'm not in the habit of standing around when some slug crawls out from under a rock and starts pounding someone a third his size."

"I'm not interested in your habits," she responded. "Please leave."

"Suppose he comes back?"

"I can handle him."

"You weren't doing very well when I saw you."

"That's not your concern." She dismissed him with a wave of her hands, and the top of the dress gaped open.

Bolan shrugged out of his jacket and offered it to her.

The young woman snatched the offered jacket and slammed it to the floor, then, as if suddenly aware of her near nakedness, bent to retrieve it, covering her breasts with one hand. She turned her back and slipped into the jacket, turning back with the lapels bunched tightly in one white-knuckled fist.

Her tone softened somewhat when she continued, but there was no lack of determination in her voice. "I don't mean to seem ungrateful, but you have meddled in something you know nothing about. You may have caused far more harm than you could possibly realize." Then as an afterthought, she added, "Thank you for the jacket."

Bolan walked over to one of the desks and perched on its edge. "I certainly didn't want to create any difficulty for you. But if I waited to ask your permission, you might have been in no condition to grant it."

"You underestimate me, Mr...."

"Belasko, Mike Belasko." He extended his hand, and she took it immediately in her own. The firm grip was surprising from so small a woman, and he realized her fragility was only skin deep. Under the delicate beauty was a skeleton of stainless steel. There was no give in her.

"Thank you, Mr. Belasko. My name is Kwan Lee."

"This is your gallery, then."

"Yes."

"You're not Vietnamese, are you?"

"Chinese extraction, but my family lived in Cholon for several generations. I am, for all practical purposes, Vietnamese. Why do you ask?"

"Because I think you can help me."

"But only if I am Vietnamese? I don't understand."

"What can you tell me about Cao?"

"There is not much to tell. A crude and brutal man, who works for another more crude and still more brutal. Somehow I don't think that is news to you. So how can I help?"

Kwan Lee looked at the women in her office. "Why don't you take an early lunch? Come back at one." As if they had been waiting for just such orders, the young women vanished immediately through the office door, a lingering faint perfume the only evidence they had been there.

"Would you excuse me for a moment, Mr. Belasko?"

"Of course."

Kwan Lee stepped through a door behind her desk and closed it halfway. Bolan heard a click, and a band of light spilled out through the opening. He moved to a chair at one end of the desk and sat down. Beyond the door, one edge of a full-length mirror was just visible. Trying not to watch, Bolan's eyes kept wandering back to the silvery band. Kwan Lee had removed his jacket, then stepped out of the remains of her dress. Bolan turned his back. The woman was definitely beautiful, and certainly seemed to be unconcerned whether or not he was able to see her.

A few moments later she reappeared, dressed in a faded denim work shirt and blue jeans. She was barefoot and moved with a silent, sinuous grace. Pulling a wheeled chair from behind another desk, she dragged it to a position directly in front of Bolan, turned its back, and sat down cowboy-style, propping the delicate oval of her face on crossed forearms braced on the chair's back.

"Tell me about Cao."

"I think I should tell you about myself, first. My father was a successful silk merchant under the French, and we were what you Americans call well-to-do. In the early years of the war, he sent me to Europe, where I studied art for several years. When he died, I came back to help my brother and sister run the business. It did not survive the war. Neither did my brother. He was killed by a Vietcong rocket attack while having dinner at a restaurant in Saigon.''

"I don't see the relevance."

"You will, Mr. Belasko. Just be patient. My brother died in 1973. As the Americans began to withdraw, my sister and I tried to sell the business, to salvage whatever we could. Naturally there were no takers. When Saigon fell, we were unable to get out of the country. Then, when the Vietnamese began to harass the ethnic Chinese, we knew we would have to find a way to escape. We paid thirty thousand dollars for passage on a small boat designed to carry twenty people. We had seventy-one fellow passengers.''

Bolan, of course, knew the horrors endured by the so-called "boat people," but to hear this lovely young woman relate her story so dispassionately was unnerving.

"We made it to Indonesia, although not all of us survived. The Indonesians didn't want us and sent us to an internment camp, then shipped us to Thailand. I left the camp and made my way to Bangkok. I had no money, no friends and nowhere to turn. I spent two years as a prostitute, servicing high-rolling international businessmen. That enabled me to save enough money to get to the United States.''

"And to open the gallery."

"No, not really. That took far more money than I had at the time. I had made it a habit to keep the business cards of my clients in Bangkok. When I got to New York, I began to look them up, one by one. Most refused to see me, others thought I wanted to blackmail them or to resume my former business relationship with them. What I really wanted was a sponsor, someone to advance me the money to open a gallery in exchange for a participation in the profits. Some misconstrued the proposition, and others refused to give me the one prerequisite I insisted on.''

''Which was?''

''The right to buy out their interest for a specified amount. When no one was willing, I was forced to resume my former occupation. I managed, after four years, to accumulate enough money to share space at the gallery. Two years later, I had enough capital to go out on my own. This is where we are now sitting. And that, unfortunately, is how it was achieved. But the important thing for you to understand, Mr. Belasko, is that it is *mine*, all of it. And no one, not Cao, and not the ones who control him, are going to take it from me.''

''But you are willing to pay protection money. Why?''

''I'd rather not tell you that.''

''Do you know who Cao works for?''

''Yes.''

''Will you tell me?''

''No.''

''Why not?''

The set of her jaw and thin, tight line of her lips were obstacles he couldn't hope to overcome.

''You mentioned a sister. What happened to her?''

Kwan Lee shook her head, rested her forehead on her forearms and said nothing.

''Is that why you won't tell me who Cao works for?'' Bolan reached out and gently raised her head. Her eyes were closed tightly, but there was no mistaking the tears welling up from behind the quivering lids. She said nothing.

She didn't have to.

"Kwan Lee, before you make up your mind, there are a few things you should know about me." He sighed deeply, trying to decide where to begin. "My name isn't Belasko. It's Bolan."

CAO SAT STIFFLY, his broken arm immobilized by a cast and sling. Ky Xuan sat back in a heavy leather chair, his immaculate shoes propped on the desk. He hadn't said a word for several minutes. Cao could feel a cold sweat trickling between his shoulder blades and beading on his forehead.

Finally Ky dropped his feet to the floor and sat up with a sudden jerk. The slap of hard leather on the tile floor sounded like a gunshot, and Cao flinched in spite of his resolve.

"How do you expect me to tell Nguyen about the money? What am I supposed to tell him? More to the point, why should I tell him anything at all? Why shouldn't I let you tell him yourself?"

"He'll kill me," Cao whispered.

"And you think he won't kill you if *I* tell him?"

Cao said nothing.

"By my calculations, you must have had nearly fifteen thousand dollars in that briefcase. Nguyen has had men killed for fifteen dollars. I know, because I have seen it."

"But it wasn't my fault. It's not as if I took the money myself."

"But it was entrusted to your care. You are responsible. You know that. You also know you are expected to defend that which is not yours."

Cao bent his head. "What can I do?"

"You have done enough already. I will have to bail you out. I will need some time to think about it."

"Thank you."

"Fortunately for you, the money is not due for a day or so. We still have some time."

"What do you want me to do?"

"Try to remember everything you can about the man. Every detail. In the meantime, we will have to watch Kwan Lee. If she has hired this man to protect her, we may be able to settle the matter rather quickly."

Cao stood, bowed stiffly and left without being told. He didn't have to be told. He knew his place. And right now it was an eyelash from the edge of the highest cliff he'd ever seen. A little breeze and he'd be history. Out in the hallway, he saw his reflection in the mirror. For a moment he didn't recognize himself. The customary arrogance was gone, replaced by an abject terror he thought long left behind.

He moved closer to the glass, his mind in a turmoil over the insult to his manhood. That was worse than losing the money, as far as he was concerned. He had been made to look like an idiot, an incompetent fool. He would remember the man who was responsible. He would remember, and he would get even.

As he backed away from the mirror, a little of the old fire returned to his eyes. It wasn't much, but it was a start. And, thankfully, Ky understood. Ky would help him as he had helped Ky so many times in the past. Even now, Ky was on the phone. Cao could hear the soft murmur of his voice through the heavy oak door. Ky wasn't wasting any time. He never did.

Perhaps, Cao thought, that was why Ky gave the orders and he followed them. But at least he was a reasonable man. Nguyen was a different story. He remembered nothing, saw only what he wanted and thought only of how he would get it. Except insults to his honor. Those he did not forget. Those he saw, and the memory grew like a cancer until it consumed the very thing it sought to defend. Nguyen was so single-minded that he had been known to neglect business in pursuit of revenge.

Cao shuddered involuntarily. The frightening thing was that Nguyen, too, took orders. Cao didn't want to think about the man who gave them. He closed the door softly and stepped out into the street. It was beginning to rain. He thought briefly about running, but dismissed it almost immediately.

There was no place to hide.

8

The building at 427 Cunningham Place was almost too anonymous. Its faded brick exterior had been sand-blasted recently, and the masonry repointed, but the wooden window frames needed a paint job badly. The front door was scarred, the brick steps cracked and a heavy coat of paint was worn away from the steps and peeling away in scales elsewhere. The only thing distinguishing it from a dozen other buildings on the block was a wrought-iron grate on each of the four first-floor windows.

Bolan, dressed in his work clothes, was a study in black. He climbed over a high wooden fence that blocked the alley between 427 and 431, snagging his shirtsleeve on the rusting barbed wire strung in loose coils across the top of the fence. Once over the barricade, he found himself in a narrow alley, scarred by faint blocks of light from windows in either wall. The concrete of the alley felt cracked and broken under his shoes.

A squat shadow loomed suddenly out of the darkness, and Bolan dropped to one knee before he recognized the outline of a trash bin jutting out from one corner of the alley ahead. Regaining his feet, Bolan pushed onward, feeling more comfortable as the alley widened out. At the foot of the yard, another wooden fence, again strung with loose coils of barbed wire, separated the yard from a wider alley intersecting at right angles. A low wire fence marked the property line between the two buildings.

Moving parallel to the trash bin, Bolan kept one hand on the wall's rough brick, his leather gloves catching occasionally on sharp projections from the new mortar. Somewhere ahead, he knew, was a metal stairway leading up one flight. At the top of those stairs he would find a metal fire door, always left unlocked when the occupants of 427 were conducting business. At the first sign of trouble from out front, the door would be flung open and a human river would flow down the metal stairs, skip over the low wire fence and disappear into the alley.

Nguyen Tho Duc was too confident of his ability to buy and sell people like used cars to worry about a police raid. His solitary concern was an incursion from the competition.

He had never heard of Mack Bolan.

Not yet.

Bolan found the railing of the stairway, a dark rod of shadow in a gray mass huddled in the corner. Shifting his Beretta 93-R to his left hand, he hugged the wall to his right as he ascended the steps. The door was dimly outlined by a narrow band of white paint, and behind the door, he knew, was a dark room, the sole purpose of which was to serve as an escape hatch. The last thing Nguyen wanted was a block of light to outline each of his escaping patrons.

Bolan reached the metal platform at the top of the stairs. The door handle was missing, and he had to feel along the outside edge of the door, hoping to get enough of a grip with his fingertips to pull it open. Failing in that, he pulled a serrated combat knife from its sheath on his hip and slid the blade into a narrow crevice. Pressing the knife sideways, he was able to pry the door out a bit, but when he pushed a blade in to get a more secure purchase for its teeth, the door closed.

Bolan cursed softly, then tried again, this time rotating the knife and driving its point into the sheet-metal door just enough to pull it all the way out. He slid his fingers in and pulled the door open before resheathing his knife. Then, dropping to his knees, he hauled a small coil of piano wire out of his back pocket. Using a hinge pin as an anchor on one side, he searched inside the dark hall for a place to anchor the other end. He found a radiator against the wall and gave the wire several quick turns around the steam valve, then knotted it securely.

Bolan then crossed the six feet to the inner door. The house was deathly quiet. He placed an ear against the door's central panel. A soft murmur hummed and throbbed through it. Turning the knob slowly, pulling it toward him at the same time to dampen any rattle, he opened the inner door a crack, just wide enough to peer through.

A tall, slender man stood at the foot of another set of stairs, facing away from Bolan, his ethnicity betrayed by long, straight black hair. He was talking to someone out of Bolan's view. Over the guard's shoulder, the warrior spotted a group of people in evening dress gathered around a table. The table itself was all but obscured, but from the rapt attention of the onlookers, it was obvious that something was going on. Bolan pulled the door wider, sliding through sideways, the Beretta, set for single shot, gripped tightly in his hand.

Once inside, Bolan let the door close quietly, slowing its spring hinges with back pressure from the palm of his free hand. His soft rubber soles were silent on the wooden floor as he crossed a narrow landing to stand at the head of the stairwell. His plan, sketchy as it was, depended on there being no more than four hardmen. Any more than that, and he wouldn't be able to move fast enough to accomplish his purpose without putting relatively innocent people at risk. He was not interested in the gamblers, only those they gambled with.

Working his way down the stairs two at a time, Bolan got within grasping distance of the cranelike sentry when a woman on the outer edge of the crowd turned and saw him. She said nothing, but something in her expression caught the guard's attention. As he turned to look over his shoulder, Bolan bounded down the last four steps and snaked an arm around the startled man's throat.

Pressing the muzzle of the Beretta to his captive's temple, he continued down to the floor itself. A second guard, the unseen conversationalist, reached inside his jacket.

"Don't do it, friend," Bolan warned, resting the muzzle of the Beretta against his prisoner's skull. "Not unless you want to be mopping brains off the ceiling for a week."

The guard froze, his eyes darting from Bolan to the crowd and back again. He was looking for a particular person, someone to make the decision for him, and when he failed to find him, he slowly raised his hands into the air.

Simple as it was, the delay answered Bolan's principal question—Nguyen was somewhere in the house. The guard wouldn't have dared to make a move without the man's approval, and if he wasn't in attendance, he wouldn't have looked at all for guidance.

Bolan shoved the captive roughly forward and got within reaching distance of the second hardman. A smaller version of the man in front of him, he was wiry rather than muscular. A thin pencil mustache crawled across his upper lip like the world's slowest caterpillar.

As the warrior reached out, the shorter man's face tightened and his fingers curled. Before he could make the move he was contemplating, Bolan lashed out with the Beretta, raking its barrel across the man's forehead, plowing an angry furrow in the unwrinkled skin. The man fell to the floor, both hands pressed over his injury, moaning on the edge of consciousness.

Prodding again with the Beretta, Bolan whispered into his captive's left ear, "When I say three, we're both going to bend down, and you're going to get his pistol out with only your fingertips. Place the gun on the floor, muzzle first. If I even think you're going to try something, I'll kill you. Do you understand?"

The pinioned man nodded slightly.

"Good. One...two...three." Together, like a well-rehearsed ballet team, they bent to the floor, Bolan keeping the man's frail body between himself and the crowd. Quickly the prostrate guard's pistol was removed and placed on the floor. Bolan picked it up and stuffed it into his pocket. Then, like a motion picture in slo-mo reverse, they rose again to a standing position.

"Ladies and gentlemen, don't be alarmed. Just raise your hands above your heads and keep them there." Bolan waited until they had done so, then continued. "No one is going to be hurt as long as you do what I say. I want you all to gather at the far corner. No exceptions. Move slowly and keep your hands above your head at all times. Is that clear?"

Like a chastened children's chorus, they nodded in unison, their hands sliding still higher in the air.

Prodding his captive, Bolan stepped farther into the room. "Gentlemen, I want all three of you to walk over to the metal door on the far wall. Walk backward, facing me at all times. And don't forget where your hands are supposed to be.''

The three gunsels did as they were told. The one Bolan had hit stumbled and fell to the floor. ''Help him up,'' Bolan snapped.

When the tumbler had regained his feet, Bolan urged them all backward. The three men stood in a semicircle across the doorway. Placing the gun near his prisoner's ear, he guided him toward his comrades in front of the metal door.

Once inside, Bolan quickly withdrew several sets of handcuffs from the slit pockets of his black suit. He cuffed his captive to the door frame and patted him down, keeping one eye on the remaining three. He tossed the cuffs to the nearest member of the trio. ''Put these on. Cuff yourselves to that heat pipe over there in the corner.''

''How you expect us to do it, man? We supposed to be magicians or something?''

''I don't care how you do it. Just do it.''

''Damn, man...''

Bolan watched impatiently, glancing through the doorway from time to time. The patrons were getting restless, but so far no one had ventured to put his hands down or to move away from the crowd.

When the cuffs were on, the three men bent awkwardly toward the corner. Bolan patted them down one at a time, removing four handguns, two switchblades and an ugly-looking pair of brass knuckles. He piled most of his collection in a wooden chair, keeping the brass knuckles for himself, then released his first prisoner, still cuffed in the doorway.

''I hope you have a good memory, friend.''

"What? What are you talking about?"

"I'm talking about the combination to the safe."

"I don't know it."

"Too bad." Bolan rapped him sharply behind the ear with the brass knuckles. The man fell like a bag of wet cement. Bolan stepped over the unconscious man and approached the trio in the corner. "Anybody over here got a better memory than your friend on the floor? How about you?" Bolan addressed the man in the middle. "You going to tell me, friend?"

"No way, man. I tell you and they tell Nguyen. I'm a dead man."

"You want to die?"

"Better you than him kill me, man. You do it fast."

"You sure?"

The man faltered.

"You aren't, are you? If you tell me the combination, I'll let you walk away. No questions asked."

"And if I don't?"

Bolan shrugged. "Who knows? You want to gamble? Have it your way." Bolan raised the Beretta and slowly brought the muzzle up under the man's nose. The pistol wavered slowly, like a Cobra undulating with flared hood and unblinking stare.

"All right, all right. I'll open it. You swear you let me walk?"

Bolan nodded. He unlocked the cuffs, and the anxious gunner raced to the wall safe. Bolan stood in the doorway while the other man worked. The nervous gunman lost his place and had to spin the combination wheel a few turns to start over. A minute later the last tumbler clicked, and the door swung open.

Bolan rushed to the open safe and peered inside. He reached in, took a fistful of banded bills without counting and backed away from the gaping safe. Gesturing with the Beretta, he said, "Help yourself."

He backed through the doorway and sprinted to the stairs. A moment later he was in the alley, mission accomplished. Nguyen would be boiling. When he compared notes with Ky, it would be obvious to both that the same thorn plagued their sides. The resulting dissension would be useful. He wasn't sure how yet, but it had to be.

In the dark at the end of the alley, he watched two gunmen pitch headlong over the concealed piano wire. Then he backed into the shadows. He had to get the attention of the top man, whoever was working this end for the kingpin. Knowing who it was wasn't good enough. If you wanted an audience with the king, you better have something to offer him.

Bolan knew he wasn't there yet.

But he was close.

9

Eleventh Avenue after midnight was not to be believed. Bolan's Oldsmobile, rumbling with a muffler in need of some attention, cruised along the broad dark street lined with towering warehouses and crumbling housing. Ahead of him loomed the great white elephant of the Javits Convention Center, its thousands of glass panels glittering in the moonlight like the facets of a gargantuan insect eye.

South of Thirty-fourth Street, the street grew more depressing still. Nearly every block featured a half dozen hookers in various states of undress, some tottering in a parody of seduction on stiletto heels, others leaning indolently against the nearest wall. Small knots of women seemed to materialize out of the very masonry as his car approached, shouting proposals as he rolled past, then cursing him for his lack of interest as he continued on by.

Stopped at a traffic light, the only car on the block, he was approached from both sides at once. Young women leaned through the open windows, their heavy makeup struggling to conceal the ravages of time and trade. They made suggestive remarks and offered to outdo one another in debatable skills in an obscene parody of free-market competition. Like stereo gone mad, they chattered in both windows. Bolan did his best to ignore them as they leaned farther into the car until, unable to control his emotions, he gunned the engine in warning, then sped through the still-red light. The women scurried away to their respective curbs like crumpled scraps of colorful paper.

South of the helipad at the Hudson River's edge, he spotted what he was looking for. A great, gray whale of a warehouse, its twin piers occupied by nondescript freighters flying Liberian flags, lay against the New Jersey skyline to the west. Four eighteen-wheelers, their twin stacks breathing a light gray mist into the moonlight, had backed into place along the southern edge of the warehouse.

Bolan rolled on past, slowing to a crawl, but saw no movement. He hung the next left and sped down the block, just making the light at the next corner for another left, then ran the next light to head back toward the river. The street was dark, its commercial properties long since shut down for the night. The glass in the streetlights had been broken long ago, making the street a black hole in the middle of darkness itself.

Bolan jammed the Olds between two delivery vans and got out. Ahead, he could just see the southern corner of the warehouse, but the trucks were beyond his line of sight. The street was so deserted he could hear the whisper of his crepe soles on the pavement as he trotted down the block between corrugated doors and the hulks of trucks, which were parked in defiance of every conceivable regulation.

His greatest exposure would be in crossing the broad expanse of the avenue. Brilliant moonlight bathed the entire scene in a silvery wash. Just short of the corner, Bolan stopped, pressing in against a corner of jagged green wood. Surveying the area around the trucks through binoculars, he saw no one. It was possible, he knew, that he had been misled about the projected rip-off, but so far his intelligence had been solid, and everything had panned out. Each link in the chain, when squeezed hard enough, popped open, releasing the next link. Sooner or later, he would have to face the possibility that he was being set up, deliberately brought to some out-of-the-way location where he could be ambushed. Was this it?

Bolan had decided to chance it. So here he was. He slipped the flat binoculars into his hip pocket and raced across the avenue. Keeping his eyes on the trucks, he still saw no movement. The parking area in front of the warehouse was nearly a hundred yards wide. Bolan kicked into high gear, like a quarterback breaking into the open. He elected to head for a corner of the warehouse, rather than the trucks themselves. As he approached the building, the moon, low on the horizon, disappeared behind the high edge of the building and offered a frail cloak of shadow. It wasn't bulletproof, but it would offer him some measure of security.

Leaning against a wall while he caught his breath, he surveyed the avenue itself. Up and down, as far as he could see, the traffic lights changed in sequence red to green and back again. An occasional car sped by, pacing itself to the timed lights, trying to cover as much ground as possible with as little interruption as possible.

To the north of the warehouse, a high chain-link fence surrounded another parking area, this one for a shipping company and its headquarters. Bolan looked at his watch. It was one-thirty. The rip-off should already have been under way. Pushing off from the wall a bit, Bolan looked up at the eaves, nearly fifty feet above. The upper half of the wall was a sheet of wired windowpanes, many damaged by stones thrown by passing vandals.

Some of the glass lay at the base of the wall, crunching as he walked over it.

Bolan stepped to the corner of the structure and peered around the edge. The trucks were unoccupied, their engines running.

Cautiously Bolan crept between the warehouse and the nearest truck. He stopped at the trailer's rearmost tires and dropped to one knee, Big Thunder in hand, and peered under the vehicles. He saw nothing but shadows. Getting cautiously to his feet, he continued on to the back of the truck. He briefly considered opening the rear door, but the noise was certain to alert someone.

The doors of the next two trucks were also closed, but the fourth truck yawned open, its trailer only partially filled. It looked as if the hijackers had left in a hurry, but he couldn't even hazard a guess as to why. Hoisting himself up into the truck bed, Bolan approached the palleted, stacked cartons warily. He lit a match and peered at the labels on the front rank of boxes. Each contained either stereo equipment or a television. They were the Korean brand he had been told to expect, easier to move on the illegitimate market because the Koreans were tyros in handling the huge volume demanded by the American consumer.

Bolan shook the match out, then left the truck, unwilling to gift wrap himself for the hijackers should they return, as the running engines gave him every reason to suspect they would. When his feet touched the asphalt, he heard tires squeal, out toward the edge of the parking lot. The warrior ducked under the truck and dashed toward the wall of the warehouse, keeping low to make it under the remaining trucks.

He flattened himself against the wall, watched headlights spear through the shadows and dance wildly as a van bounced over the rough surface of the lot. It skidded to a halt on the pebble- and litter-covered pavement. The lights went out and the engine died. Two short, dark-haired men got out of the front, laughing loudly. They walked to the rear of the van and yanked its double doors open. A woman, naked from the waist down, sprawled through the open doors, landing hard on the pavement and sliding for several feet. Three more men, also apparently Orientals, followed her out of the van.

The shortest of the three prodded the fallen woman with the toe of his heavy work shoe. "Go on, bitch, get out of here."

The woman struggled to her knees. Bolan could see that her palms were bleeding, torn by the ragged pavement.

"What about my money?"

"Honey," the short man said, "you just had me. That's better than money. Now beat it."

"What about my clothes?" For a moment, her face came out of the shadows, and Bolan could see she'd had a rough time of it. Her makeup had been smeared, and its ruined remains were streaked with tears. A thin trickle of blood from one nostril ran down over her chin.

The short man grabbed her hair and yanked her head back roughly. "You know, I could cut your throat and dump you in the river. You think anybody would miss a piece of trash like you?"

"My babies... I have two...children. I...please..." The words were nearly unintelligible, but it didn't matter. The man wasn't listening, and Bolan had seen enough.

"Give the lady her clothes." The voice was razor-edged and as cold as ice.

The five men whirled as if their movements had been choreographed.

"Who the fuck—"

Bolan stepped partially out of the shadows, his hands at his sides. "I said to let her go."

"You better haul ass out of here, pal. This is none of your business."

Bolan pumped a round into the chamber of his .44. The click spoke volumes. It was as if time had stopped for the briefest of moments. Then one of the men went to the van and reached in.

"Real slowly, now," Bolan cautioned.

The man nodded, withdrawing his hands slowly, a white skirt and pair of sling-backed shoes in one, and a small ball of underwear in the other. He handed them to the woman, who turned her back to struggle into them. She continued to whimper.

"Now," Bolan continued, "I want you to empty your pockets, one at a time. You first." He waved the AutoMag at the short man, who seemed to be the leader of the group.

Bolan slid the Beretta from its holster and sheathed the AutoMag, while the head goon made a show of reaching into his pockets, one of the others shuffled slightly, drawing Bolan's eye. One arm was out of sight, and Bolan shifted the Beretta subtly. If the guy was stupid enough to make a move, he'd be ready.

Suddenly the man dived to one side, and Bolan squeezed off a shot. The 9 mm stinger tore into the guy's left eye, leaving a yawning red canyon in its wake. The others scattered, not sparing their fallen comrade a passing glance.

Bolan dived under the nearest truck, looking for the woman while maneuvering for cover. He spotted her legs, still bare, and behind them a heavy pair of work shoes. A second man crouched behind the open driver's door of the van. Bolan took careful aim and punched two quick holes through the door, the 9 mm parabellums tumbling through the thin upholstery and fragmenting on their way through the sheet metal of the door.

The crouching man fell to the asphalt, his left arm extended as if trying to ward off the impact. Bolan needed one man alive in order to get to the next link in the chain, and, noticing a small pool of blood oozing from under the sprawled figure, he turned his attention to live quarry. Backing away from the heavy tires of the tractor, he rolled quickly to his right, out in the open for an instant and behind the wheels of the second truck. A shower of sparks danced just behind him. With a roar, the outer tire blew out, showering him with shredded rubber.

The man he wanted to keep alive was going to be the toughest to get to. He had the woman hostage, and even the denizens of the night weren't expendable as far as the Executioner was concerned. He'd have to take the stubby boss without exposing her to harm. He stuck one leg out for a second, drawing fire. The flash revealed the shooter's location, and Bolan, beyond caring about noise, drew Big Thunder.

An inch or so of shoulder projected beyond the wall at the corner of the warehouse. Taking careful aim, Bolan fired twice, first at the edge of the warehouse and then shifting to the right, hoping the first shot would expose a little more of his target.

It worked.

Three down and two to go.

The fourth man had run to the rear of the trucks. Bolan heard the guy's feet scrape on the crisp old papers littering the parking lot, and he spun around. The man, crouching to peer in under the trucks, held a machine pistol in one hand and a flashlight in the other, which he waved back and forth under the first truck.

Bolan firmed his grip on Big Thunder, waiting for a clear shot. As the target moved beyond the first truck, he was dead in the clear for an instant, but passed behind the rear tires of the second. He was now straight ahead of Bolan. The big guy caressed the trigger once, the heavy slug slamming into the target just above the left hip and snapping the spine on its way out. The hardman fell to the pavement, flopping aimlessly like a landed trout, then lay still.

Bolan spotted the fifth and last man, just backing into the rear of the van, still shielding himself with the hapless hooker. This was the one he needed.

Alive.

Bolan slithered to the right, moving into the open momentarily, and drawing a shot from the squatty body in the van. Rolling under the next truck, Bolan drilled both rear tires of the van as its engine roared into life. He got to his feet and raced to the passenger's side, careful to stay out of range of the sideview mirror. The van started to roll as Bolan yanked open the door. He grabbed the woman by the arm and tugged her free of the driver's grasp. She tumbled to the asphalt as the vehicle began to move faster. Bolan dived inside, the AutoMag butt-first in his hand, and slammed it into the driver's temple. The van sputtered once as the unconscious man's foot slipped from the accelerator, then died.

The woman backed away, her clothing still clutched in a trembling fist. Bolan sat back and waited for the driver to wake up.

They had a lot to talk about.

10

Kwan Lee moved with grace. Watching her from the austerity of a Scandinavian sofa, Mack Bolan wondered whether she actually walked or had somehow managed to defeat gravity. The huge loft in which she lived was as stark and white as her long dress was black.

From behind she could have been anyone or someone special. That, in a way, was what made her so intriguing. As Bolan contemplated the delicate beauty of this Oriental woman, the ambivalence welling up in him made him restless. He shifted nervously on the sofa, hoping she would turn around, reassert her identity and chase away the ghost her silence had summoned.

Leaning back and closing his eyes, he realized it was the voice, after all these years, that most haunted him. Late at night, he could hear it, whispering through the motionless curtains of an open window, its rhythms in the hiss of bus tires on a rainy pavement.

Cam Minh Canh, Mindy—the memory of her lingered in him, a scar on his soul. He didn't want to think about the last time he had seen her, that was too painful. And the time before that had been too special. Instead, he remembered the first time, threading his way through the clutter of Saigon, the bars on the strip blaring their odd amalgam of Rolling Stones and Hank Williams, all of it so loud it took a musicologist to tell one tune from another.

He hadn't known her very long, six weeks or so, but it had seemed an eternity then...and now. Six weeks of long walks and longer talks. The beach, the long nights lying under a fan. At the time, there had been no time. They were lost, frozen in an eternal moment like a fly in amber, a crystal, their relationship so perfect all motion had ceased. It was extraneous, unnecessary.

And then it all had come tumbling down.

Bolan shook his head from side to side. Suddenly something cool brushed his forehead. He wanted to open his eyes but was afraid to, afraid the pleasant sensation would stop. Instead, he tried to guess what it was. It wasn't cold enough to be ice, or hard enough to be the frigid glass of a drink.

Opening his eyes, he saw Kwan Lee drawing back from him, and realized the source of the sensation had been her lips. That explained the softness, but not the coolness. Then he noticed her drink was half gone as she extended another toward him. Bolan accepted the drink and closed his eyes again.

He felt the weight of her on the sofa beside him. A faint scent of flowers drifted toward him on the current of conditioned air.

"What's wrong?" The question was so softly uttered, he wasn't sure he'd heard it.

He turned his head and stared at her a long moment before answering. The bruise, still swollen, but artfully concealed under a thin layer of makeup, brought him back to the present.

"I was just thinking."

"She was Vietnamese, wasn't she?"

"Yes."

"And beautiful...." It wasn't a question. "I remind you of her, and it is painful for you. I'm sorry."

"It doesn't matter."

"It always matters, Mr. Bolan. Always. And it does no good to pretend otherwise."

Bolan closed his eyes again, preferring not to answer.

"What do you really want?"

"I'm not sure."

"But you have an idea?"

"Yes, I have an idea."

"And you think I can help."

"Yes." He spoke more harshly than he intended. "I think you can help."

"In what way?"

"You can start by telling me the whole truth."

"The whole truth is not something any of us knows. I have told you as much as I think you need to know, based on what it is I understand you want to accomplish."

"I want it all."

The warm pressure of her thigh on his vanished. A moment later, Bolan felt the sofa shift slightly as she stood up. He still refused to open his eyes. In her agitation, the sylphlike glide seemed to desert her. He heard her pacing nervously back and forth, as if trying to make a decision she preferred to avoid.

When he finally opened his eyes, he found her staring down at him. Her silence pressed on him like an invisible weight. In the dim light, he thought he saw a trickle of tears on one cheek, but she turned abruptly away before he could be certain.

"I have already told you a great deal. More than you have any right to ask."

"I know that, and I appreciate it. But I need to know more. Call it a favor, call it a show of gratitude, call it what you like. But tell me."

"I owe you a debt, true. Even though you have no idea of the kind of trouble you may have caused me, I know it was unintentional. But you have even less of an idea what you ask."

"Tell me about your sister. . . ."

Kwan Lee stepped back, bending away from him. Then, drawing on some inner strength, she turned back, drawing herself up to her full height, which, despite her diminutive stature, projected great dignity.

She tilted her head, and Bolan noticed the flare of her finely chiseled nostrils . . . and a dark bruise under her chin, no doubt another legacy of her encounter with Cao.

"You are a brave man, Mr. Bolan. But I am not sure you are brave enough to hear what you ask me to tell you."

"You have been brave enough to live it, haven't you?"

She nodded. "Yes. But I have had no choice. That is always the difference, isn't it. You can walk away. How can I walk away from my own life. It comes with me, like a turtle's shell. It is at the same time the source of my strength and of my vulnerability."

"You've done all right so far."

She nodded again. Turning her back, she walked back to the bar. Bolan heard the clink of ice and the burble of liquid being poured. Kwan Lee took a long pull on her drink, added to it, then turned back.

She placed her elbows on the polished mahogany bar, the first time he had seen her do anything that betrayed her past. It didn't cheapen her, but it seemed to give her some additional toughness, her features hardening, their lines becoming sharply etched, as if thinking about her past physically transformed her.

"I told you we were separated in Thailand. I didn't tell you how."

Bolan waited patiently. Kwan Lee looked at the glass in her hand, then, without warning, hurled it to the floor. The crystal shattered into a hundred fragments and skittered across the floor in a pool of liquor, the slivers of glass indistinguishable from the shattered ice.

"You are familiar with your Mafia?"

Bolan nodded. "What does that have to do with anything?"

"If you want to hear, then you must listen. It has everything to do with it. Everything. You know that your CIA had been involved in smuggling heroin out of the Golden Triangle. It was the price they had to pay to keep certain of our less honorable generals interested in the war. The techniques used were not new. There were interesting wrinkles added, of course. Flexibility is the key to success, after all."

Kwan Lee walked toward him slowly, the broken glass and ice chips crunching under her feet. It was the only noise in the huge loft. She stopped suddenly, and Bolan thought for a moment she would turn and walk back to the bar. Instead, she resumed walking, dropping onto the sofa at its far end. She kicked off her shoes and tucked her feet up under her.

"Such a lucrative business could not be allowed to vanish simply because the war had been lost. After all, the machinery was in place, the expertise available, the techniques of proved utility. When your CIA lost interest, there were other Americans ready to step in...and they did. Unlike the CIA, they had no political motives. It was just business."

"The Mafia?"

She nodded.

"But how?"

"It was quite simple, really. Obviously Americans couldn't hide all that easily among the Vietnamese. But that wasn't true of the generals. I know for a fact that two of them are still involved in the smuggling operation. And that having learned the techniques of the Mafia, they have taken control of the network. The Mafia is no more than a distribution arm. And even that is likely to change."

"Where does your sister fit in?"

"I am coming to that."

Kwan Lee reached into a pocket and pulled out a pack of cigarettes. She lit one with a plastic lighter, inhaled deeply and tossed the pack on the sofa. "Since there were no more body bags in which to hide the drugs, some other method was needed. You might have noticed I specialize in Oriental art. Most of it comes from Thailand, although it is gathered from all over the Far East."

"The drugs are concealed in your shipments." Bolan nodded. It was all starting to make some crazy kind of sense.

"Yes. And you are interested in the man who murdered your friend, Mr. Mackenzie? And Ambassador Tranh?"

Bolan agreed.

"I don't know who he is, but I know who he works for."

"Who?"

"An American. An American colonel. Thomas Griffith."

Bolan sat up abruptly. "What?"

"Yes, I know. He is supposed to be dead. But I assure you, he is very much alive. And he is responsible for the assassination of Ambassador Tranh. Therefore, he is also responsible for the murder of your policeman friend."

"You are contradicting yourself, Kwan Lee. First you say the Vietnamese have taken over the smuggling operation, then you tell me it is being run by an American. You can't have it both ways."

"Did you know Colonel Griffith?"

"Only by reputation. He was in the mountains, mostly. A rogue elephant. He had carte blanche for his operations. It was like something out of Conrad, almost. He spent so much time with the Meo tribesmen, he almost became one of them."

"So he did."

"Where does your sister fit in?"

"You don't think I would willingly cooperate with something so onerous as drug smuggling, unless I had good reason, do you?"

Bolan stared at her. "You mean...?"

"Yes. He has my sister. As long as I cooperate, she will remain alive. The minute I stop..." She drew a slender finger, its bright red nail like the tip of a bloody stiletto, across her throat.

"Then why did you tell Cao no more? What was that all about?"

"Cao and his boss were running their own operation. They were putting the squeeze on me. I have paid several thousand dollars a year for the past few years. I have paid enough. It is that simple."

"But why now?"

"Because I have learned, through my own sources, that they were not the ultimate authorities. They were simply taking advantage of their connection for their own purposes. For Colonel Griffith, my continued cooperation in the smuggling operation is sufficient. The extortion is of no concern to him."

"You're certain of that?"

"Yes."

"How do you know?"

"I won't tell you. I can't."

"But you're sure your sister is still alive?"

"Yes."

"How?"

"I can't tell you that, either. But I am certain of it. I know it is true. It has to be, and so it is."

"That's not a particularly convincing argument."

Kwan Lee didn't respond. She was crying soundlessly. Then, when she'd got herself under control, "Mr. Bolan—" the voice was hesitant, that of a child afraid of the dark, the toughness gone "—please, do me a favor... Hold me?"

11

The Tribeca streets were deserted. At 3:00 a.m., even the chic were reluctant to be out and around. Bolan had parked two blocks from Kwan Lee's loft, in an all-night lot. The dark, refurbished buildings seemed somehow all the more deserted than the abandoned shells of the Lower East Side.

He stopped to look north, toward Canal Street. Busy during the day, lined with shops open to the street and the stalls and tables of sidewalk vendors, it was quiet at night, an occasional cab drifting across town with a late fare. Turning south again, he picked up his pace.

Huddled on a doorstep across the street, a bundle of shadows moved restlessly—probably a drunk. The buildings, some of them a dozen stories tall, stood side by side. No alleys cut the block, so Bolan had to be concerned only with doorways and open windows. On this hot, muggy night, there were plenty of the latter. The co-ops, mostly converted office buildings, were air-conditioned, but some of the older buildings, having somehow escaped the developer's magic wand, still housed the struggling artists who had pioneered residential settlement of the area. They would soon be gone, forced out by the desirability their presence, spawned by desperation, had created. In the meantime, they slept with windows open behind iron gates, padlocked in the choice between safety and fire regulations.

Bolan cut down Mansard Street, heading toward Broadway. He glanced in each doorway as he passed, his hand under his jacket resting lightly on the butt of his Beretta. What Kwan Lee had told him had changed everything. The scope of his search had grown to transoceanic proportions, and potential trouble had increased accordingly.

Mack Bolan was no stranger to syndicates, regardless of origin. Kwan Lee had been right to call his attention to the Mafia, since they were the perfect working model. The Corsicans she had mentioned, if anything more ruthless than their Sicilian-American counterparts, had a long history. Their association with Southeast Asia was decades old, but their tutelage had hardly been necessary for the Vietnamese, who had developed their indigenous variety of organized crime by the judicious grafting of modern techniques onto ancient, tribal vines.

During his tenure in Vietnam, Bolan had seen more of heroin and opium than he cared to remember. As the war gradually wound down and Turkish supplies had been interrupted, everyone—the Corsicans, the Mafia and the Vietnamese exporters—had turned to new channels. Three-quarters of the world's supply of opium was grown in the Golden Triangle, so it was no surprise it had been more than able to fill the Turkish void.

The surprise had been in who was at the top of the heap. Rumors had circulated for years about Colonel Griffith. He had become the focus of a complicated web of stories, half hearsay and half-shadowy glimpse. Eventually an entire mythology had grown up around him. Some said *Apocalypse Now* was about him, others said it couldn't have been made without his cooperation. Another version had him long dead, but still presiding, like Jeremy Bentham, in preserved serenity, at convocations of his successors.

But to learn that he was not only alive, but actively involved in a smuggling operation so lucrative that assassination had been a necessary tool, was a shock. Musing on the situation, Bolan thought for a moment about calling his old friend, Hal Brognola, at the Justice Department. Hal would likely have access to some useful intel, but this was a personal affair, and he wanted to keep it that way if at all possible. Hal would be there if needed.

A second shadow caught his eye, this time high up on a fire escape to his left. A sudden flash threw a bearded black face into sudden relief as the man lit a cigarette. The movement was too natural to be surreptitious, just a man taking the night air in city fashion. Bolan stepped into a doorway to make certain. As the man continued to puff, the rising and falling glow reassured Bolan. After the fourth drag, he stepped out of the doorway. The glass behind him shattered, and Bolan hit the pavement.

Peering back at the door, the warrior spotted the neat round hole at the center of a spiderweb of cracks. Shoulder high in the left door panel, the shot would have taken his head off. Bolan quickly skittered on hands and knees to the next doorway, a little deeper than the last. He had seen nothing and heard nothing. The sound had been suppressed, and so had the flash. That meant a pro. But how did they know where to find him?

He immediately thought about Kwan Lee. Could she have called someone? No, she had no idea where his car was parked and his visit had been unannounced. That meant they were watching her. But who the hell were they? Was it Cao or Nguyen? Or someone bigger, someone with more on his mind than a broken arm and a little high-velocity vengeance?

The doorway wasn't deep enough to offer much cover, but the rifleman hadn't fired again. He was either gone, or he was waiting patiently, like a good professional. Bolan tried the door behind him. The knob rattled but didn't turn. The door was locked. He felt the glass with his fingers, keeping his eyes on the roofline across the street. The glass was pebbled, and probably wired, but his options were limited. He slammed at one corner of the glass with the butt of the AutoMag, the heavy gun bouncing off without inflicting any damage. He tried again, this time hearing a slight squeal, as if the glass had begun to crack. The third blow confirmed it, as several chunks ground their broken edges against one another with the eerie sound of pack ice breaking up in a sudden thaw.

Still watching the street, he felt the corner of the window with his fingers. A few gaps in the glass were evident, but the wire embedded between the double panes was still intact. Rapping repeatedly with the gun, Bolan cleared a rough five-inch square out of the corner. Satisfied he had enough clearance, he turned quickly, kicked sharply at the wire then ducked back flat against the doorway.

The second shot slammed into the wooden door, just above his left shoulder. It was close, so close he felt a slight tug on the material of his jacket. But the wire was free. He only hoped the sniper wasn't using an infrared scope. Stretching his arm out along the bottom of the door glass, he could just reach through to the inner knob. It, too, rattled but wouldn't turn. He'd have to leave cover while he felt for the latch. The alternative was to make a run for it, but he still had no clue to the shooter's location and didn't even know whether the man was alone.

What the hell? What real choice did he have? Bolan leaned out and groped upward, finding the latch with the tips of his fingers, then ducked back. Now he knew where it was, but could he get it open?

A rush of footsteps up the block told him it was time to find out. He stepped to the center of the door, reached in and twisted. The latch gave and the door came open with a click. Yanking it open all the way, he dived through as it slammed shut behind him, landing on chunks of glass at the base of a marble stairwell. To his left a hall disappeared in the darkness. As far as he could tell, it was an office building.

Bolan got to his feet and latched the door, then backed into the dark hall until he reached an open elevator. He ducked inside and watched the door. The pebbled glass was only translucent, but he could make out a cluster of wavy shadows thrown by the streetlights. Three, maybe four men huddled to one side of the doorway, and, as he expected, one shadow suddenly stepped front and center. Bolan could just make out the hand groping through the broken glass for the latch.

He squeezed off a shot, aiming slightly left of the shadow to compensate for the angle of the streetlight. The Beretta hissed, as silent as death itself, and a hole appeared in the other door's glass panel. Something heavy crashed into the door, and the hand stopped groping, twisted awkwardly once, turned palm up then slid down and out of sight. Bolan winced involuntarily as he remembered the sharp edges of glass at the bottom of the opening. They would have ripped and shredded the back of the hand as it slid heavily over them. That was all the proof he needed that he'd hit his target.

Both windows of the door disappeared in a burst of gunfire, which Bolan recognized as suppressed automatic weapon fire, probably an Ingram or Uzi. As the slugs ricocheted off the stone walls of the corridor, Bolan pressed himself against the back of the elevator. When the hail of fire stopped, he peered out in time to see the doors implode and two men stand shoulder to shoulder, each with an SMG held waist high.

Bolan aimed quickly, sighting on an imaginary triangle with the target's head as the pinnacle. The Beretta was now set for a 3-shot burst, and he pulled the trigger. One of the shadows flew backward, as though a rag doll tossed away by an angry child. The man fell on his back, arms flung out over his head.

Bolan pushed the largest button on the panel and heard a hum as the power surged on. He got no response when he pushed one of a pair at the bottom. But with his second choice he was rewarded by the grating sound of the door closing. He pushed the top button and one in the middle of the panel. If the floor indicator over the elevator bank was lit, he wanted to keep them guessing.

He got off at seven. A small light in one of the offices cast weak illumination into the building to his left, but it wasn't enough to light the whole corridor. Opting for the left, Bolan raced down the hall to find himself face-to-face with a grainy glass door. There was no outlet at that end. Going back past the elevator, he found a metal door at the other end of the hallway. The red exit light above the door was unlit. Bolan walked onto the landing of the fire stairs and stopped to listen as he guided the door softly closed.

He leaned over a railing and, two or three floors below, spotted a single low-wattage bulb casting shadows up and down the stairwell. High above, probably at the top floor, another bulb poured shadows down the stairs. Going down was too risky, but staying where he was was riskier still. That meant he had to go up, and hope the hit men were anxious enough to take a ride to the top on the elevator. Step by step, he climbed the stairs, feeling the months of accumulated dust and grit grinding under the soft soles of his shoes.

On the tenth-floor landing, he turned and went part-way up the stairs, stopping at a position that gave him a clear shot from the knees up at anyone coming through the top-floor door. A dull echo boomed from below, and he knew someone had entered the stairwell on the ground floor. Either the guy was stupid or he intended to be heard. Bolan took the latter position. It was tough to plan when you didn't know the size of the opposition, so Bolan wanted a free-form plan of attack with plenty of room for improvisation.

A burst of gunfire whined up the stairwell, the slugs shattering the skylight overhead, glass raining into the stairwell with a tinkling delicacy that contradicted its origin. While the glass showered over him like flakes of temperate ice, the twelfth-floor fire door slammed back into the wall. A rush of footsteps brought two shadows to the railing. Bolan fired once, then again. The dark mass of shadow to the left crumpled.

It fell toward him in a graceful dive, preceded by the heavy metallic clack of the man's weapon. The body seemed to snag for a moment, perhaps caught by its feet on the railing, then jerked free and plummeted down-ward. Shoes clattered once, then again against railings on lower floors. The thud at the bottom seemed to echo up forever.

Someone shouted from below, and Bolan recognized the language as Vietnamese. He couldn't hear the words, but the tone spoke volumes.

Suddenly a soft yellow glow suffused the stairwell from above. Bolan looked up just as a clump of oily rags, enveloped in flame, dropped over the railing. He fired again, aiming low, under the main bannister. One shot pinged away off an iron upright, showering sparks down the stairs. The second struck flesh, the scream of the wounded man sharp and quick. Bolan charged up the stairs, stopping halfway between eleven and twelve.

The wounded man lay halfway through the fire door. He gritted his teeth and inhaled in short, sharp gasps. Both hands were wrapped around his wounded thigh, blood streaming between his fingers wrapped like a tourniquet around the wound. Bolan charged up the final few steps to kneel beside the man. He placed the muzzle of the AutoMag on the center of the wounded man's forehead. In Vietnamese he said, "Call your friends. Tell them you got me but you need help."

The man spit at Bolan, ignoring the cold, heavy steel threatening to tunnel slugs through his brainpan. Bolan twisted, bearing down sharply on the AutoMag, then repeated his command. This time the injured man did as he was told.

Bolan pressed into the shadows at the base of the wall and waited. Footsteps drew closer, getting louder and louder, and then slowed as the ascent began to take its toll. After what seemed to be an eternity, two men, two snow peas from the same pod, bobbed into view. Bolan waited until they were nearly at the top of the stairs.

"Stay right there," he commanded. They chose to ignore him, as he had assumed they would. Firing four shots in rapid succession, he lay back and listened to the echo of dying thunder. When it had faded into a whisper, the quiet, leathery rasp of shoes on four twitching, newly dead feet followed it into oblivion.

And another link in the chain snapped open.

12

Central Park was crowded. Like any hot Sunday, this one spilled over into the streets, people leaving their steaming apartments for the open spaces and green grass. The entrance at Seventy-ninth Street was clotted with vendors selling sno-cones and Good Humor, papaya juice and lemonade squeezed on the spot.

Bolan eased through the mob and started to walk downhill, using the asphalt drive where the pedestrian traffic was thinner. The police barricades were in place, and the drive was off limits to automobiles. In the humid heat, Bolan caught the accumulated scent of a thousand walked dogs and a hundred incontinent winos. The drive curved to the right, and he crossed all the way over to get on the sidewalk.

He stopped to light a cigarette under a grape arbor, its rustic benches full of lounging street people. They were crowded together, keeping out of the sun as if it were fatal. They were vampires of a sort. One of the more alert hit him up for a smoke, and Bolan obliged, tapping a couple of Winstons free of the pack. As usual, the guy had his own matches. With a "God bless you" that might have been recorded for all of the conviction it conveyed, the man slithered back to his seat, muscling in among the others who had already begun to reallocate the space.

If Kwan Lee was right, he was about to make his last major contact, hitting them in the largest, deepest pocket of their capacious and multisubsidized wallet. According to her sources, Cao was to deliver three kilos of street-grade heroin, many times stepped on and probably no more than six- or eight-percent pure. It was the kind of deal that went down day in and day out in the country's largest city, and the one with the largest addict population. The street value of the three keys was somewhere near seven figures. This would be a dent they'd notice, a tug on their coattails they couldn't ignore. And, best of all, it was of direct concern to Griffith. It was a dangerous game he was playing, but it was the only game in town.

The events of the preceding night had proved he already had their attention, but Bolan wasn't satisfied. He wanted it undivided. Already toying with the notion of a trip to Southeast Asia, he still wasn't sure it would be necessary. But if he snatched the heroin, and further embarrassed Cao, he could get what he needed—a face-to-face meeting with Cao's immediate superior, and on his own terms. Anything less wouldn't cut it.

The tree-lined walks wound like the strands of an unraveled sweater through the parched green of the park. Small knots of people gathered around groups of musicians playing the ethnic music of their choice. Everything from an amplified polka band to the keening swirl of a *klezmer* group vied with all the others for the attention of the dollars of passersby. It was an eerie sensation to pass from one zone dominated by the spicy riffs of a full-bore salsa ensemble into the no-man's-land between it and a punk trio, cooking through battery-powered amps with the frenetic minimalist rhythm accompaniment that was the hallmark of the style.

All Kwan Lee knew was that the deal was to take place on a stone bridge in Central Park. Heading toward the lake at the heart of the park, Bolan kept a weather eye peeled for Cao, but the ethnic carnival tumbling all around him would make it almost impossible to spot a lone Vietnamese. The crowd began to thin as he approached the center of the park. Even in broad daylight, there were sections seldom used. Some had been appropriated for specific use, like the tangled undergrowth of The Ramble, much favored by cruising gays, and the southeast corner, which was one of the easiest places in town to score a little crack, some rock and roll or grass. Not to mention the pill of your choice.

The bridge, arcing at a gentle angle over a thin strait connecting the two large sections of the lake, was a beautiful spot, but seldom heavily peopled. Ideal for the lazy strut of young couples or a welcome pause for someone walking across the park in no hurry, it afforded anyone who used it a good view of every approach. Its scenic vista of the West Side skyline also made it a frequent site for high-fashion shoots, but never on Sunday afternoon in this kind of oppressive weather.

Bolan crested a hill and looked out over the lake stretching away to east and west. He had a straight downhill walk of a hundred yards or so to get to the main path taking him onto the bridge. He was undecided whether to take Cao before or after the exchange. Either way, he'd have a substantial bit of leverage. Cash or dope, it was money in the bank.

Bolan sat on a rock half buried in the grass and watched a few casual strollers amble across the bridge. Checking each approach one by one, he noticed nothing out of the ordinary. The woods on the slope beyond the bridge were fairly dense, and the dozens of benches scattered throughout the area were perfect lookout points if you knew who or what you were looking for. But Bolan was in the dark.

As he turned to scan the West Side approach, he spotted something out of the corner of his eye, just over his left shoulder. Turning quickly, he found himself looking at one of the most muscular women he'd ever seen.

"Sorry, didn't mean to startle you," she said. Her voice was much softer than he would have expected. A red string bikini did little to hide the bulging product of dedicated iron pumping. At her feet, which were bare, a towel and a bold orange dress lay in a heap.

"No problem," Bolan replied, preparing to leave.

"Wait a minute, don't go." She seemed genuinely apologetic. "I come here to work on my tan. There's usually no one else around, so I don't have to deal with the geeks, you know?"

"I don't want to interfere. I can sit anywhere."

"I don't think so."

"What do you mean?"

"You were waiting for somebody. I could tell that. I never would have gotten as close as I did, if you weren't wrapped up in something."

As she chattered, she dropped to one knee and folded the dress before stuffing it into her purse. Then she spread the heavy beach towel into a smooth, perfect rectangle. Pressing the few tiny wrinkles flat with both hands, she went to both knees and leaned forward, lowering herself in a reverse push-up.

Once on the ground, she cocked her head to one side, staring at him through large, amber-tinted sunglasses. "You work out?"

"In a way."

"I thought so. You look like it."

Bolan turned away from her to watch the bridge.

"I'm sorry," she said. "I guess I must seem like one of the geeks I supposedly come here to avoid. I usually don't talk this much, I swear. Sit down and do whatever you were doing. I'll just shut up. I promise."

Reluctant to stay, yet even more reluctant to surrender the ideal vantage point afforded by the rocky hill, Bolan decided to take the woman at her word. He checked each of the approaches again, and still saw no sign. He looked at his watch and began to wonder whether Kwan Lee had been misled. It was already one o'clock, and the drop was scheduled for twelve forty-five.

Bolan stood, then walked over to lean against the rough bark of the single tree on the hill, a large fir nearly two feet in diameter at its base. From his new location, he was able to survey the woman, now apparently absorbed in her tan. In repose, her form was less stylized, the musculature less prominent. Her long legs were almost graceful as she changed position and rolled onto her back. The taut breasts, flattened by her position, were larger than he had at first thought. Long, coal-black hair, spread out behind her head in loose coils, gave her an Oriental cast, and her eyes, just visible through the dark amber lenses, added to the impression.

To her right, a capacious vinyl purse gaped open on its side, and Bolan noticed something that gave him pause. He couldn't see much, but there was no doubt it was blued steel. A gun. He began to wonder whether she was there by happenstance—or if something more sinister had brought her to this place.

He walked casually past her, then dived to the ground alongside her, grasping her wrist as her right arm snaked out to reach for the purse. She was as strong as her initial impression suggested, the muscles taut and wiry.

Struggling to hold her still, Bolan reached into the purse and pulled out the small hunk of blued steel. In the harsh sunlight, it was even uglier than he had imagined—a Colt Woodsman .22-caliber target pistol. The dark blue suppressor snagged on the lining of the purse as he tugged it loose.

"You pump a little lead, as well, I see," Bolan observed. "And don't try to tell me you carry this for protection. I know better."

"What's it to you?"

"I know an assassination special when I see it. Who do you work for?"

She swiped at him with her left hand, just grazing his cheek with her open palm and fingers. "Give me that. It's none of your business."

Bolan released the clip and tucked it into his jacket pocket. He worked the action and snagged a cartridge as it arced away. "One in the chamber, too. You *are* serious, aren't you?"

"Bolan, you're such a paranoid ass. I swear to God."

"How do you know my name?"

"I know more than your name, pal. I know a few things about you and your wanting to find the main man in a Vietnamese extortion ring."

"Kwan Lee sent you."

"Of course! You think lying around here in a bikini is my idea?"

"Why?"

"She thought you might need some help."

Bolan tucked the gun back into her purse. "She could have done better."

"You think so? Then why did I get close enough to blow your brains out? You might be getting old, slipping a little. You know how it is in our line of work. The reflexes go a little, and you don't even notice it, at first.''

''That's a long way off for me yet.''

''Are you sure?''

''That's *your* clip in my pocket.''

''Listen, if you want to take Cao, you just might need my help. Why don't you give me the magazine?''

''Why should I?''

''You could have used a little help last night, on West Broadway, couldn't you? You think that was a coincidence?''

''No.'' Bolan stared at her silently for a long moment. When he spoke, it was more like he was thinking out loud than carrying on a conversation. ''Of course, it could have been Kwan Lee who set me up. Who else knew where I was? Then again, if they were watching her place, why didn't they try to take me there?''

The questions were addressed to himself, but the young woman answered him. ''Kwan Lee is more valuable to them alive than dead. The same can't be said of you, can it?''

''No, it can't.''

''Then let me go so I can get dressed. It's almost time for the drop.''

He let go of her arm, and she got to her knees, slipping into the loose-fitting dress she had yanked out of the purse.

''My name is Margot Blaine.''

13

"I think we ought to take a stroll," Margot suggested. She took Bolan by the arm, swinging her purse in her free hand like a young girl on a date. Bolan, responding stiffly, followed her lead. They stepped onto the path, and Margot leaned her head on Bolan's shoulder. She nuzzled his ear, and whispered, "Try to act naturally. We're supposed to be in love." She bit his ear, then continued, "Cao is across the bridge, under the second clump of trees."

Bolan snaked his left arm around her waist, again impressed by the sensation of strength she projected. Her entire body seemed to hum with the tension of steel springs waiting to be released.

Among the trees, Cao stood stiffly, trying to seem interested only in the scenery. And it was obvious that the man was uncomfortable. The arm Bolan had broken was supported by a light blue sling; the right arm dangled at his side, a nondescript briefcase clutched tightly in his hand.

"We'll split up once we get to the bridge," Bolan said. "You stay on the bridge, and watch your back. I'll circle around to get past Cao."

"You sure that's a good idea?"

"Look, you said yourself that they know more about me than I do about them. If this is a setup, I want to have a fallback position."

"You going to take Cao before or after the exchange?"

"After. I think his boss cares more about money than drugs. Dealers never count the cash until it's in hand. It'll hurt more, make him angrier, when I tell him I've got his man and his money."

They began the gentle ascent to the center of the bridge, Bolan keeping his eye on the loitering courier. They stopped for a moment at the crest of the bridge and leaned over the stonework wall. Bolan squeezed her, and she whispered in his ear again, for all the world a not-quite-young couple feeling their oats, perhaps feeling younger than their years, enjoying each other on a summer stroll.

"Be careful."

Bolan nodded, then turned and walked off the bridge, stepping into a tree-shrouded asphalt path angling off to the right. He hurried up the steep incline, temporarily losing sight of his quarry.

At the top of the hill, he turned to look back down at the bridge. Margot was still leaning on the wall, now facing the inside of the bridge. The purse dangled loosely in her hand, slightly open. Bolan could just make out the colorful towel, which covered the .22.

From his detached perspective, Bolan watched her for a minute. She was good. She seemed perfectly at ease, but knowing her purpose, Bolan could tell she had not taken her eyes off Cao, despite the casual turns of her head, the occasional toss of her long hair. Bolan slipped into the trees, losing sight of Margot as he worked his way to a spot behind Cao.

The trees were tangled in dense undergrowth, vines and shoulder-high shrubbery struggling to control all the available space, fighting for the occasional scraps of sun filtering through the dense foliage overhead. The going was slow. Bolan felt as if he'd been thrown back a decade and a half, and was once again duelling both a jungle and a deadly enemy. In fact, the feeling was not that far off the mark.

As the warrior neared the place where Cao had been waiting, the undergrowth thinned a bit. Through a gap in the trees, he caught his first glimpse of the Vietnamese since leaving Margot on the bridge. Worming forward another few feet, he could see Margot herself, still dallying on the bridge, but now walking slowly, with no apparent urgency, toward the near end. She must have seen something.

Bolan ducked behind a large oak. Directly in front of the tree, a wooden bench—half its slats missing, its concrete standards chipped and broken—afforded him some cover, and he dropped to one knee and inched forward. Now between the bench and the oak, he was fifty yards uphill from Cao, who had begun to pace nervously.

Some overhanging branches at the far end of the bench would allow Bolan to sit without being seen by Cao. He slipped behind the bench and ducked around its far end, then dropped to a precarious seat on the remaining slats. He picked up an abandoned newspaper and spread its pages.

Footsteps behind him, on the asphalt, caught his ear. Two men curved into view, descending the path from Bolan's right. Both were wearing long, sleeveless T-shirts, and one carried a ghetto blaster on his left shoulder. They whispered as they walked, and Bolan wondered why the radio was silent. He wondered even more about the prominent bulge on the hip of the man closest to him as they passed.

Bolan was about to follow, when he heard a twig snap in the undergrowth across the path. Instinctively he dived to the left, landing hard on his shoulder. The few remaining back slats of the bench splintered into a shower of toothpicks as he squirmed into the brush just ahead of the hellfire. The shooter was firing blind from somewhere in the woods, or would have nailed him in the first burst—which had to mean it was someone who had been moving into position in the past few moments.

The strategy was sharp, if poorly executed. Bolan thanked his lucky stars as he rolled to his right to take cover behind the ancient oak. Whether meant as a diversion or an assassination, it had delayed him. The two muscle men had not stopped or turned, all the proof he needed that they were expecting the gunfire. He now had two choices: he could ignore Cao for the moment and try to take out the hidden gunman, running the risk of losing Cao altogether, or he could expose his back to the shooter and try to take Cao down. Neither proposition was attractive.

The muzzle of an SMG poked through the leaves. Training his sights on it, he waited a beat, then squeezed as a flash of blue appeared among the leaves. The spitting Beretta found its mark. A round man in a blue oxford button-down pitched forward through the shrubbery, landing on his face on the asphalt. He didn't bother to try to protect himself with upraised arms. There was no point.

Crouching low behind the gun had been his first mistake. Letting Bolan catch a glimpse of him had been his second. The 9 mm advice the Executioner had tossed his way took out the back of his skull. The shattered bone now gaped up at Bolan like the exaggerated smile of a surprised clown.

The muscle men had disappeared, and so had Cao. Bolan couldn't wait to see if the dead man had friends. He got to his feet and raced down the path toward Cao's position. The path was empty. A dozen half-smoked cigarettes were the only trace left by the nervous courier.

Sprinting around a second bend in the path, Bolan spotted the two muscle men, now lounging on the bridge. Cao was gone and so was Margot. Bolan dashed forward. The hardmen, each watching an end of the bridge, had placed their radio on the wall between them. The warrior charged straight ahead, provoking a shout from the man looking his way.

Bolan drew a bead on the first muscle man as he yanked a gun out of his belt. Firing once, Bolan drilled him just above what was probably an assiduously cultivated pec. The heavy-lifter grabbed his shoulder and pitched backward, slamming into the wall and knocking the radio into the brown water below.

The second kid, a small automatic in his hand, lost his chance when he hesitated, unable to decide whether to look after his friend or take Bolan head-on. They were amateurs, picking up some spending money for a weekend's work, and Bolan had no particular reason to kill either one. He barreled ahead, throwing his shoulder into the second kid, just below the rib cage. The kid grunted and went down, the gun flying from his hand and skittering down the gentle incline of the bridge.

Two old men had stopped in their tracks, bewildered, frozen in fear as Bolan rushed by. Near the top of the hill, he caught a flash of Margot's dress, its bright orange almost impossible to miss. Margot wasn't alone. She and Cao were walking swiftly toward another stand of trees, down along a finger of the lake. Cao still had his brief-case. They were bracketed by two additional men, both in dark suits, one of whom also carried a briefcase.

Although moving briskly, they seemed unconcerned about being followed. No doubt they assumed Bolan had been permanently waylaid. As they neared the bottom of the hill, Bolan was only fifty yards behind. Suddenly Margot wheeled, striking the man on her left in the throat with the edge of her hand. It wasn't a polished move, but it did the trick.

The stricken man gagged, and Margot spun him into Cao and the other suit. She broke for the trees, and the second suit raised his hand. Bolan raised his weapon and fired off a shot from a distance that didn't guarantee ac-curacy. He hadn't stopped running, and the shot went high, but it caught the man's attention. He turned to-ward Bolan as Margot made it into the trees.

The warrior dived to the ground, taking a steadier aim and squeezing off two shots. The man in the suit dropped to one knee. Bolan saw the bright red spot on his left shoulder and fired again. This time the 9 mm stinger punched between two ribs and into the man's heart. The suit sprawled backward, his gun flying in a bright arc to-ward the edge of the lake. It landed just beyond the grass with a small splash in the shallow, muddy water.

Cao made a break for it, first yanking the second briefcase from under the dead man. The movement was almost comical, Cao with his arm in a sling, carrying two briefcases in his free hand, waddling through the thick weeds along the fringe of the lake.

The other man, now recovered from Margot's assault, had drawn his own gun. He lay prostrate, taking careful aim. The tree behind and to the left of Bolan's head was chipped by the first shot, and the second ripped up some grass just to his right. Bolan couldn't afford to give him a chance for a third.

The prostrate man presented a small target, and Bolan drew careful aim. The man pressed himself to the earth, squeezing himself into as compact a target as possible, then suddenly erupted in a roll to the left. Bolan's first shot went wide, ripping through the weeds.

The hardman continued to roll to his left, and Bolan fired again. This time he scored, the slug slamming into the target's shoulder from above, breaking the collarbone and bringing the rolling man to a halt.

Bolan got to his feet and scanned the area for Cao, who was now laboring heavily around the edge of the lake. A bright flash of orange darted through the trees, then Margot was out in the open. She slipped off the dress and waded into the mucky water. Waist deep, now, she leaned forward, and dived into a brisk crawl toward a small peninsula ahead of Cao.

A moment later, her sleek body streaming with muddy water and algae, Margot climbed out of the lake just as Cao reached the peninsula. He seemed startled for a moment and stopped short. That was all that Margot needed. She lunged at him, her head down, and struck him on the left shoulder, using her skull like a battering ram.

Bolan sprinted into the clear and reached the peninsula as Margot, sitting astride the fallen courier, wrestled a small automatic from his grasp. Winded from the exertion, Bolan leaned over and placed a hand on her shoulder. "You are really something. You don't fool around, do you?"

Margot arched her eyebrows in a mock leer and smiled. "I might, with the proper inducement. What did you have in mind?"

14

Getting Cao to talk had not been easy. Getting him to reveal the name of his immediate superior had been harder still. But he had, after some strenuous persuasion, relented. Bolan paused, about to drop a quarter into the pay phone. This call was his trump card. Playing it exhausted his last stateside option. If it went nowhere, he was left with an empty barrel, there was nothing else he could do.

He took a deep breath and dropped the coin. He heard the clanging of the phone's internal chimes, the usual clicks and buzzes, and, finally, a ring. Then a second and a third.

The dim light of the street corner cast shadows on the sidewalk beside him. He studied his own faint umbra as the phone continued to ring. The oblique angle stretched him out flat on the sidewalk to more than four times his actual height. It also made him a dream figure, pale and insubstantial, something you could step on or over, as you preferred.

There had been times when his entire career had seemed end-stopped, exhausted and, ultimately, pointless. The frustrations, the countless blind alleys, the accumulated anger at the boundless evil of the savages had begun, like a corrosive acid, to eat away at him. It was not a pleasant feeling.

The pauses between missions had been short because he couldn't live any other way. But the pauses during missions were the worst—always had been. They cut right to the heart of his existence. How could one man make a difference? That was the question he sought constantly to answer. And when a friend, himself a professional bastion of civilization fending off the hyenas of the world, dies in your arms, it's hard to believe anything you do matters to anyone, even to yourself.

After the eighth ring, Bolan was about to replace the receiver in its cradle. Angry at Cao, angrier still at himself, he wanted to go back to Kwan Lee's loft and put a bullet through Cao's head. But that wasn't the right way, and it sure as hell wasn't his way. To adopt the hyena's code was to become one yourself. Blood on his hands was something Bolan had learned to live with. He'd be damned if he'd spend the rest of his days exhaling the fetid stench of dead meat.

Absorbed in his thoughts, he almost missed the click. The voice on the other end of the line put a stop to his reverie.

"Hello?" It was a woman, by the sound of her a young woman.

"May I speak to Mr. Quang, please?"

The hesitation was expected. The question was not. "Whom shall I say is calling, please?"

"A friend of Mr. Cao."

"One moment." The muffled clack of the receiver being set on a tabletop was followed by the same voice, at some distance from the mouthpiece, calling out, "Father, it's for you."

In response to an apparent question, she said, "I don't know. He said a friend of Mr. Cao. That's all he told me."

A second later she was back on the line. "One moment. My father will take it in his office." Then she was gone.

In a way, Quang's daughter answering the phone defused the explosive potential quivering in his gut. It always amazed him how wide was the gulf between a criminal's public, professional behavior and his personal life. They, too, were husbands and fathers, worried over bad grades, a child's illness. And yet how schizophrenic, not to give a damn about the humanity of their victims, as if suffering were reserved for the arrogant few.

And a moment later, it was all gone. The acid voice of Quang sounded as if it would dissolve the miles of cable connecting them and spew poison in his ear. "Where is the money?"

"Wait a minute," Bolan snapped. "Don't you want to know how your man is?"

"I want the money or the merchandise."

"What about Cao?"

"Does the elephant want a flea?"

"Have it your way."

"I always do. Who are you?"

"Does it matter?"

"If I get what I want, not a bit."

Bolan pushed a little harder. "And you want the money or the merchandise?"

Quang waited a long moment. Bolan outwaited him. "Yes."

"How about both?"

"And what do you get in return?"

"Maybe I don't want anything."

"Then you wouldn't have called."

"All right, but the price is high."

"Tell me your demands. We will see whether there is a point to further discussion."

"What alternative do you have?"

"I could have you removed from the competition."

"No great shakes so far on that one."

"I am a patient man, but don't push your luck."

"I want the man who killed Aloysius Mackenzie."

"And what makes you think I have him? I don't even know who Aloysius Mackenzie is."

"You wouldn't. The point, though, is that I do. And I want the man who killed him."

"Perhaps we should meet to discuss this further. I am not entirely comfortable using the phone for such... delicate matters. It is a secure phone, but..." Bolan could visualize the shrug of his shoulders.

"You call it. I'll be there."

Bolan glanced at his watch. He could hear Quang mumbling to someone, his hand over the phone. It was nearly midnight. When Quang got back on, he sounded less sure of himself.

"The Cloisters? In one hour?"

"I'll be there. Come alone."

"Make sure you bring the money and the merchandise."

"You bring what I want, and you'll get what you need."

"I am counting on that. Please don't disappoint me."

THE CASTLELIKE TURRETS of The Cloisters loomed against the lights of New Jersey across the Hudson. On a hill at the northern end of Manhattan, it housed the medieval collection of the Metropolitan Museum and sought to replicate structures from the appropriate era. The surrounding hills were given over to a park and featured thick stands of trees and narrow, winding paths among dense patches of shrubbery. It was an ideal place to meet someone you only wanted to see in the dead of night.

It was also an ideal place for an ambush.

Bolan stood in the trees, watching the parking lot. The only automobile access was from the Henry Hudson Parkway up a steeply circuitous roadway comprised of granite blocks. As Bolan waited, it began to drizzle.

He'd made the trip in twenty minutes, ignoring posted speed limits and running every light. Dealing with the likes of Quang, it was best not to be overly punctilious about something so trivial as traffic regulations. There was access to the park on foot, but Bolan was less worried about that, since it would be almost impossible to find him in the dark.

Lights speared up the roadway, and Bolan steeled himself. A large Cadillac loomed out from behind its headlights, its tires slipping a bit as it negotiated the sharp angles of the incline. Bolan waited patiently as Quang got out of the passenger door. So, he'd brought at least one man with him. All bets were now off. If one rule was broken, they were all fair game.

Quang looked around, stooping somewhat to peer into the shadows. Satisfied that he'd arrived first, he waved to the car, and two men emerged carrying submachine guns. One immediately vanished into the clotted shadows against the iron grillwork closing off the museum to the public. The other headed straight for Bolan's position.

The second man, a reedlike Vietnamese with bony hands and fingers, stepped behind a large maple, directly to Bolan's left. He checked his SMG and, satisfied, squatted to present a smaller profile to the parking lot.

Bolan waited until the man settled in, then slipped behind him, sliding a forearm around the man's neck to choke off his air. Using his other arm as a lever, Bolan snapped the man's neck. The body dropped to the ground.

It was 1:20, which gave him ten minutes to circle around and take out the first man. Margot was supposed to arrive on the dot of one-thirty. If he was in position by then, that distraction would provide him with an opening. But he had to be there to take advantage of it.

Melting back into the shadows, Bolan half ran and half slid down to a set of stairs, angling to his left. He climbed up the steps, made slippery by clotted leaf mold, and reached a flat asphalt path circling the north end of the building. It was bordered by two stone walls, each shoulder high, so he ducked between them and sprinted in a half circle, until the building was between him and the parking lot. The maneuver took half his ten minutes. He paused briefly for a quick look at the Palisades across the river, then climbed over a stone parapet.

He was now on a platform fifteen feet over the iron grille, and spotted Quang lounging against the right front fender of his Cadillac. The crime lord was facing away, looking down the approach road, crossing and uncrossing his arms. Bolan leaned over the stone wall at the edge of the platform and saw the remaining hit man below him, about three feet to his right.

Quang was getting impatient. He had started to pace back and forth in the area between the Cadillac and the building. The strut was regular, and the timing seemed almost precise. Bolan watched three more circuits, and when Quang still didn't vary the pattern, Bolan made his move.

When Quang came as close to the wall as he normally did and made his turn, Bolan flung himself over the wall, landing on the sentry feetfirst. The unsuspecting hardman pitched forward onto his face, landing with a sharp crack as his nose and chin struck the pebbled asphalt pad.

Bolan got to his knees and grabbed the half-conscious man around the neck, squeezing until he stopped breathing. The man collapsed in a heap, and Bolan stood just as Quang made his turn at the far end of his circuit. The guard was not dead, but he'd be out for a while, long enough, Bolan hoped, to conduct his negotiations with Quang. He crouched in the shadows to wait for Quang's approach.

The Vietnamese hadn't noticed anything, and strolled in a stiff, birdlike strut back toward the stone wall. He stopped just before he reached it, as if he sensed something he couldn't put his finger on. Moving cautiously, one step at a time, Quang whispered into the darkness, leaning forward at the waist. "Duc? Are you there? Duc, what's happening?"

He was now more than fifteen feet away, and Bolan coiled his legs, ready to spring at the first sudden movement. Quang edged forward a little, taking tiny steps. His expensive shoes crunched on the pebbles with a sharp, rasping sound. When he started to reach into his jacket Bolan made his move.

Rushing headlong, he careered into the much smaller man, knocking him onto his back. The warrior landed heavily atop him, pinioning the man's arms with his knees. Quang continued to search inside his jacket, and Bolan grabbed the probing arm by its wrist, yanking it back and twisting it painfully. The tendons ground faintly against the bones of the wrist, and Quang moaned, then cursed his larger adversary.

"Settle down, Quang. Save your strength. You're going to need it."

"I see I was wise to expect treachery from you." Quang actually smiled. The look on his face was controlled, bordering on the serene. Bolan wondered whether the man might be on some sort of drug, but his eyes were clear and sharply focused. The tranquility was not chemical in origin. It was, instead, the manifestation of that arrogance all crime bosses seem to have in common. It seemed to be the one prerequisite to holding such a position.

"You weren't exactly true to your word, Quang."

"How do you think I have managed to get where I am? As you Westerners say, there is no honor among thieves. You were wise to take precautions. It is unfortunate that I underestimated you, but there will be another time."

"Don't count on it."

"I don't have to count on it. Waiting for good fortune is the hobby of the fool. The wise man makes his own luck."

"Maybe so. But yours is on the verge of running out."

"YOU ARE EVEN BETTER than I thought. Are you going to shoot me now, or later?"

"I don't shoot defenseless people, Quang. That's the difference between you and me."

"And I suppose you are going to give me my money and the heroin, if I tell you what you want to know."

"That was the deal."

"So it was. But as I told you, I don't know Aloysius Mackenzie. How can I possibly tell you who is responsible for his death, however untimely and unfortunate it might have been.''

''Because whoever shot Ambassador Tranh, also killed Al. And you know who did it, or better yet, who paid for it.''

Standing under the trees in the rain, Quang, unarmed, still managed to convey more than a little of the jungle menace Bolan remembered all too well. The captive seemed wary, but not frightened. He reached into his coat, and Bolan tensed. He had already patted the man down, but some weapons weren't easily detected.

Bolan relaxed a second later as Quang ripped open a pack of Camels. The smaller man made a ritual of lighting the cigarette, and when he had finished, he exhaled the first drag with a kind of smug vehemence. ''I am a practical man. Even if I can believe you are willing to deal honorably in this matter, which, as I am sure you can understand, is an open question, I need something more than your word.''

''Such as?''

''I can't help but notice that you have no briefcases with you. How do I know you can even have what it is you propose to give me in exchange for the information you desire?'' Quang punctuated the question with a sharp pull on the cigarette.

Bolan nodded. ''A fair question.'' He backed toward the car and leaned in, watching Quang from the corner of his eye.

''Margot, give me the key to the trunk, will you?''

She snapped it free of the key ring and passed it through the window. Bolan walked to the rear of the car, opened the trunk and reached in. Straining a bit, he removed a large object that turned out to be Cao. Prodding the courier with the Beretta's muzzle, he herded the bound and gagged man back to Quang.

"Is this convincing?" he asked, indicating Cao.

"Somewhat. But how do I know you have anything but Cao? A dozen of him is not worth the contents of either briefcase, as I'm sure you can appreciate."

"If you don't think I have what you want, why did you agree to meet me?"

Using another drag on the cigarette as an opportunity to frame his answer, Quang paused reflectively. When he spoke, it was with more self-assurance than he had so far demonstrated. "What did I have to lose? I was reasonably confident I had nothing to fear."

"Strike one, eh, Quang?"

"You might be able to use the cash, but I know enough about you to believe you have no use for the drugs, except as a bargaining chip."

"True."

"So I took the chance. I also assumed the whole thing might very well be a bluff. So far, I am not convinced I was wrong."

Bolan grunted. He walked back to the car and yanked two briefcases from the recesses of the trunk, then slammed the lid shut. Dangling them in one hand, he walked back toward Quang, this time keeping some distance between them. He dropped the two cases into a puddle. The splash ruined the careful crease in Quang's immaculate trousers. "Strike two. . . ." Bolan said.

"You Americans are so obsessed by sports. They seem to govern your entire view of the world," Quang said, mixing bafflement with distaste. He took another drag of his cigarette, then looked at it disdainfully, as if it were somehow implicated in Bolan's naïveté. He tossed the butt to the ground, where it sputtered out in a shallow puddle. "You seem to think rules govern everything, that winners and losers can be determined by looking at a scoreboard. Where I come from, no one keeps score."

"You're in my ballpark, Quang, and you'll play by my rules," Bolan answered, prodding the cases with his foot. "Or I'll take my ball and go home."

"May I open the cases? You will concede, will you not, that they are unremarkable. By design, of course. No need calling attention to transactions best left off the business pages, eh?"

"Be my guest."

The latches clicked, and Quang used his cigarette lighter to explore the contents of the case. Bolan, looking past the open lid, could see the stacks of wrinkled, well-circulated hundreds, bound in ten-thousand-dollar bundles. There were, he knew, eighty-one such bundles in the briefcase.

"So far, you seem to be honest. Let us say...half honest, at any rate."

"Check the other case."

Quang did so, hefting each of three thick blocks wrapped in black plastic and duct tape. Rain water dripping from the trees above beaded on the plastic, like small phosphorescent beetles.

"Open one if you want," Bolan said.

"No need. I am convinced." Quang closed the case carefully, making sure the latches caught securely. He set each case upright, then moved both out of the puddle into which Bolan had tossed them.

Quang stood and walked off a little way, his hands folded behind his back. He seemed half tempted to make the deal Bolan was proposing, but the risks, Bolan realized, were significant. The odds for the warrior being able to do anything with the knowledge were slim. Quang might even take the chance of feeding him some false information, a risk Bolan had factored into his own approach.

Pivoting smartly, the crime lord walked back to stare at Bolan silently.

"Very well. I accept the terms you offer."

"Who killed Aloysius Mackenzie?"

"If, as you say, it was the same man who assassinated Ambassador Tranh, it was Albert Carlucci."

Bolan whistled. Carlucci was as expensive as they came, a hired gun of the old school who was willing to kill anyone, anywhere, anytime, as long as the price was right. And for Carlucci, the right price started in the middle six figures. He hadn't been heard from in more than two years.

"You're sure of that?"

"I am."

"How?"

"I myself made the initial contact with him," Quang said, raising a hand to cut off Bolan's anticipated reaction. "But it was for the purpose of eliminating Ambassador Tranh only."

"I understand. But you didn't make the payment?"

"Oh, no, that was beyond my humble level, I assure you."

"Then who?"

"I don't know."

Bolan raised an eyebrow, skeptical.

"I swear it."

Instead of answering him, Bolan shifted the Beretta.

"Don't," Quang screamed, holding up both arms as if to ward off the bullet's impact.

Bolan flicked his wrist again, squeezing off a shot. The Beretta coughed discreetly, slamming a slug through one corner of the heroin-filled briefcase. A thin trickle of whitish powder began to leak onto the wet pavement.

"All right, all right. Wait a minute," Quang begged. When he was certain Bolan would indeed wait, he smiled. "You can't blame a man for trying. That, too, is part of the rules, is it not?"

"Who paid?"

Answering the question with one of his own, Quang said, "You have heard of Colonel Griffith? Colonel Thomas Griffith, MIA and presumed dead?"

Bolan said nothing.

"Have you?"

Bolan's nod was almost imperceptible, but Quang continued. "I suppose he is still MIA, in a way. Insofar as your government is concerned, anyway. And I assure you he is in action. Very lucrative action. Mr. Carlucci has been an exclusive employee for almost three years now. He is well paid, as you might imagine, for such dedicated service."

"Where is Griffith?"

"I don't know."

Bolan snapped off a quick shot at the briefcase. The 9 mm slug tore a chunk of material out of the case, enlarging the hole and accelerating the trickle to a steady flow.

"Wait! I don't know—not exactly. He moves around. Always in the Golden Triangle, mostly in the mountains, in Laos, just over the Vietnamese border. That's all I know."

"Sorry, Quang, it's not enough."

"But it's all I have. I cannot give you more than I have."

"How do you contact him?"

"I don't. I am a small cog in a very large, very well-oiled machine. He contacts me, when he needs to."

"Come on, Quang. You know and I know that he needs two-way intelligence. You have to be able to send him information. Even if you don't speak to him personally, there has to be a contact point, somebody you go to with information. Who is it?"

"Another American, living in Bangkok."

"Name?"

"Garfield, James Garfield. A Negro. Named after one of your presidents, I believe."

"How do you contact him?"

"By courier. I have a telephone number, but I have never used it. It is for emergencies only."

"Give me the number."

Quang reached into his jacket and withdrew a heavy-looking Cross pen, from its heft probably solid gold, rather than gold plated. For a small fish, Quang was living rather high on the hog. He scribbled something on a sheet of notepaper and passed it to Bolan, who glanced at it quickly then stuffed the paper into his pocket.

"I know where you live Quang, and you can't run far enough to hide. You understand me?"

The Vietnamese nodded.

"Then I am free to go?"

"As far as I'm concerned."

Quang bent over the briefcase and stuffed a handkerchief into the large exit hole, and a ball of notepaper into the smaller entry hole. Ignoring the still-gagged Cao, whose hands were tightly tied behind his back, he ferried the two cases to the Cadillac, dropping both into the back seat.

Bolan prodded Cao toward the car, then into the passenger seat. Walking around to the driver's side, where Quang fumbled with his seat belt, Bolan poked the Beretta into his temple. "I want a five minute lead. You stay here until we're out of sight. We're going to back out of here, so I'll be able to keep an eye on you. Got it?"

Quang nodded. "I understand."

Bolan walked backward to the rented Oldsmobile, keeping the Beretta trained on Quang. "All right, Margot, let's get the hell out of here."

The car was already running, and she threw it into reverse, backing down the hill with the skill of an Indy driver. Once they'd cleared the first turn, Margot stopped the vehicle. "Let's see how seriously they take us," she said. After a minute, she seemed satisfied and resumed the backward descent. Around the second curve, she stopped again, reaching into her handbag for a small black box, roughly the size of a compact.

It was unadorned, save for a small green button at its center. Watching her long fingers handle the mysterious box, Bolan was fascinated by the colorful contrasts of her meticulously done red nails with the bright green button. The long, almost serpentine fingers accentuated the miniature tableau.

She seemed to hesitate a second, then shrugged. She pressed the button. A fireball blossomed among the trees, sharp yellow and dull orange quickly fading to black, leaving only a broad column of gray smoke to waft up among the trees and on into the rainy sky.

Bolan looked at Margot in amazement. Never in his life, not even in his own mirror, had he seen a more baleful smile. Raising her right hand, thumb prominently extended over her right shoulder, Margot said, "Strike three. You're outta there."

15

Bolan picked up the phone reluctantly. He started to dial, but his fingers felt thick, as if the phone itself were trying to tell him something. He replaced the receiver in its cradle and looked around the hotel room, wondering what his life had come to, wondering whether he'd made a wrong turn somewhere along the way. Thinking back to the beginning of his lonely crusade, the rudeness of its start, the cruelty that prompted it, he sighed.

Breathing deeply, his head spinning just the least little bit, he stared at himself in the mirror, its phony gilt frame an echo of a hundred similar glasses, and he saw a shadow in the heart of a void. The shadow, he knew, was himself. The void was...what? His life? His purpose...or lack of one? Who knew? The life he had chosen seemed destined, with almost Biblical inevitability, to end as violently as it had begun. The things that fueled it, courage, a rage for justice, a passionate hatred for the oppression of savage beasts who had no more compunction than a shark at rending human flesh, with their guns and knives, bombs and rockets, seemed like an exercise in futility. On a grand scale, certainly, but when the end came, and the bullet destined to put an end to his crusade finally found him, what would be left behind?

Wearily Bolan ran a hand across his eyes, pressing fingers tightly against the lids. He saw the bright fire of phosphenes and shook his head to extinguish them. Then he picked up the phone again, this time ignoring that part of himself that didn't want to make the call.

When the call went unanswered, Bolan hung up. He'd tell Brognola about it when he came back.

If he did.

Bolan drew the plastic chair close to the table that held his weapons and sat down. As he cleaned his guns, he realized it was nearly impossible to anticipate what was to transpire during the next few days. The war, so long off the front pages, was part of what he was. Memories of the horror of Vietnam simmered beneath the surface of his consciousness. Flashes, bright green, the sound of a chopper, could bring it back. He knew about the adjustment problems of his fellow veterans, understood the pain they suffered. And he realized how he had dealt with his own—how he continued to deal with it. Bolan was fortunate—if one could use that word—in having an outlet for all those unresolved conflicts that was denied his fellow veterans.

He hated to read the papers when some guy lost control. How many times had he seen the words Deranged Viet Vet in print, as if they were as inseparable as q and u? And when did you ever see Deranged Korean Vet, or Berserk Conscientious Objector? The plain fact was that the war wasn't over, no war ever was for those who had managed against the odds to go through hell and out the other side. Vietnam was, if anything, worse than all American wars before it—with the possible exception of the Civil War—in that the transition was too abrupt, brutally so, and the real world into which you were thrust, in as little as twenty-four hours, had no use for you.

But the Executioner was going back. He wondered how he would react to having the jungle close over him again, feel the heat, hear the incessant hum of insects, like the sound of a dynamo keeping the world alive. And then he knew he couldn't possibly anticipate it. It would happen, and he would know.

Whether he wanted to or not.

The pungent fragrance of gun oil filled his nostrils, like a narcotic made just for him, and the smell of cordite was gradually overwhelmed by the light oil.

He finished the Beretta 93-R, then wiped it clean before reassembling the parts and slipping it into its holster. As Bolan stood to put on the shoulder rig he heard a gentle rap on the door. He wasn't expecting anyone. He kept well to the left as he approached the door, so he could reach out and grab the knob without exposing himself to sudden fire.

"Who is it?"

The soft voice said something almost inaudible. It sounded like "room service." He wasn't expecting any.

"I didn't order anything."

"Open up! It's me!"

He sighed and opened the door.

Margot stood in the doorway, framed by two suitcases. She lifted them easily and sidestepped through the narrow doorway. Once inside, she dropped them with a thud and turned to face her surprised host.

"Going on a trip?" he asked.

"Uh-huh."

"Where?"

"Where do you think?"

Bolan stepped back. "You can't be serious."

"Absolutely."

"You're talkative tonight."

"Just dispensing with the pointless in order to get to the essential. How's the bed?"

"Like a rock."

"Good, it's better for my back, yours too."

"What do my bed and your back have to do with each other?"

"What do you think?" Margot sat on the bed, bouncing once or twice as if to test his assessment. "Come on, sport, hurry up. We only have all night."

She pulled the zipper down the front of her black silk jumpsuit with one hand, and reached for the light with the other. In the darkness, she was just a dim outline on the stiff white chenille.

Bolan didn't mind.

THE MORNING LIGHT WOKE HIM. Margot, one arm draped over her eyes to ward off the glare, still slept. Bolan rose carefully, closed the bathroom door and showered. When he stepped out of the bathroom, swathed in steam, Margot was sitting up in bed, the sheet drawn up over her breasts.

"Good morning," she said, stretching her arms over her head. The gesture caused the sheet to slip down, and Bolan grinned.

"It's getting better all the time."

"What time's the flight?"

"Ten o'clock."

"And what time is it now?"

"Too late for what you have in mind."

"Shucks."

"Midwestern girl, huh?"

"Iowa."

Bolan looked at her, his head cocked to one side.

"Don't ask."

"What?"

"How'd a nice girl like me, et cetera, et cetera...."

"Some day you tell me yourself, when you're ready."

"I promise."

"You better get dressed. I'll put you in a cab."

"Like hell."

"Why not?"

"I'm going with you."

Before he could argue, Margot charged in. "You think I always bring two suitcases for one-night stands? I don't need that much makeup. In case you haven't noticed."

"I've noticed. But you can't go."

"Give me one good reason."

"It's ridiculous."

"I can help."

"I don't need help."

"Like hell."

"Look, Margot, I appreciate the offer. But I can move faster alone."

"I'm a professional...and don't you dare say anything." She raised her fist in mock anger.

Bolan sat beside her on the edge of the bed. "Margot, look. I don't have any idea what I'm getting into, and I don't want anything to happen to you."

"I'm a big girl, Mack. And I can take care of myself, in case you forgot. Besides, there's nothing you can do about it."

Bolan stood, his back to her. She reached tentatively for him, then dropped her hand when she realized it was the wrong approach. Logic would convince him, or he couldn't be convinced at all. She was certain of that.

Without facing her, Bolan said, "How could I justify it to myself if anything happened to you?"

"That it was bad luck, that I was too slow, that I was too smart for my own good…that you'll miss me. I don't know. But, nothing will happen. At worst, I'm not a liability. You know that. And I think I can help. I've been to the Far East before."

"Not where I'm going."

"Oh yes I have. I did two tours as a nurse in Nam. Nothing you'll see there is new to me. I have a little bit of Vietnamese, and I can pull my own weight. What have you got to lose?"

Bolan turned, reaching for her shoulder. The big hand rested lightly on her skin, and she looked at it as if a rare butterfly had just landed on her arm.

"All right."

"You won't be sorry."

"I hope you're right."

"I know I'm right." She tossed the sheet aside and stood, pressing herself full-length against him. He wrapped her in his arms for the briefest of instants, feeling his blood rise as her breasts flattened against his chest. The pounding in his ears was deafening.

Looking over her shoulder, he admired her form in the mirror. The long tapered legs, the slender waist and broad, almost powerful shoulders. He liked what he saw.

16

Margot dropped back into her seat. It was her third trip to the rest room since the flight began. Bolan eyed her curiously.

"Nervous?" he asked.

"Not until now." Margot smiled. "I think we have unexpected company. Don't turn around now, but go to the head in a few minutes and see what you think."

"What've we got?"

"Two Viets, business-suit types, apparently, but I'm not sure. They don't look comfortable."

She snuggled down in the seat, tucked her legs up under her and closed her eyes. "I think I'll get some rest. I didn't sleep much last night."

"Oh, really? I didn't notice."

Margot didn't say anything, settling for an elbow carefully planted in his ribs. She didn't apologize. Bolan twisted a bit in his seat, restless, now that Margot had raised the possibility they were already being followed.

Stalling, as Margot had suggested, Bolan studied her face. In repose, it was more striking, as if some aspect of her personality, consciously suppressed, were allowed to come out for a little fresh air. The bones of her finely sculpted cheeks were high and prominent, giving her a hint of Amerind. The skin, too, seemed more exotic,

taking color from the bone structure. He had known she
was beautiful.

It hurt to look at her. Thinking of other women he'd
allowed himself to get close to, to care for, to care *about*,
always tinged him with melancholy. They were all gone,
in one way or another, from his life. Margot, too, would
soon be a painful memory. He knew it as surely as she
seemed not to. There was no room in his life for that kind
of vulnerability. The more you cared, the tougher it was.
And the danger, either to himself or to the woman, was
elusive, but incalculable.

When a reasonable time had passed, he squeezed her
hand and stood in the aisle. As he moved toward the rear
of the plane, he tried hard to control his curiosity about
his fellow passengers, looking, instead, like a vacationer
more interested in the limitless expanse of clouds sliding
beneath the giant wings of the 747.

Two rows from the rear bulkhead, in the right-hand
section of seats, Bolan spotted the men Margot had
meant. They had their faces buried in newspapers, yet
talked softly to each other. They seemed uninterested in
the papers, using them more as a screen than reading
matter. Bolan eyed them casually across the center section of seats, then moved up the left aisle to the rest
room. Stepping inside, he locked the door and turned on
the water.

Quang had not tried that hard to conceal his knowledge of Colonel Griffith. Maybe he'd thought to alert the
colonel that Bolan was on the way, but Margot hadn't
given him the chance. That meant the information was
either false or that it was intentionally given to him as
part of an earlier plan. There was, of course, a third
possibility—perhaps the two men following him were not
connected to Quang or Griffith at all, perhaps they were

working for someone else altogether. But that was a can of worms too large to be opened now, and until he learned something to the contrary, he'd assume they were Quang's, and, ultimately, Griffith's goons.

He splashed some cold water on his face and wiped his face and hands with a couple of paper towels from the dispenser. Regardless of whom the two reported to, they were on the plane. There was nothing he could do about it now. In this most complex of all possible worlds, their presence was just one more wrinkle to be dealt with.

THE PLANE TOUCHED DOWN with a jolt. The pilot reversed his engines, and the plane shuddered as it bounced over the asphalt strips in the concrete runway. Much of its grace gone, the 747 lumbered clumsily toward the terminal. Don Muang Airport was as modern and antiseptically impersonal as any major international air terminal. Bangkok was thriving, and the relative tranquility of Thailand when compared to her neighbors made it a major transcontinental business center. Don Muang reflected that.

Debarking to the usual inanities from the flight crew, Bolan took Margot by the elbow and steered her quickly through the throng waiting to meet arriving passengers. He was still uncertain about the men apparently following them, and the only way to eliminate those doubts was to force them to show their hand.

Hustling across the huge, high-ceilinged terminal's tile floor, he headed for the escalator that led to the baggage carousels. As they drew away from the gates, the crowd thinned out. Jumping onto the slow-moving stairs, Bolan began to walk down them, dragging Margot behind him.

"What's the rush?" she managed to ask.

"I want to see if our friends are in as big a rush as we are."

At the bottom of the escalator, Bolan glanced up at the omnipresent signs, found the arrow he needed and set off in that direction. Halfway down the corridor leading to the baggage area, he ducked into a newsstand, crouching behind a magazine rack and pulling Margot down beside him.

A moment later, the two diminutive shadows sprinted past, each of them watching a side of the corridor, glancing in through the shop windows as they ran. Bolan had seen enough.

"You wait here. If I'm not back in fifteen minutes, meet me at the hotel. We have reservations in the name of Stoneman."

"What are you going to do?"

"I'm not sure. But I think I want to get to know a little bit more about our fellow passengers." Bolan was twenty yards behind the two men. As they entered the baggage claim area, the Vietnamese split up and made a circuit of the huge room. Bolan stood at one corner of the arched entrance, watching them. He ducked behind a rack of paperbacks standing outside a smoke shop, averting his face from the men, who stood scanning the room, paying particular attention to each cluster of new entrants.

They seemed to be running out of patience. At long range, Bolan was able to distinguish them only by the difference in hairstyles, one affecting a late-sixties, long, straight cut, while the other wore his hair closely cropped, almost military in its severity.

Bolan, unlike many Occidentals, did not believe all Orientals looked alike. He had known too many, good and bad, to be so blind. And his close pass while still on the plane had etched the features of each clearly on his brain. The longhair was, paradoxically, the older of the two, maybe stuck in the sixties like the aging hippies so noticeable on the streets of America's large cities, now that the tide of hair had receded and style had become more varied, less emblematic of politics.

The younger man also moved with more precision. That he had done time in some form of disciplined organization was beyond question. Where and for whom were the questions that most interested the big American.

As the luggage started to pour through the dangling rubber ribbons from the receiving area onto the pickup carousels, the men concentrated their attention on the bags. Baggage from the incoming flight was concentrated on one carousel, and the two men moved in among the crowd gathering around it. They seemed to be as interested in the bags as they had been in locating him. His height made it difficult for Bolan to get too close, but as the area filled up, he crept closer.

Moving into the rearmost fringes of the crowd, he spotted Margot's red suitcase emerging from the rubber strips, then sliding down the polished metal shoot to the revolving wheel. A moment later, his bag appeared. The younger Vietnamese nudged his older companion, indicating Bolan's bag.

They spoke to each other, shuffling impatiently as the wheel made its big, slow turn. Bolan stepped closer. The younger man leaned forward, snatching Margot's bags as they reached him. The other man got a firm grip on the handle of Bolan's bag. As he started to tug it from the carousel, the warrior grabbed both men around the neck from behind, squeezing tightly.

"Those are mine," he hissed. "Take them off the carousel and set them down. Now!"

The Vietnamese did as they were told, setting the bags gently on the apron beside the carousel. "There's one more, a blue one," the younger Vietnamese said.

"We'll wait for it."

Neither man struggled in his grasp, and Bolan began to wonder what was going on. When the blue bag appeared, he allowed the man on his right to bend and yank it from the wheel.

"All right, let's go someplace where you can tell me who you are and what you want with my luggage."

Letting them go, Bolan watched as they obediently picked up the remaining three bags. As they pushed through the crowd, they said nothing, either to each other or to him, and made no attempt to break free.

At the claim gate, Bolan showed his tickets, and the three of them passed through the turnstile under the indifferent eye of the attendant.

Bolan pointed to a small alcove and lounge where the rest rooms were located, and they walked silently toward it. The lounge was vacant, and the men were directed to set the bags on the floor.

Neither man gave Bolan an argument as he patted them down. As he expected, neither was armed. The security at Kennedy was too tight for someone to get a gun through, and neither man seemed to be carrying anything more lethal than a fountain pen.

When he had finished, Bolan directed them to sit on the Naugahyde bench in front of him.

"Obviously you know who I am. That gives you a temporary advantage. Who are you?"

It was the younger man who spoke. "I am Tran Can Giap, and my associate is Pierre Minh Bo."

Bolan raised an eyebrow. "Pierre?"

"My mother was French," the older man explained.

"And what do you find so absorbing about me?"

"We know why you have come to Thailand. We are prepared to offer our assistance."

"I don't need assistance. And what makes you think you know why I'm here?"

Ignoring the question, the younger man withdrew a pack of cigarettes from his jacket pocket. "Do you mind if I smoke?" When Bolan nodded acquiescence, the man tapped a cigarette from the pack, then took a lighter from his pocket. He flicked it once, then again. The small wheel sparked, but refused to light the butane. "I should give it up, anyway. It's no more than another example of Western decadence."

Bolan now knew with whom he was dealing. At least now they were getting somewhere. Something sharp stabbed into his shoulder. The sting vanished almost immediately. He reached to the shoulder, turning as he did so. His fingers brushed feebly at a small, hollow dart embedded in the material of his jacket. He felt groggy and started to fall to the floor.

The two Vietnamese caught him and lay him gently on the clean tiles of the lounge. The younger man leaned over him, his face expressionless. "Don't worry, Mr. Bolan. We mean you no harm."

17

Margot never could follow orders. Restless waiting for Bolan's return, she checked her watch, dutifully counting the minutes. At thirteen she'd waited long enough. She left the newsstand and walked rapidly toward the baggage-claim area. By the time she reached the carousel, she was nearly sprinting.

Skidding to a halt, Margot ducked in behind a book rack and surveyed the carousels. Bolan wasn't there. Neither were the two Vietnamese. Small knots of people stood around each of the revolving wheels, but the crowd had thinned enough that she could tell her quarry was not among them.

Racing into the nearest ladies' room, Margot entered a stall, sat on the toilet and opened her purse. Piece by piece—and with purpose—she went through her small makeup bag, her wallet and the jumble of items at the bottom. Five minutes later, she had a fully assembled Glock .45-caliber automatic in her hands, a little dusty, but functional nonetheless.

It had taken more than a little ingenuity to conceal the metal parts among other metal pieces, in some cases hiding them inside, in others merely combining two or three with the clutter of lipstick, nail clippers and loose change. It had been enough to fool the X-ray machine at JFK.

The masterstroke had been the ten-shot magazine and the ammunition. Lining a vibrator with sheet metal and slipping the loaded magazine inside to replace the working parts, she had managed to eliminate the telltale contours. She played a hunch that no security guard alive, man or woman, would take too close a look at such a device in public.

Margot smiled as she rammed the clip home. Stuffing the Glock back in her purse, she let the stall door bang shut behind her and pushed out into the corridor. It was less busy than it had been, and the desultory traffic was easily scanned. Poking her head back into the carousel area, she noticed a man standing in the doorway of a lounge off to the right. Before it fully registered what he was doing, he had raised the tranquilizing gun and fired.

Margot padded softly across the floor, her joggers almost noiseless on the polished tile. The man who had fired the dart stepped into the lounge. Margot veered to the left and raced to the wall. No one seemed to notice her, just as no one but she had seemed to notice the gunner. Pressing flat against the wall, trying to appear casual all the while, she crept along it until she was two feet from the lounge entrance. From her angle, she couldn't see what was going on, and the hurried conversation—in whispered Vietnamese—was just a low mumble. She could hear nothing.

Stifling the impulse to barge in, Margot took a deep breath. Before doing anything, she at least had to know the odds. For all she knew, the target of the gunner hadn't even been Bolan. She watched the carousels spin while she tried to glean a few words of the conversation. Neither her bags nor her companion's were anywhere in sight.

She couldn't stay where she was all day, and there was no point in leaving until she knew what had happened in the lounge. Turning her back to the people in the claim area, she pulled the Glock out of her purse. With its plastic shell, it didn't look like much more than a toy, but the stopping power of a .45-caliber slug was unaffected by such perceptions.

Dropping into a crouch, Margot stepped into the doorway, brandishing the automatic before her in a two-handed grip. Sweeping the lounge with her eyes, the first thing she noticed was Bolan sprawled on the floor, two men leaning over him almost tenderly. A third man, the one who had fired, stood with his back to the entrance.

"Sit down, gentlemen. We have a few things to discuss," Margot said. She was conscious of a quaver in her voice, but the three startled Vietnamese seemed intent only on the ugly little weapon in her fist. Gesturing with the gun, she waved them away from the unconscious Bolan.

Cautiously, as if afraid a sudden move might have a sympathetic effect on Margot's trigger finger, the three men raised their hands to shoulder height and stood in a row. Bolan lay between them and her. She waved them back and knelt beside him, shifting her grip on the Glock to one hand, and reaching for Bolan's throat with the other.

She never took her eyes off the three men. The steady throb under her fingers was reassuring. She stood and backed toward a wall of the lounge, stopping only when she felt its steady pressure against her.

"Sit down," she ordered, a little louder than she had intended.

The Vietnamese looked at one another, then did as they were told.

The youngest man, who seemed to be the leader of the trio, said, "We meant no harm."

"I can see that. I guess it's just an old Vietnamese custom to drug a total stranger when visiting foreign capitals."

"Mr. Bolan is no stranger, Miss Blaine."

"Oh?" Baffled by the entire scene, Margot wasn't sure what to say or do next. "Do you have an antidote for whatever you used to knock him out?"

"Of course."

"Then give it to him."

"Here?"

The tallest of the three, the one who had used the tranquilizer gun, glanced to his superior for direction. The latter nodded, and he reached into his jacket. "Easy, now," Margot warned, pointing the gun at him. "This little baby has some unpredictable side effects you don't want to know about."

The man reassured her with open palms, then slowly withdrew a small leather pouch. He unzipped it with a crisp jerk of his delicate hands, and it fell open. A small syringe, some disposable needles and three rubber-topped ampoules lay snugged under small leather bands.

"You even think about using the wrong stuff, and, so help me, they'll need a month to clean your brains off the wall. Understood?"

The man nodded. He fitted a needle to the syringe, then tilted the pouch to insert the needle into one of the ampoules, not bothering to remove it from the pouch. He drew several cc's of a pale yellow fluid into the syringe, then pressed the plunger to force the air out. A small rainbow of the yellow fluid arced from the needle.

"I don't want to risk an embolism with so volatile a nurse in attendance."

He knelt beside Bolan, yanked the sleeves of his jacket and shirt up to the elbow and sought a vein in the prostrate man's forearm. "This should do nicely," he said. Deftly he inserted the needle, injected the fluid and removed the hypodermic, pressing the small cotton ball to the puncture.

"How long do we have to wait?" Margot demanded.

"A few minutes, no more than that."

Margot nodded.

"Now, why don't you tell me what the hell is going on here?"

"We wanted to talk to Mr. Bolan," the young, crew-cut leader said.

"You have a funny way of striking up a conversation."

"The discussion was...sensitive. We could not do it here."

"You people ever hear of a coffee shop?"

They stared at her blankly.

"What do you mean?" the crew cut asked. If he wasn't as puzzled as he seemed, Hollywood was missing a sure thing.

"You introduce yourself, ask for a few minutes of his time and go sit down in the coffee shop. You order coffee or a Coke, or whatever you drink, and you talk. Very simple, really. Very...civilized. No needles necessary."

Margot snapped her jaw shut. The look on her face foreclosed further conversation. She stared at the three men, arrayed in decreasing height from right to left. They looked like some bizarre parody of the see-no-evil monkeys. The deep black eyes had seen more than their owners could ever tell.

Bolan groaned. For a few seconds his limbs convulsed, then he lay still. Margot stepped forward, dropping to one knee again to feel for his pulse. It was as strong and steady as before. She felt his head move, and he struggled to sit up. Firmly, in that finely tuned nononsense way of hers, she pressed him back to the floor.

"Give yourself a couple of minutes, Mack. Don't sit up just yet. Everything's under control."

"What happened?" His voice was barely recognizable. His tongue felt thick, his mouth coated with a pasty film. He was thirsty.

"A few friends from the East wanted to introduce themselves."

"My head feels like it's split open."

"You see, I told you," the tallest Vietnamese said. "Headache is a normal reaction to the antidote."

Margot glared at him. "You got any aspirin in that little bag of yours?"

"It will not help. The headache will go away in a few minutes."

"It better," Bolan growled.

He shook his head vigorously, but the pain shot through his skull like ricocheting .22 slugs, then zipped down along the back of his neck. He lay back, covering his eyes with one hand.

Margot stood, backing to the wall again. Her concern for Bolan was interfering with her concentration. She didn't want to get careless, now that they were almost in the clear. As soon as the big guy was able to walk, they could get the hell out of the lounge. It was only then that she noticed their luggage on the floor by the other bench.

Bolan sat up, and Margot walked back to the middle of the room. "You feel well enough to watch these guys for a minute?"

"Yeah."

"Good." Margot handed him the Glock. He looked at it and smiled at her.

"You think of everything, don't you?"

"All the time."

Margot went to her baggage and unlocked the combination lock on the larger bag. She reached inside and pulled out a small automatic. It was a Smith & Wesson .32, with an 8-shot magazine, and a stubby suppressor already screwed in place.

As she closed the bag, Bolan got to his knees then struggled to stand up. He almost lost his balance, and one of the Vietnamese dashed forward to catch him by the arm. Margot fired once at the wall, the impact of the slug louder than the weapon's discharge.

"Stay where you are," she grated. "The next one will be for real."

"I only wanted to help," the man explained. "I thought he was going to fall."

"I'm okay," Bolan said. "I think we should go someplace and talk."

"How about the coffee shop," the crew cut suggested, glancing at Margot.

"That'll do."

Like a bizarre United Nations parade, they marched into the coffee shop of the airport terminal. Margot ordered coffee for them all before joining them at a corner booth.

"All right." Bolan's voice was quiet, but Margot noticed the undertone of high voltage. "You wanted to talk. Make it quick. And it better be good."

"As you know, Mr. Bolan," the crew cut said, "plain speaking is not a habit in the Orient. But out of respect for the immediacy of your concern, which, not coincidentally, is identical to our own, I'll be direct."

"I'd appreciate it," Bolan snapped. "You can start by telling me who you represent."

Crew cut looked at his two companions. "The Democratic Republic of Vietnam." He paused for effect, but Bolan remained impassive. When it was evident there would be no response, the man continued. "It is our understanding that you are interested in Colonel Thomas Griffith."

"Go on."

"We would like to lend our assistance."

"No thank you." Bolan's jaw snapped like a bear trap.

"But why? We want the same thing."

"I wish I could believe that."

"You can."

"What's in it for you?"

"Two things. First, the elimination of a source of illicit heroin, a plague to which my people is no more immune than your own."

"And the second?"

"A faction within my government is, at least indirectly, involved with Griffith."

"Indirectly?"

"At least. If they are not directly benefitting in financial ways, they are using him for their own ends."

"I don't follow you."

"It is quite simple, really. By allowing Griffith to continue his operation unimpeded, they have a source of unbudgeted revenue to pursue their own adventures and to ensure their own continuation in power."

"That is of no concern to me. Internal politics, or international politics, for that matter, are totally beside the point. I have my own reasons for wanting Griffith eliminated. I don't care to discuss them with you, and I don't care to continue this discussion any longer. Good day, gentlemen." Bolan stood abruptly, taking Margot by surprise, as well as the Vietnamese.

"I am sorry you feel that way."

"Ever since I started looking into this mess, I've been tripping over Vietnamese. I haven't bothered to ask any of them their political philosophy. It is irrelevant to me. As is your offer of assistance. I will handle this in my own way."

"If you should change your mind . . ."

"I won't!" Bolan grabbed his bag and was out the door before Margot managed to slide out from behind the table. She rushed after him, not certain he had made the right decision.

She was even less certain how to suggest that possibility to him. If he gave her an opening, she'd be ready, but she doubted it would matter.

She wondered whether he might be tunnel blind. Perhaps it was too personal a matter. That was bad enough.

Worse still, it might get him killed.

18

Bangkok was a blend of contraries. Bolan remembered the teeming markets and the traffic threatening to overwhelm the streets with its clamor and choking exhaust. Through it all, pedicabs managed to zip along, swerving in and out like a halfback in broken-field drill. Imminent contact, time and again, was averted by the narrowest of margins.

The worst aspect of the snarl, for a man in Bolan's position, was the immobility. Trapped in a cab or stuck behind the wheel of a rental car, you were a choice target. Shooting fish in a barrel would seem like competition shooting for an assassin in the back seat of a small Honda or Kawasaki. Like the Parisian and Roman punks who hired themselves and their guns to the highest bidder, the hit kids of Bangkok knew that maneuverability was the highest virtue. Fifty bucks or fifty thousand, it was all the same, useless as a pocketful of small change, if they nailed your ass.

But a bike gave you the speed and mobility to split the tangled traffic like Alexander cutting his knot. It was simple, direct and total. If you did it right, nobody would bat an eye, taking the small spit, if they heard it at all, for a balky carburetor or a leaky muffler.

This evening, Bolan was going to a part of the city where every shadow might be the one to split your skull or slip a razor-sharp blade between your ribs. The down scale avenues of nighttime Bangkok were no place for the squeamish. Its underbelly was as bloated and rotten as that of any major city. Add the mazelike wilderness of narrow, winding streets, alleys and blind courtyards, and you were asking for trouble.

Bolan, togged in black, hurried through the unlit back alleys, blending with the shadows. He traveled on foot, in this city the only way to go. Jimmy Rogers was an old friend, but he'd fallen on hard times. His address was all the proof Bolan needed. But if you wanted something, anything, in a hurry in Bangkok, Jimmy was the man to see. If he didn't have it and couldn't get it, you were out of luck. Nobody got things quicker, and with fewer questions asked, than Jimmy. And what Bolan needed was best left unquestioned altogether. If the price was right, Bolan would have it by morning.

Moving into the shadows of an alley, little more than a slit between two shuttered vegetable stands, Bolan slipped into the first doorway he passed. He'd been hearing slight noise behind him for several blocks, as though someone was in stealthy pursuit. Casual glances over his shoulder had so far proved fruitless. If anyone *was* tailing him, the guy was little more than the sound of a pair of rubber soles whispering in the neon-splattered dark.

The far end of the alley was a dull red rectangle. Suddenly it was gone. Somebody had followed him into the narrow passageway and was none too cautious about it. Bolan pressed back into the doorway. The whispering rubber soles were hissing now, sibilant in the quiet. Faint street noise from the late-night crowds on the main avenues drifted in, like signals from a distant star. Against that background, the pursuer's shoes were deafening. Bolan slipped the Beretta from its holster, thumbed off the safety and waited. A round already chambered.

The blocky shadow, faltering slightly, drifting from side to side in the narrow alley, drew closer. Its pace was steady and its form was indeterminate. It could have been a man or a woman. Shapeless and arhythmic, it drew ever closer, still seemingly unconcerned about the possibility of discovery. Raspy breathing hissed against the dirty blocks lining the alley, the rough edges of the sound sharpened on the soft stone, cutting through the night like an unsteady saw.

The shadow was big, and not more than ten feet away when it stopped. Bolan could now see clearly enough to tell it was a man, dressed in a dirty naval uniform. It was unfamiliar and much the worse for wear. The sailor mumbled something, weaving unsteadily on his feet. He started to move, seemed to lose his balance, then tripped and bounced off the far wall. He fell to one knee, scraping at the brick with his nails as he struggled to regain his feet.

Bolan was beginning to breathe a little easier. The guy seemed harmless enough. The warrior started a count and, on reaching ten, was about to step into the center of the alley when another shadow appeared at its mouth. In quick succession, two more shadows joined the first. Bolan pressed back into the doorway. The three newcomers were keeping well back against the wall, avoiding the center of the alley as if they feared being targets for someone or something they believed lay waiting in the darkness ahead of them.

The sailor seemed oblivious to them, still mumbling as he tried to pull himself up. The front-runner reached the man, now prostrate on the damp, paper-littered pave-

ment of the alley. His back was against the wall, and he
continued to mumble incoherently. The first shadow
knelt and shook the sailor roughly by the shoulder. A
burst of profanity, slurred and nearly unintelligible, was
the only response.

The remaining two men, short and slender like their
precursor, had remained several yards back, closer to the
mouth of the alley. At a signal from their leader, they
moved cautiously forward, their feet gliding soundlessly
over the damp alley. A small rivulet, a fluid of some unknown origin, ran down the center of the alley, which
sloped away from the wall on either side. Bolan didn't
care to speculate on the source of the small stream,
knowing sanitation was a low priority in most of Asia
and was inefficient at best, even in the most modern
cities, once you got away from the main tourist areas and
enclaves of the wealthy. The deeper you probed into the
bowels of the cities, the closer to the surface seeped raw
sewage. The scent assaulting Bolan's nostrils told him
more than he cared to know about the shallow stream in
the alley's deepest part. Here and there it glistened dull
red, taking its color from the mouth of the alley, and
rippling like cold liquid fire.

The three men stepped past the drunken sailor and
moved ahead, fanning out like fox hunters drawing close
to their prey. Bolan wondered at his good fortune. If it
hadn't been for the seaman, he might have ignored the
threat that came creeping along behind him. These guys
were as silent as the night.

They were abreast of him now, and Bolan flattened
himself against the hard wooden door behind him. The
metal handle dug into his ribs, and Bolan shifted un-
comfortably, the Beretta cocked and ready. The slight
sound had been enough. The nearest man wheeled and

flicked his arm out, like the tongue of a lizard casually snapping at a fly. Bolan ducked instinctively, just under the *thunk* of something hard burrowing into the wood where his shoulder had been. The knife twanged, singing its deadly song with the cold clarity of a tuning fork, until the vibration died, swept away by the clatter of the Beretta, and it jarred loose as the Executioner's forearm struck the edge of the hard brick wall of the doorway.

Bolan cannoned into the man, knocking him to the ground and rolling over into the seemly dampness at the center of the alley. Another of the hit men sought a target as Bolan got to his knees, balanced precariously on the chest of his struggling would-be assassin. Then he drove his right hard into the face of his opponent. The fist plopped wetly into soft flesh, crunching hard into the bone beneath. The nose, now smeared like a dark plum across the man's face, bled profusely.

Bolan dived to one side as the spit of a suppressed automatic hissed off the wall. The slug slammed into the prostrate hitter, who groaned once, then shrieked in pain. The gunner fired a second time, deliberately aiming at his fallen comrade to quiet him. The ugly splat of the slug smashing through bone and brain sounded final in the dark alley.

Bolan rolled to the base of the wall. He reached for Big Thunder, felt the butt of the .44 and tugged. The gun was jammed into his hip, pinned by his weight. The gunner spun around, looking for his quarry. A sudden explosion tore open the desperate silence, and the gunner pitched forward, facedown, landing in the polluted gutter. Puzzled by the blast, Bolan didn't waste time trying to figure out where it had come from. He rolled, hauled the AutoMag out and up, flicking the safety off with his thumb. He drew a bead on the third man.

Before he could squeeze the trigger, another blast slammed into the third assassin, knocking him forward. This time Bolan saw the flash. The sailor, scrambling to his feet, rushed forward, stood over the man and brought his foot down on the back of his neck. With a sudden pressure, he forced the neck down until the sharp crack of a vertebra sent a sudden spasm through the fallen man. The splayed legs rose slightly off the ground, shivered a second, then went limp.

"Slimy bastard," the sailor mumbled.

Bolan brought the AutoMag to bear on the suddenly sober sailor. The seaman waved casually with his left hand, tucking a squat, chrome-plated automatic back into his loose-fitting tunic.

"You don't need that cannon for me, lad," he said.

"Who the hell are you?" Bolan demanded.

"Oh, never you mind. That makes no difference. The question is, who are these fellas?"

"I suppose you already know."

"I have a good idea. A certain Mr. James Garfield, middle initial A, I believe. No relation, though, in case you were wondering."

"You were waiting for them, weren't you? You knew they would be here..."

"I knew *somebody* would be here. People have been sniffing after you for two days, even before you got here. News travels fast, nowadays." He shook his head, as if baffled by the technology that made it possible. "But what I don't know is why."

"Who sent you? That's my immediate concern," Bolan snapped.

"Jimmy sent me, you bloomin' idjit. Who the hell else?"

"Jimmy Rogers?"

"Himself."

"Why didn't he just warn me?"

"Because there were too many possibilities. Besides, laddie, sensitive sources have to be protected."

"Sensitive sources?"

The seaman waved the question off.

"You took a big chance, laying there like that," Bolan suggested.

"Not really." He whistled shrilly, the harsh sound lancing out into the shadows. A moment later, two men appeared in the mouth of the alley. They sprinted forward, stopping just to the rear of the seaman.

The taller of the two carried a small machine pistol in his left hand. Even in the gloom, Bolan recognized the unmistakable contours of a Skorpion, the finest Czechoslovakian weapon made. It was available by the thousands on the black market and was a favorite of Soviet-bloc assassins.

"Everything all right, Seamus?" The big man's voice seemed to come from the bottom of a well, echoing up from his diaphragm, reverberating among his ribs and emerging as a dull rumble. The accent was flat and vaguely Eastern European. Bolan would have guessed Poland or the Ukraine, if he had to make a choice.

"Fine, me lad, just fine."

"You want us to follow you awhile longer?"

"No, lad, that won't be necessary. I will be just fine now, just fine. I'll call you in the morning. Go on home and get some rest."

The shorter of the two newcomers had said nothing. At Seamus's dismissal, he turned on his heel and was halfway down the alley, when he stopped and turned. "Watch your ass, Seamie."

There was no mistaking the origin of that voice. It had Philadelphia written all over it.

The two men disappeared into the blocky shadows then turned out of the alley and into the dull red hell beyond.

"They're good lads, both of them. But we'll be better off on our own. We can move faster that way. And Mr. Rogers doesn't have too much time tonight. Not even for an old friend like you. We better get a move on."

Bolan nodded but didn't answer. He didn't know quite what to say.

19

"You must be out of your mind."

Bolan sat quietly, letting Jimmy Rogers have his say. The big, raw-boned Irishman was pacing like a hyperkinetic tiger in a cage. His feet were shod in combat boots that shone with light reflected from the ornate chandelier in the center of the room, and they thudded with every step. His khaki shirt—sleeves cut off well above the elbow—strained at its seams. His muscular forearms flailed the air with every word, the tattoos rippling like things alive.

When he had finished, he whirled to face Bolan, as if waiting for applause. It was an impressive display, but Bolan was unmoved.

"Are you finished?" he asked.

"Damn it, Mack, didn't you hear a word I said? My God, man, you don't stand a chance out there. Griffith knows those mountains like the back of his hand. You haven't been up there in a dozen years. It's not like it was. Not at all."

"It doesn't matter. I want him, and I'm going to get him. If you won't help me, I'll have to find someone who will. I'll start with Garfield and work my way back to him somehow."

"Mack, Mack, Mack...." Rogers sat heavily in his battered leather chair, the frame creaking with the sudden weight. "Nobody was fonder of Al Mackenzie than I was. Not even you. And you know that's true. But this is a whole hell of a lot bigger than one man. Griffith has an army out there, and they damn near worship him. I'm not just talking about the hill people, either. He's got about half a dozen Americans, AWOLs and bloodthirsty cutthroats you won't find in the worst ghetto in America. These are guys with nothing to lose, and they like killing people. You hear that? They *like* it. That's why they're with Griffith, and that's why he has them around."

Bolan stood abruptly. "I guess I'll have to look someplace else then, Jimbo. Thanks anyway."

"Hold on Mack, don't go off half-cocked. Now, I didn't say I wouldn't help you. I just want you to know what you're letting yourself in for, that's all. Besides, Garfield is dead. Word is, Griffith blamed him for letting you get this close. And I can't tell you how Byzantine this entire business is. It's more complicated than you can possibly guess."

"I already know how tough it's going to be. What I don't know is whether you're going to make it any easier for me." Bolan sat again, crossing his arms in front of him, settling down to wait until hell froze over, if it took that long for his old comrade to make up his mind.

When Rogers didn't answer immediately, Bolan prodded him. "Are you?"

Rogers let his breath out in a single explosive sigh. "Yes, I'll help. But don't blame me if I don't come to your funeral."

"Don't worry about it, Jimbo. I won't be there, either."

"You son of a bitch. You're crazy, you know that? Crazy as a fucking loon."

"I love you, too, Jimbo."

"You want a beer?" When Bolan nodded, Rogers cracked his palms together, the way an H. Rider Haggard potentate might have done. That was Rogers all the way, playing his fanciful role to the hilt. He didn't need Haggard to give him the idea, because it was probably already deeply ingrained long before he could read. Even now, Bolan wasn't sure Rogers ever opened a book.

But if he got what he came for, it wouldn't matter.

The beaded curtain to Bolan's left clacked as a slender young woman in a red silk dress parted the strands with one delicate arm, then stepped through the opening with a fluid grace.

"Lee Wong, two beers. Chop chop!"

"Jimmy, where the hell do you get that crap?"

"What crap?"

"Chop chop!"

"Hell, I feel like a jerk when I do it, and I sure as hell know I sound like a jerk. But I have an image to live down to. A white man in these parts is *supposed* to sound like that. We all have our stereotypes to conform to. Just because you brought a woman along on this jaunt, doesn't mean I have to embrace the ERA. I have the right to do things the old-fashioned way. And I earned it."

"Since when have you been a sociologist?"

"Ever since I got the hang of making a buck out here. Most of my business is with wide-eyed romantics. They come out here looking for something shady, something with a hint of the illicit. I have to play Sydney Greenstreet for them, or they walk. Hell, I never had much pride to begin with, so it was easy enough to bag the rest of it. The money's good and the work is easy."

The young woman was back before Bolan could offer an argument. He watched her as she poured the beers, her light bronze skin taking on a reddish tint under the bloody glass of the stylized chandelier. When she'd finished, she bowed and left, the beads clattering behind her. And when the room was quiet again, he knew there was no point in arguing with Rogers. Whatever he was, he wasn't a stupid man. If he felt this was the way he wanted to live his life, no argument from Bolan would change his mind. If anything, it might tip Rogers to the wrong side of the fence. He was too important to Bolan's plans to take that risk.

"All right, Mack, let's talk turkey." Rogers lifted his glass, draining half the beer in a single gulp. "What do you need?"

"Not much. I need a chopper and pilot, three dependable men and some weapons."

"The chopper is easy. I'll fly you anywhere you want to go. You know that. What kind of weapons?"

"Nothing too heavy. But I want some real firepower. I want the best bang I can get for my buck. I want some submachine guns—six, I think—plenty of ammo for them. I'll need some plastique, too. I imagine Griffith is dug in pretty tightly out there."

"You got that right. You ought to use a nuke on him and forget about trudging through the jungle. Hell, that's what I'd do."

Bolan smiled. "You never change, do you, Jimbo?"

"Not unless I have to, and I haven't had to for a long time now, Mack. Anyhow, guns and plastique I can get you. The three men, I don't know."

"Any possibilities?"

"Sure. But it'll cost, and I never liked turning my back on hired help. A guy does what he does for money, there's always somebody with more who can buy him. Taking a salary is like advertising you're for sale. The high bidder walks off with him every time."

"If you've got a better idea, I'd love to hear it."

"You mind shaking hands with the devil?"

"I've done it more than once in my life."

"Your nickel, Mack."

"What do you have in mind?"

"I know a few guys who probably want Griffith as bad as you do. I'm sure they'd love to help. I'm also sure their motives are a lot less noble than yours, but if you don't care to be particular, I think you'll be a whole lot better off. And they'll work for nothing."

"How soon can you set it up?"

"You have another beer, and I'll get it done before you're finished."

"Make your call. But hold the beer."

Rogers stared blankly at him for a minute. His face seemed suddenly petrified, as if Bolan were a Gorgon. Then, after the longest minute Bolan could remember, Rogers shook his head as if to toss aside a hypnotic spell and got to his feet with a groan. "Wait here."

When Rogers left the room, parting the beaded curtain with a lot more noise and considerably less grace than his servant, Bolan stared into the dark corners of the room. Even the deepest shadows were tinged red by the ruby glass of the chandelier. The effect was that of a slaughter house that hadn't been hosed down in years. Bolan hoped it wasn't an omen, but nothing about the past week gave him reassurance on that score.

Rogers came back with another swirl of the beads. "It's all set. Get your hat, man, we have to get moving."

"What's the hurry?"

"The men you want to see don't like being seen. They told me where to be. They'll check us out and, if they aren't offended by what they see, will let us know."

"And if they are offended?"

"Most likely we'll never know."

"They'll walk?"

"No. They'll blow us away. Humor is not their long suit. And since there's not much funny about what you propose, it's not too likely we'll offend their tender sensibilities."

Bolan nodded. He tilted the glass back to drain the rest of the beer, then cracked it down on the marble table in front of him. "You driving?"

"No way. We're both walking. Less chance of getting into trouble that way. Besides, I like knowing there's someplace to run."

"Maybe, but you're forgetting one thing, Jimbo."

"What's that, Mack?"

"There's no place to hide."

"Hiding ain't your style, Mack, and it ain't mine, either. I been thinking about this a little. You know, I owe Mackenzie. I'll never get a chance to tell him that, now. And the last time I had the opportunity, I wasn't ready to admit it. I'm not proud of that. But I'll make it up to him somehow, even if he don't know it."

"Then let's go."

Rogers stood stock-still, his head cocked as if listening to a distant sound. Bolan didn't need to be told what was running through the other man's mind. He couldn't count the number of times he'd cocked his own head that way to replay, like a reel from an inexhaustible film library, scenes from a past that seemed simultaneously eternal and all too brief.

"I guess we might as well." Rogers sighed. "But you let me do the talking. I know how to handle guys like this. Two years on the bomb squad does wonders for your antennae. Nothing like knowing the wrong move can turn you into a smear of jelly on the wall to teach you patience."

"I don't have time to be patient."

"You got no patience, then you got no time at all, and even less of a chance to get Griffith. Mack, I'm telling you, the man is wired. And the dudes you're going to meet are about as tight as he is. You make one false move, you're history. Shit, man, we go back a long way. And you were always one of my favorite crazy men. But you want to go out in a puff of smoke, these guys are the ones to see. And by God you won't take me with you. I got a soft gig here. I aim to keep it awhile yet."

Bolan nodded. He understood only too well what Rogers was telling him. He'd already made up his mind. There was no turning back. He needed Rogers, and Rogers knew it.

Just how much it would cost him remained to be seen.

20

Marlowe's Bar and Grill was a nightmare. The phony bamboo facade looked plastic even under the dull green neon announcing the bar's existence. A slab of granite in a Grateful Dead T-shirt leaned against the door frame, arms folded across his chest. When Rogers pushed past, he nodded, and the granite flipped a casual hand before giving Bolan the once-over. Apparently satisfied, he eased back a little for Bolan to pass through, and was already checking the street for the next patron.

Inside, the lighting was even dimmer. The bar, with its full-length mirror framed by flashing lights, gave the entire place the look of a game-show set. Four men, as big as the doorman, worked behind the elevated bar. The room was twice as long as it was wide, its far end featuring a bandstand and small dance floor, the rest crammed with round tables and battered cane-backed chairs.

Marlowe's hummed like a dynamo, dozens of conversations congealing into a dull roar. Rogers pushed through the throng of merchant seamen, bar girls and seamy has-beens, looking for a table.

Finding one with a single chair, he sat down, then leaned back to grab a vacant chair at a nearby table. He shoved it toward Bolan, who sat with his face to the door, which was just visible over the teeming horde.

"What now?" Bolan asked.

"We wait."

"How long?"

"As long as it takes, Mack. If I know these guys, we won't have to wait long." He snaked an arm around the waist of a passing waitress in a skimpy skirt and halter top. "A couple of beers, darlin'."

He slid his palm over her hip, its rough skin rasping on the skintight cloth. She smacked him playfully on the side of the head and disappeared.

"You seem right at home here, Jimbo."

"A man has to have someplace to do his serious drinking. This is where I do mine."

"How do you stand it?"

"Mack, after an hour's serious drinking, you could stand hell, if you had to."

"This place is good practice, I guess."

Before Rogers could answer, a burst of static rumbled through the sound system, and the crowd quieted for a second. Bolan followed the gaze of a number of heads that swiveled to look past him. A band made its way onto the stand. Two Caucasians and three Orientals fumbled with their instruments. The drummer adjusted his stool, accompanying himself with a few snaps of the high-hat. An organ arpeggio and a couple of guitar licks, followed by the crack and rumble of a bass being plugged in, thundered through the crowd.

With no fanfare, the band broke into a raucous rendition of an old Freddy King instrumental. The guitars were loud and overloaded with fuzz and phase shifters, but the musicians were competent. The tune ended abruptly, and an ominous minor-key riff took its place as a tall Oriental woman in jeans and an Elvis Costello T-shirt slipped onto the stage. She closed her eyes, sweeping her shoulders with long, straight black hair, then picked up on the modified reggae rhythm, undulating her hips in slow synch. When she felt the groove, she leaned into the mike, still with eyes closed, and did a passable version of "Watching the Detectives."

Bolan turned back to the door while Rogers continued to ogle the singer, mumbling something about her having big tits for an Oriental girl. Bolan was getting impatient. After glancing at his watch, he tapped Rogers on the shoulder. "I'm giving this five more minutes, then I'm going."

"Mack, you got to be patient. These things take time. We didn't even get our beer yet."

"I didn't come here for a drink."

"It's part of the big picture. Relax. They'll be here. And here comes the beer."

A moment later the waitress was back, a pair of mugs on a small tray in her left hand. She slapped the tray down with practiced nonchalance. "You running a tab, Jimbo?"

"Not tonight, Honey." He stuck a bill in the back pocket of her skirt, letting his hand rest a moment. "You're putting on weight, Honey. You better do something about that. It's crowded enough in here. Maybe you should work out a little."

"How the hell am I going to work out when you assholes won't quit drinking? This place is open twenty-four hours a day, and I'm here more than half that. Besides, I'm not putting on weight."

She grabbed Bolan's wrist and stuck his hand into her other pocket. "That feel fat to you, gorgeous?"

Bolan smiled.

"See," the waitress concluded, "your friend doesn't think so."

"Yeah, yeah. But he doesn't know how good you *used* to look."

"I'll remember that, Jimbo, next time you want a drink on the house." She swaggered off with a toss of her hair and an exaggerated motion of her decidedly trim hips.

Rogers watched her admiringly. Bolan turned away after a moment to look at the door. He tensed almost immediately as a tall man with a sallow, acne-scarred complexion stepped back out of the doorway.

"I think we got company, Jimbo. Better get your mind back on business."

A moment later the acned face reappeared. Like a phantasm, it seemed to float above the crowd, drifting toward them with no apparent effort. Then the rest of him appeared, every bit as gawky and disjointed as the face had suggested. The man was a good six foot seven, and probably didn't weigh much over a hundred sixty pounds. Dressed in camou fatigues, he looked like a caricature. But the eyes weren't funny. Deep, empty holes, they seemed to bore through the ruined face into another part of the universe.

Right behind him a pair of more conventional-looking men, a few years younger and considerably healthier looking, stood in tandem. They sported the same attire as their gaunt companion. But there was something about the two that seemed out of place. There was a softness to them that had nothing to do with their physical appearance, almost effeminate, but not in any overt way. Bolan wondered about the relationship between the two young men and their reedlike mentor.

The tall man nodded, then looked for a chair. He snatched one from a nearby table and sat down like a crane collapsing. "Jimbo, how you been? I was surprised to hear from you. Thought you weren't talking to me no more."

The younger men, at closer range, looked like cherubs on steroids. They positioned themselves on either side of their leader, like a pair of bookends.

"Times change, Garth. Times change."

"They do that...."

"You drinking?"

"You buying?"

Rogers nodded.

"Beer, then."

"All around?"

The squatty bodies nodded in unison.

"I'll get Honey. Hold on a minute."

Bolan sat quietly, Garth staring at him with the detachment of a sated python watching a rat. His eyes went flat, as if he'd completed his appraisal, and only then did the lids blink once. He reached into a flapped pocket on his shirt and removed a pack of cigarettes. He lit it with a slender wooden match from a box tucked into the cellophane wrapper, then let out a long stream of smoke. Everything seemed to echo his physical traits, from the twiglike match to the cigarette and its slender tube of smoke.

Rogers rejoined them, sitting down with a stiff motion that reeked of tension. "Honey'll be here in a minute. Mack, this is Roland Garth. Garth, meet Mack Bolan. He's the straw boss on this gig."

"What's the deal?" Garth addressed the question to Rogers, but his eyes never left Bolan.

"I want Colonel Griffith," Bolan stated flatly.

Garth went pale. Bolan wasn't quite sure of the emotion, but he knew it wasn't fear.

"Why?"

"Does it matter?"

"If you want to meet him, it might. If you want his balls in a jar, not in the least."

"I gather you have no great love for the colonel," Bolan said.

Garth blinked. He took another drag on the cigarette, then ground it in the grubby ashtray on the table. "You could say that. What's your interest?"

"He's responsible for the murder of a good friend."

"How much you paying?"

"Expenses only. You want in, I foot the bills. That's all."

Honey interrupted with the beers, and Rogers paid her. She backed away from the table as if she sensed something deadly lurking in its vicinity, continuing to stare at Garth all the while. Bolan noticed and decided to ask his friend about it later.

"I'm interested."

"Tell me why," Bolan pressed.

"You don't need to know that."

"Like hell."

Garth fidgeted in his chair. His long fingers twitched, and he interlaced them, trying to bring them back under control. "I have my reasons."

"I don't doubt that. What I asked you was what they are."

"I owe the bastard something."

"What?"

"I said you didn't need to know that."

Bolan stood, pushing back his chair with finality. "Then we have nothing to discuss."

He started to walk away, and Garth shot out his right hand, clamping his fingers around Bolan's wrist. The grip was surprisingly strong. Bolan twisted his hand, grabbing the man's wrist in his own fingers. Dispassionately he squeezed until tendons started to hum. Garth let go, rubbing his wrist with his uninjured hand.

"Don't ever grab me like that again."

When one of the muscle boys tried to stand, Bolan rapped him sharply on the skull, and the kid sat down heavily. "Let's go, Jimbo."

Rogers stood, and Garth reached out to grab him, hesitating for just a second, then letting his hand drop. "Wait a minute. All right, all right...sit down, for Christ's sake."

Jimbo dropped back into his chair, but Bolan remained where he was. "I'm listening," the big guy said.

Garth swallowed, then his long tongue slid over his thin lips with a sound like dry leaves in the wind. "This ain't easy, and it ain't for broadcast. Sit down. I'll tell you what you want to know."

Bolan resumed his seat. He stared at the tall man dispassionately and waited.

"Griffith had me court-martialed."

"Why?"

"Rape and murder. Two counts of each."

"Were you guilty?"

"He framed me."

"Were you guilty?"

Garth nodded. "Yeah. But I wasn't the only one. A bunch of guys in the unit were doing it. It was like a game we played. We called it the real body count."

"Griffith knew?"

"Yeah, but he didn't give a fuck. He had his own thing going."

"So why'd he roll over on you?"

"I nailed some broad he had his eye on. Blew her away when he was getting ready to put the blocks to her. He was pissed."

"And he had you court-martialed?"

"Yeah. Five fucking years in the stockade at Fort Benning. Five years, man. I owe the bastard something."

"And what about your choirboys, here?"

"What about them?"

"Where do they fit in?"

"They do what I tell 'em."

Bolan stood again.

"We in, or what?"

"I'll get back to you. Let's go, Jimbo." He turned on his heel and pushed through the crowd. He knew before he got to the door that he was going to use Garth. He had no choice. The thought of it made his stomach turn, but the thought of letting Griffith go was even worse.

He waited for Rogers on the pavement outside. The idea of letting Margot and Garth be swallowed by the jungle in the same gulp was repellant. Margot could take care of herself, of course, but something about Garth gave Bolan the shivers. It wasn't fear, and it wasn't simple revulsion. It was more than that, more like what an unarmed man must feel staring into the flat, unblinking eyes of an angry cobra. The certainty of dispassionate malevolence was unmistakable. And he was going to agree to have it covering his back.

21

The truck jounced through a rutted track, its canvas cover whipped by branches from both sides. Margot, Bolan and Jimmy Rogers sat up front, Garth and his two companions in the rear. All Bolan had been able to learn about the latter was their names, Don and Bruce. It was as much as he cared to know.

The chopper jump into the highlands would be a long haul, near the outer limit of the decrepit Huey's range. Rogers claimed he had a fuel supply at the landing zone, but Bolan wasn't so sure. It had been tough enough to resupply with the entire U.S. Army in line behind you during the war. True, the war was over, at least technically, but it was also a fact that the gargantuan apparatus of war had been disassembled. The sporadically reliable had been replaced by the luck of the draw. And luck was the one thing Bolan hated to rely on. The old axiom about it being the residue of design was never truer than when you found yourself chest high in muddy water with bugs the size of small butterflies strafing your head and shoulders. Throw in accident, ineptitude and outright malevolence, and you had a recipe for disaster, plain and simple.

Bolan was in no mood to tempt fate.

Margot stared in awe through the bug-splattered windshield of the truck. Like Bolan, she had been away too long to remember how bad it really was, and this jungle was, theoretically, peaceful. But everyone in the truck knew the Thai border was an international fiction, about as visible as the equator to anyone who didn't care to see it, and about as impenetrable.

Laotian, Kampuchean and Vietnamese refugees continued to pour through the supposed cordon preserving Thailand's territorial integrity. If you wanted to get through, there was nothing to stop you.

Bolan leaned back against the Plexiglas window between the cab and the cargo bed, but if Garth and the others were talking, they weren't saying much, and it wasn't loud enough to be heard over the roar of the engine. Rogers stopped the truck in a small clearing and stepped out to relieve himself. While he was out among the trees, Margot spoke for the first time since they'd left the staging area.

"I didn't remember how green it was," Margot whispered. "And how quiet it could be." She slid behind the wheel to listen to the rain forest. The birds and monkeys had been silenced by the engine's roar. Everything else that lived there made a practice of keeping silent. If you wanted to eat, or to avoid being eaten, noise was your worst enemy.

"It gives me the creeps," she said, sliding back toward Bolan and wrapping his left arm around her shoulders.

"Sorry you came along?"

"No..."

"But?"

"But I don't like your new friends very much."

"Jimmy's all right. A little rough around the edges, but he's a good man."

"I didn't mean him."

"I know," Bolan said. "But look at it this way. Ever since human beings developed the opposable thumb, they've used whatever came to hand. That's what tools are for. When you're done with them, you put them away."

"Mack, don't be coy. I know all about tools. My grandfather was a carpenter. Even a buzz saw is harmless if you take precautions. But how the hell do you defend yourself against a slug like Garth? And those geeks he has with him! How do you know what not to do?"

"I'm not sure."

"Are you sure it's even possible to be careful?"

"No...."

"Then why?"

"You already know the answer to that question."

Margot slid away from him. She wrapped her arms around herself, shivering despite the heat. "I don't like it, that's all. I'm sorry."

"Don't apologize. I don't like it any better than you do. And as soon as I do what I came here to do, I'll drop him like an empty can. But right now I need him. You don't think that you, me and Jimmy could have done it on our own, do you?"

Margot didn't answer. She didn't have to. They were once again trampling in the muddy ruts of well-traveled terrain. They'd spent half the night going around in circles. And when, on the fifteenth go-round they had still come up with only one answer, she had reluctantly agreed. She resented being backed into a corner by circumstances, but no more than Bolan himself.

He reached out to take her hand, but she resisted, shrinking from his touch. Rogers wrenched open the door before Bolan could ask her to be patient one last time.

Climbing up into the cab, the Irishman sighed. "God, I needed that. I hate like hell to stop out here, too damn many bandits, but nature calls." He shrugged and turned the ignition key, and the grinding of the starter put a stop to any further conversation.

The engine caught, and the truck jerked forward, its huge tires slipping on tall, damp grass in the rutted road. It didn't take long for any unpaved surface to disappear under the wild proliferation of the jungle. Rogers kept his eyes glued to the windshield, knowing a fallen tree or a washout was a likely possibility during the remaining five miles. Despite the laboring engine, progress was slow. The incessant slapping of the leaves and branches was deafening.

Bolan leaned in front of Margot to yell at the nearly comatose driver. "How much longer, Jimbo?"

"Fifteen, maybe twenty minutes. Just keep your shirt on. Not you, Margot."

She nailed him with an elbow, and he laughed. "God, I hate driving in this shit. The only thing worse is doing it in the rainy season. Then, you can't see more than a few yards."

"When's the rainy season?" Margot asked. "I'd forgotten all about that. It should be soon, shouldn't it?"

"Any day now."

The implications of the impending seasonal deluge weren't lost on any of them. But no one wanted to discuss them.

Rogers drove on in silence, the engine struggling to drown out the jungle drumming on the canvas. Five minutes later, he shouted to Bolan, "Should be right up there, around the next bend."

"You sure? I don't know how the hell you can recognize anything in this mess. Half these plants weren't even alive the last time you were out here."

"Mack, me lad, some things you forget at your peril. I been out here too long to let myself forget. Sometimes I think it gets engraved on the brain, like a built-in atlas. You must have been that way when you were out here."

Bolan didn't answer. There was too much truth in his friend's observation to warrant comment. He tried not to remember what it had been like, day after day in the rain and the heat. There had been many times when he felt like nothing more than ambulatory food for whatever cared to rip a piece out of him. The worst was always the night. The flutter and hiss of things in the dark was a noise he'd never forget.

Thinking about it in spite of himself, he stared out the window at the jungle and remembered how every clump of shadow, every trembling leaf, might be the last thing he saw on God's green Earth. Death came in so many varieties, some native to the jungle, some the fiendish fruit of the brains of desperate men. A viper and a punji stake both could kill you. A spider or a claymore mine could spirit your life away in an instant.

But the worst thing had been the uncertainty. There was no innocence and no guilt in the rain forest. Those were pointless judgments made after the fact, long after it ceased to make a difference. The innocent you forgot, the guilty took you by surprise and you never even knew it.

The trembling leaf might conceal a harmless monkey or a man in Goodyear sandals with a Russian rifle in his hands. That small depression in the forest floor might be a place to rest or a place to die. Never had the distinction between momentary and eternal sleep been more elusive.

And then the green hell exploded in flame. Just ahead, a towering tree leaned precariously then swept away everything in its path as it fell to Earth.

"We got trouble," Rogers said, standing on the brakes. "Wake the guys in the back, just in case they didn't hear it."

Bolan ripped the plastic window aside and leaned into the cargo bed. "Somebody blew a tree up front. Grab your weapons, and check the rear."

Garth cursed, and Bolan heard the three men fumbling in the dark for their rifles. Bolan snicked the safety off his M-16 while the Irishman pushed the collapsible windshield forward, where it clattered over the hood. For a moment, Bolan wished he had a Commando, instead of the longer Armalite, but in the trade-off of convenience for accuracy, he'd known what counted most for the coming struggle.

"Bandits, most likely," Rogers guessed. "And probably not too many. They wouldn't bother with the tree, otherwise." A second blast, somewhere to the rear, punctuated the sentence. Bolan looked into the back of the truck and could see the bright green jungle through the unzipped canvas flap. Two dark shapes, one on either side of the opening, must have been Garth's men.

"Garth?" Bolan whispered. "You there?" No one answered. Suddenly two figures darted alongside the passenger door, and Margot screamed. Bolan turned in time to see the flashing arc of a descending machete. He leaned back, crushing Margot back into his friend, who faced the opposite side of the truck. Bolan squeezed, and a tight arc of fire coiled into the short man standing on the running board. His machete flew free, clanging off the hood before it disappeared from view. The green curtain, just behind the would-be assailant, dripped red gore, the blood slowly splashing from leaf to leaf, thinning as it ran, picking up moisture from the leaves.

Bolan slammed the door back and stepped out, his M-16 thrust forward. "Stay here, Margot. Watch Jimbo's back." Then he was gone.

She slid over to the door and jerked it shut. Somewhere behind them, someone cut loose with a blood-curdling scream that terminated abruptly in a harsh gurgle. Bolan looked past the rear of the truck, but saw nothing. Don and Bruce—their puffy shapes giving a whole new meaning to the word *doughboys*—crouched just inside the tailgate and had not yet fired a shot.

Bolan slipped into the forest, then wormed his way toward the blasted tree. He was surprised at how quickly the old reflexes came back. It was as if he'd never left. And then he understood, in a way he never had before, that it was not possible to leave the war behind. To survive it, as he had done, was to carry it on your shoulders forever. Like Atlas groaning under the weight of the world, he, and all those who had fought beside him and were lucky enough to rejoin the World with skins intact, carried the whole freight.

Bolan felt comfortable, at ease... at home. And he hated the way it made him feel.

Dropping to one knee, he tilted his head to get a better look through the jungle, trying to avoid the slashing green swords of light dancing off the leaves and lancing away into the forest. A frond moved, somewhere to the left, and Bolan didn't think twice about firing off a controlled burst through the leaves. A howl of pain confirmed the hit, then a small man in ragged clothing

pitched forward, flashing briefly into view before landing facedown on the mulch-littered floor of the jungle.

Off to the left, a sustained burst of gunfire brought
Bolan running. He waded through the undergrowth, letting his sixth sense take the reins. A minute later, he broke
into a small clearing, and what he saw brought him up
short.

Garth and the two pretty boys stood over a small cluster of corpses, huddled in a bloody mass at the center of
a rough circle. Obviously surprised by Garth, they had
never had a chance. Sickened, Bolan stepped to the perimeter of the massacre, walked around the circle until he
stood alongside Garth. The stick man grinned. He stank
of sweat, the kind of passionate perspiration that comes
from two human activities—sex and the joy of killing. In
Garth's case, they seemed to be one and the same.

Bolan swung the butt of the M-16 up in an arc, catching Garth on the side of the head. The man fell backward, his hand wrapped over the already-swelling knot
on his temple. Quickly Bolan swept around the muzzle of
the carbine to cover the acolytes. They looked back at
Bolan with flat, emotionless faces. It was as if Garth were
a total stranger to them.

"You bastards," Bolan snarled. "I ought to shoot the
three of you."

"Garth said they were bandits."

"They're old men and women. Even a couple of kids.
They're refugees, for God's sake."

"They started it."

"They had nothing to do with the attack. Where are
your eyes? Can't you see anything? Get out of here, and
take him with you," Bolan said, cocking his head toward the still-unconscious Garth. "When he wakes up,
tell him this—he's dead if I ever see him again."

"You can't leave us out here." The protest was emotionless, as if read from a script by a bad actor.

Bolan turned and stepped into the jungle. "Watch me."

22

The Huey coughed, its rotors clinging desperately to their inertia for a few seconds before grudgingly beginning to spin. Then the sky erupted into the all too familiar *whup-whup-whup* no American who served in Southeast Asia will ever forget. The chopper's engine groaned, and the bird began to lift. It slipped to the side a little, drifting to the edge of the small clearing, then cleared the trees.

Bolan looked out and down, watching as the ground fell away beneath him. It seemed as if that small, treeless expanse were all that remained of civilization. As the spot grew smaller, then vanished altogether behind the lip of the jungle canopy, he felt like the last man on Earth. Unconsciously he reached out and patted Margot's knee. He felt her hand enfold his, the strength of her fingers reassuring, comforting him. But lurking under that reassurance, he could feel the tremors of her fear. She, too, felt stripped of convention, stripped of that protection at the heart of a shared set of rules.

In the jungle, there *were* no rules.

And what did that say about a man who chose to stay behind when everyone he knew had gone, taken with them all ties to his past. Bolan tried to imagine what must have gone through Griffith's mind as he made his decision to stay, but it was too great a leap. Logic played no part in it. The elemental pull of nature must certainly have been a factor, but the warrior understood that, was himself tempted by it, and yet he had resisted. The real source of Griffith's decision had to be the absence of rules, the complete freedom from restraint.

And it scared the hell out of Mack Bolan.

The KGB, the mob, the worst band of terrorists, had codes of behavior. Each group lived by rules they shared, rules they understood and accepted. No matter how at variance with more conventional codes of behavior they might be, they were understandable to a detached observer. But Griffith was a case apart, a man who had turned his back on all restraint. And it was that absence that made him so dangerous. No one could predict what he might do, because no one, probably not even Griffith himself, knew what he believed, what he held sacred, what he would fight to protect.

When nothing matters, when nothing is holy, there is no vulnerability. Terrorists understood that. It was the source of their strength. But they professed to believe in something, to be fighting for a higher set of ideals. Those beliefs could be challenged, they could be used against those who held them. But Griffith was a shark, an eating machine, cruising the deepest human waters. There was no reason to what he did—at least none Bolan could comprehend. It was almost as if Griffith did what he did because he didn't know how *not* to do it.

Shifting his gaze to the terrain ahead, Bolan saw the mist-shrouded Wuliang Shan fifty miles to the north, a blue-gray smear above the green waste below. And somewhere to the west lay the border between Laos and Vietnam. He had expected the Plain of Jars to twist his guts, but as the Huey droned above it, he had felt nothing.

Instead, it had been the mountains that ripped at him, poking with their blunt teeth at his ribs, trying to get at his heart like the ravening jaws of a thing alive. And it was where Griffith waited for him—in the desolate corner where the mountains reached ten thousand feet, where Laos and Vietnam cowered beneath the heavy weight of China pressing down on them, and where people who knew no flag, recognized no border, made their home.

Like a scene from Milton's Hell, the clouds swirled in slow, torturous tangles. He'd seen it a hundred times and more, and every time it was the same—an adrenaline rush so powerful it pounded through his veins, jumped from nerve to nerve, bridging gaps and setting every last neural circuit afire.

The chopper droned on, and Bolan closed his eyes. Sleep was preferable to dredging up old memories. But when he closed his eyes, the old images came back. In rhythm with the chopper's rotor blades, scenes from his past danced as if alive on the canvas of his sleep. Brilliant flowers of fire, red and garish orange, bloomed and died. Jungle erupted into green splendor and wasted to gray ash as if he were present both at the creation and the apocalyptic death of the planet.

Through a barren landscape littered with lifeless shells of buildings, their very frailty a testimony to the brutality of war, and their continued defiance of gravity a monument to some purposeless spirit that burned in every human heart, Bolan could see a dark hunter, a shadow stalking other shadows—and he knew the hunter was implacable. And he knew, too, that even the hunter does not go unhunted.

He saw the hunter in an umbral ballet, twirling and gyrating, defying death and bringing it to others, in an endless dance, a dark figure on a darker ground. Flashes of fire—the dim illumination of a rifle's muzzle, the glint of moonlight on polished steel—threw sparks across the landscape, casting harsher shadows into every corner of every ruined building.

And as he dreamed, a bloodred ball rose into a corner of the sky. Its glow caught fire in the clouds of dust thrown up by the hunter's soundless footsteps, and it struck him that the eeriness of the landscape lay in its silence. To see and not to hear was worse than hearing everything, the gnashing teeth and percussive detonations. Only seeing made it harder to ignore the truth of what he saw.

The moon continued to grow large over the ashes, suffusing everything with bloody light. And the hunter turned, his face a small reflection of the bloody moon, its features slowly taking shape out of the scarlet aura. Looking up, as if at him, the hunter's nascent features smiled. And he knew the hunter was himself.

Bolan sat up screaming, cold sweat running down over his brow, a torrential downpour collecting in every crease and wrinkle. And down his cheeks fell a warmer, softer rain. He reached out for a bead clinging to his lip and tasted it with the tip of his tongue.

It's pungent saltiness was undeniably a tear.

Margot murmured gentle words against his cheek, calming him, but only slowly did Bolan hear her and, more slowly still, understand. It was all right. Things were fine. There was nothing to fear. The babble, so inadequate in its wisdom, was nonetheless a soothing sound. Bolan laughed once, bitterly, then lay back wearily.

"I been there, lad, more than once. It don't never get any easier, neither." Rogers reached past Margot to pat him on the knee. The hand lingered for a moment, then slowly slipped away as Bolan reached out to grab it. He caught the bulky fingers in his own and squeezed.

"Thanks, Jimbo."

THOMAS GRIFFITH, Colonel, U.S. Marine Corps, officially listed as MIA, stood on a rough stone wall, his sandaled feet clinging to the rock like an eagle in its aerie. Dressed in clean, pressed fatigue shorts and government-issue T-shirt, he looked like a military tourist. A pair of Zeiss 10 X 50 field glasses dangled from a leather strap around his neck. They had come with vinyl, but he hated plastic. The leather had been cured right there in his camp and smelled of sweat and human spittle, chewed into a soft pliability by the Meo wife of one of his lieutenants.

The camp itself looked like a pre-Arthurian ruin in the British highlands, as if it had been assembled by Picts or a swarm of proto-Gaelic tribesmen to fend off the Viking hordes. The stone in spots was worn from his pacing and his daily surveillance of the valleys surrounding his perch. Behind him loomed the ragged teeth of the Ailan Shan, mountains like a great saw ready to cut the world in two.

The hill itself was almost, but not quite, a mountain. It sloped down and away on all sides, a perfect spot to watch your butt on all sides. And with the Ailan behind him, it was a perfect place to defend.

By modern military standards, the camp was primitive. That suited Thomas Griffith just fine. Never at ease in the modern world, he perceived himself as a man misplaced in time. Patton used to claim he could hear the sounds of battle, the screams of the dying, when he visited the fields of earlier wars. Griffith went a step further. Dislocated, he had been born centuries too late.

Strangled by the chain of command, he had longed for the chance to turn back the clock, like Macbeth to rule from his own castle. The chance had come his way in the least likely of places, and when it came, he grabbed it.

Lifting the glasses, he scanned the valley from end to end. Years of practice had polished the movement to a smooth efficiency. Years of observation had heightened a sixth sense, some said even given him a seventh. No one was quite sure how he learned the things he knew. But no one doubted that he knew them.

The canopy below was smooth. No flights of frightened birds wheeling in a circle until the disturbance passed, no puffs of smoke or oily exhaust, no distant sounds of turning gears or laboring engines ruffled the tranquility. But he knew, as surely as he knew his own name, that someone was coming. They weren't close, not yet, but they would be. And he meant to be ready. This was his world, and he ruled it as he saw fit. Both the law itself and above the law he made, Thomas Griffith was not going to see his years of work go up in smoke.

The quiet efficiency of his camp, and the network of drug running for which it was the brain and beating heart, had been difficult to establish, and more difficult still to maintain. Nothing spoiled the success itself. But Griffith was a man apart. What mattered was not how much money the machine produced, although it produced more than he had ever dreamed. What mattered was simply that it was *his* machine. He had built it, he would run it and he would decide when to dismantle it. It was his and his only. The mountain of money, accumulating interest and dust alike in the vaults of a Swiss bank, was as inconsequential as morning dew. And he noticed it with about as much concern.

He heard a scuffle behind him and turned in time to see the cause of this latest threat struggling up the steep, rocky stairs.

"See anything, Colonel?"

"Not yet. But they're coming. I can feel it."

"Are you sure?"

Griffith glared at the newcomer. "If it wasn't for you, they wouldn't be here. But you fucked up, and they're coming. Take my word for it."

"What are we going to do?"

"Not 'we'—*you*. You brought them here, and you're going to send them away."

"You think I'm going down into that jungle?"

"I know you are." Griffith let the glasses drop and turned again to his lieutenant. "One way or another, I know you are."

23

Bolan, as usual, took the point. He had wanted Margot in the middle and had planned on having Garth and his henchmen bring up the rear. But all that had to be scrapped. Instead, the three of them pushed on alone, Margot following on his heels, then Rogers. He was starting to have second thoughts about bringing Margot along. It was true she was no stranger to the jungle of Southeast Asia, and she made her living behind a gun. But this was different. Whatever she did back in the States—and most of what he knew, he knew only by inference—it was not the same thing.

She had never carried a gun out here. Whether he would regret it remained to be seen. That he feared he might was indisputable. And worst of all was the secret fear, gnawing away at the back of his skull, that his concern for her safety would cloud his judgment. That was something neither of them could afford.

The jungle kept tugging at Bolan, as if to remind him of its presence, as he hacked through the dense undergrowth with a machete. It was heavy going, and the sweat streamed down his back to drench his neck and shoulders. The perspiration made the machete slippery, the rifle slung over a shoulder only slightly less so.

They were moving parallel to a well-traveled trail, but Bolan knew too much about jungle combat, and too much about men like Colonel Griffith, to take the easy way. Griffith's attitude toward the human race was rooted in contempt for its fundamental stupidity. Taking the easy way was stupid, when that's exactly what your opponent would expect you to do. Better to work a little harder and get there in one piece.

From time to time, Bolan would call a halt, and Rogers would work his way forward. They were proceeding largely by inference, substantiated by consistent rumor. On that score, Bolan could not fault Rogers or his sources. They seemed to have heard every variant of every conceivable story about the strange American colonel living on a mountaintop in the heart of the jungle.

Extracting the gold from the dross had been a laborious process, and Bolan felt a tinge of admiration for the students of antiquity who had worried over Homer and found the ruins of Troy. Griffith was no Paris, but he had his own brand of stubborn pride. Bolan only hoped his own wiles were equal to those of Odysseus.

Bolan held his carbine aloft, the signal for a conference. The ground beneath them had started to slant upward. They were heading into the highlands, now, and misdirection would be more costly. Left or right were less taxing corrections than back and around.

Bolan dropped to a squat and consulted the hastily drawn map the Irishman's snitches had concocted. So far, it had been reliable, if not precise. Rogers moved up alongside and dropped to one knee.

"I think we're right about here, laddie," he muttered, stabbing the rough chart with a thick, scarred finger. As the older man's hand rested on the rough paper, the warrior was reminded of the circumstances that had deformed it, and he shivered.

And something else began to gnaw at him. He remembered watching Garth closely, and how the tall man never took his eyes off Margot. Now the spindly animal was somewhere behind them. Bolan began to wonder just how it had come to pass that Garth, a man of dark hatreds and secret passions, had been so readily available and so eagerly agreed to accompany him.

Hatred for Griffith, as Bolan knew only too well, could be a consuming thing, growing slowly in the insides until the exterior man was a simple shell, little more than skin and a thirst for vengeance.

Rogers tugged at Bolan's sleeve, bringing him back to the task at hand as if from a deep well into the molten interior of the Earth.

"I think we have to get moving, Mack. Griffith is almost certain to know we're after him."

"You're probably right, but we can't afford to screw up, especially so close. If we make a mistake now, it could be fatal."

"Part of me wishes that slimy scarecrow was still here. I don't know half as much about these mountains as he does."

"He did seem to know quite a bit about this area. I'm beginning to wonder whether he might have been a plant. What do you think?"

"The thought did cross me own mind, but I thought it was just me. Paranoia or something." He looked Bolan in the face, but his gaze was uncertain, the eyes struggling to stay in focus. "I been here once or twice, during the war, but that's all. What I know, I know, but it ain't half as much as I'd like, and most of it I got secondhand."

Bolan looked closely at his friend, hoping to find some trace of confidence lacking in the voice. He was disappointed. Turning back to the map, he noticed a shadow move among the leaves, over his friend's shoulder. He stared at the spot, hoping for another glimpse, but the leaves were still. He debated whether or not to tell the others, but didn't want to spook them. And if they were being followed, it was to his advantage that the pursuers not know he was aware of them.

He couldn't leave Margot unprotected. If they were being followed, there was a good chance an attack might come from the rear. If the pursuers were few, they might try cherry-picking stragglers. Ground between two stones, Bolan made his choice. Leaning down toward the map, he whispered hoarsely, "Don't move suddenly. Just lean in and listen."

Rogers bent forward as if to see the map more clearly. Scarcely moving his taut, white lips, he asked, "What's up?"

"I saw something in the jungle, about fifty yards behind us. I don't know who or what, but we'll have to be doubly alert. Don't tell Margot. Fall back and play caboose, but make sure you don't put too much space between you and us."

"I don't like it."

"You'd rather take the point?"

"No...."

"Then do what I tell you. Jimbo, I don't know what the hell we're up against, here, and for all the stories your friends may have gathered, neither do you. But if they're right, then we're getting close. The closer we get, the more likely we are to run into trouble. Use your god-damned head, man."

"Laddie, I don't like it one bit. We're supposed to be such hotshots, why the fuck can't we think of something better than hanging me out to dry on the ass end of this damn crusade of yours?''

''You got any better ideas, I'm listening....''

When Rogers said nothing further, Bolan glanced again at the spot where he had seen the movement. It was quiet. And empty. Margot was moving closer, and Bolan decided against continuing the discussion.

Getting to his feet, Bolan feigned an exhaustion he did not yet feel, but knew lay just around the corner. He stretched with exaggerated motion, twisting his back until the vertebrae cracked, releasing some of the tension. He yanked his machete out of the ground and resumed hacking at the undergrowth. Peering over his shoulder, he watched the Irishman drift to the rear of the tiny column. Now he had to hope that whoever was following them didn't outnumber them too badly. With just the three of them, it wouldn't be that hard.

Hacking away, Bolan gradually widened the gap between himself and Margot. He started to work a slight curve, and suddenly he was gone. When Margot reached the spot, she saw the machete sticking into a tall stalk of bamboo and realized immediately what she had to do. Jerking the blade free, she picked up where Bolan had left off. She slashed with reckless abandon, flailing at the insistent growth with increasing violence. It was the first exercise she'd had in days, and the pain in her shoulders felt good.

The sticky sweat born of humidity gave way to the vigorous flow generated by hard labor, and she revelled in the sensation of rivulets coursing between her breasts and down over her ribs and thighs. She kept looking for Bolan, and knew she wouldn't see him again until he'd done whatever had drawn him off.

At the first whack of the blade he'd left behind, Bolan smiled. He knew Margot was good, but this good was too much to expect. As soon as her attack settled into a steady rhythm, he crossed over the trail and doubled back. He moved swiftly, finding himself now, getting into the jungle mind-set that had kept him alive through hard combat times. Those special circuits, long dormant, lay just under the skin and tingled as new current coursed through them.

The sound of Margot's machete started to fall away behind him, and he picked up his pace. Every ten yards seemed to take an eternity as he wriggled and wormed. Dropping to his stomach to get under the heaviest undergrowth, he spotted a gleaming strand of wire. It was anchored under a carpet of dead leaves to his right, snaked out across the trail and, barely perceptible, reappeared on the other side. Somewhere to his left, he knew, lay a mine capable of shredding flesh and breaking bone.

Cautiously he crawled forward until it lay beneath his stomach, then, one at a time, he hauled his legs across the trip line. He was glad his instincts had been validated, but knew now that the job ahead was going to be tougher than he had thought. The wire had been placed recently—it was too new to have been a vestige of the old war, the one that, until two days ago, had seemed to belong to prehistoric times. The war lived, and would continue to live as long as a single man who had fought it continued to draw breath. It had been a war like no other, but then all wars were that.

He remembered when, as a kid, he read the obituaries of the last few survivors of the Civil War. It had seemed so far away, so like science fiction. That a war fought nearly a hundred years before—and which lay flat and dead on the pages of his grammar school history text-

books—had been witnessed by men who still lived
seemed to fly in the face of credibility. And yet it was so.
He wondered whether the Vietnam War would someday
seem the same to some kid struggling to understand another hundred years of American history. The chances of
the planet lasting that long seemed so remote.

Once across the wire, Bolan lay still a moment, trying
to control his breathing. The rapid, shallow breaths he'd
been taking had tired him. He became aware of a tight-
ness across his shoulders, a constriction in his chest.

Forcing himself to breathe deeply, slowly, he resumed
his crawl, slower now, more intent on the smaller details
that might mean the difference between a living human
being and a pile of ragged meat and splintered bone.
Pausing to take stock, he saw the leaves move again,
across the trail. Whoever had been tailing them had allowed them to work farther ahead, almost as if he knew
where they were headed and was in no hurry to catch up.

Bolan watched the shivering leaves intently. Overhead, a deep roar that rumbled and rolled off into the
distance shook the earth beneath him. The old sensation
of instability, of a cosmos on the edge of cataclysm, rattled his bones. He dug his fingers into the leaf mold,
scratching at the litter to grab a more solid earth beneath
it. The world seemed to tilt, as it had a thousand times.
The whine of artillery shells overhead, the distant whistle of a descending bomb were both absent. And still the
planet shook as if it would come apart beneath him,
opening a hundred cracks to swallow him whole.

Thunder.

And the first hiss of falling rain, like the sound of wind
in tall, stiff grass at the Atlantic shore. The hiss became
a dripping torrent as the sky split open. Rain poured
down through the canopy, bending leaves and branches

as the collective weight of the water became too great for the delicate vegetation to support.

Bolan was soaked through. The patter of the rain masked the sound of Margot's machete. He was alone. And then, floating before him, thirty yards away, he saw a small halo of yellow-white light in a green nightmare.

A face.

One he had seen before. One he would never forget.

Not ninety feet away stood the man who had murdered Aloysius Mackenzie. Bolan froze, staring hard at the face to see whether the eyes betrayed knowledge of his presence. An aquiline nose, pale gray eyes and thin blond hair, now darkened by the rain and plastered flatter on the round skull than he remembered, were mere details, trivial differences unable to contradict the truth of what he saw.

Slowly Bolan brought his M-16 around, struggling to keep control of its weight, muffle the sound of its passage through the leaves. The rain would cover him if he wasn't reckless. The gray eyes continued to stare, seldom blinking. They seemed to glow, as if lit by some inner fire.

Bolan raised the rifle, drawing a bead on the pale phantom hovering just ahead. Then, like a spooked deer, the face turned, froze and vanished. Bolan squeezed the trigger. As if in slow motion, he could see the green halo that had framed the face shred and splinter into green confetti. When the burst had ended, Bolan listened. He heard nothing but the rain.

Getting to his feet, he sprinted toward the ruined foliage. His feet slipped on the soaking mold, and once he fell. He half crawled and half ran the remaining distance, zigzagging to avoid running right up the assassin's rifle barrel. He dived to the earth not five feet from where the face had been.

When he peered into the undergrowth, he saw nothing but a set of muddy footprints. A single cigarette butt lay in tatters, field stripped after a hasty puff. The man was sure of himself.

Standing, Bolan pushed through the last fronds into the assassin's lair. A pale pink pool, rapidly fading to filmy transparence, lay cupped in a leaf. A minute before it had been a perfect ruby, shimmering in the rain, and now it was barely blood at all.

But Bolan smiled. He'd wounded the assassin. Not badly, for sure, but he'd given him something to think about, a reason not to be so cocky, something to make him think twice before lighting the next cigarette in the next ambush.

And that there would be another was beyond question. The assassin wanted Bolan as badly as Bolan wanted him.

Almost.

24

"We must be getting close," Bolan said. Sprawled against the base of a large tree, he breathed deeply, rubbing aching muscles in his shoulder and forearm.

"Why do you say that?" Rogers was skeptical.

"Because I know I saw that man before. I know he was the hit man, the one who killed Al."

"You barely saw him, Mack."

"I'm telling you, I would know that man anywhere. I see his face in my sleep."

"Seems to me you're taking this too much to heart. I admire your determination, but, hell, the odds are against you, man. You don't seem to realize that."

"I've been hearing that all my life, Jimbo. But even if it's a long shot, it's the only one I've got. Besides, it's a little late for you to be second-guessing, isn't it?"

"I suppose so. But you're never too old to learn."

"What am I supposed to do? Give up?"

"Of course not. All I'm suggesting is that you prepare yourself for the distinct possibility that the mission will be a failure. And if it is, I don't want you bashing your head against a stone wall in frustration. Be prepared for the possibility, and it won't hurt as much if it comes to pass. That's all I mean."

Bolan stood up. "I think we're getting close, and I intend to finish what I've started here. I'll go the rest of the way on my own, if I have to."

"Why don't you both shut up?" Margot snapped. "I'm tired of listening to you. Mack's right. We have to go ahead. If we walk away now, everything is wasted. Not only the trip, but Mackenzie's death, Tranh's death. And, in case you forgot, I'm here for another reason. Kwan Lee's sister is out there with Griffith, and if nobody else cares, I do. Griffith gets away with murder every damn day. People are shooting themselves full of heroin that he supplies. You can't allow someone like that to walk around like he was God incarnate."

"Since when did you become such a moralist, Margot?" Rogers demanded. "I thought you were a hardnosed pragmatist, somebody who looked truth in the eye and never blinked."

"Maybe I've grown a little. Maybe I can see things more clearly—"

A flutter of leaves stopped her in midsentence. Bolan reached for his carbine, but the apparition in black raised a hand to signal it wasn't necessary. Bolan stopped with his hand scant inches from the rifle.

"You all talk so very much about something you seem to understand only dimly," the newcomer said. His voice was soft, the English stilted, but precise. Its clipped, staccato delivery sounded almost automated.

"Who the bloody hell are you?" the Irishman demanded.

"Captain Nho Ngu Trang, Army of the Democratic Republic of Vietnam."

"I've seen you before," Margot said.

"Quite right. We *don't* all look alike, then."

"What do you want?" Bolan asked. "I told you in Bangkok I wasn't interested in your help. Or in helping you, either. You've been following us?"

"Of course I have. I'm surprised you didn't expect that, when you rejected our previous offer of assistance. It was an offer we couldn't afford to have refused."

"I already told you, I don't need your help."

"Mr. Bolan, I can appreciate your reluctance. I know how awkward this must be for you. I will confess it is none too easy for me, either. But I believe we both have the same concern, and I think it is a matter serious enough to override both our reservations. Please, let's discuss it once again, like rational human beings, before you reject it out of hand."

"And if not?"

"Then I suppose we will have to separately pursue an identical goal. Not the most efficient method, I think you'll agree. And one calculated to give our common enemy more of an advantage than he already enjoys. This is in neither of our interests."

"If you want Griffith so bad, why don't you just send a battalion after him?"

"A year or two ago, that might have been possible. But no longer. Colonel Griffith is in Laotian territory. My country is unwilling to violate another nation's territorial sovereignty."

"Since when? You've been sticking your nose in every anthill in Southeast Asia for ten years. Why should you suddenly be so scrupulous about a little thing like a national boundary? You could always claim you didn't see it."

"Would it were that easy. Unfortunately, however, there are those in my country who see the activities of

Colonel Griffith as desirable. They are opposed to any interference."

"So why are you here?"

"Surely you are wise enough in the ways of the world to understand that no government, and therefore no governmental policy, is truly monolithic."

"What you're really saying is that you're here on your own, right?"

"Not quite. I have my official . . . sponsors, as it were. Men who are as appalled by Colonel Griffith's activities as you are. Men who believe that it is time for Vietnam to come in out of the cold, end its isolation from the rest of the world."

"You're one of them, I suppose."

"This is a volunteer mission, Mr. Bolan. The men with me have all willingly accompanied me, despite the risk of incurring disfavor. In my country, as I'm sure you can appreciate, that is no inconsiderable risk. And I should think that the departure of your friends would make a difference. Six would have been too small a contingent to achieve what you intend. But three . . . ?"

Captain Nho stopped speaking abruptly. He glanced at each of the three people arrayed before him in a semicircle. The faces of skepticism seemed to daunt him for a moment. It was obvious his argument was falling on deaf ears. It was something he hadn't expected. He raised one hand as if to implore them then, as if convinced he were haranguing statues, he waved it aside and turned smartly. In a second, he had vanished.

Bolan leaped to his feet and dashed into the jungle after him.

"Captain Nho, wait a minute. Hold on."

The Vietnamese had already vanished, and Bolan plunged headlong into the thick undergrowth, sweeping aside thorny branches that clawed and scratched at his skin and clothing. Ahead, Bolan could hear the sharp bark of the captain's voice, and he broke into a narrow defile just as a small detachment of Vietnamese regulars began to move off in single file.

"Captain, wait."

Nho turned, a quizzical look on his face. Bolan rushed forward. "I think we ought to talk about this a little bit more."

"I don't know why. I have nothing further to add to what I've already told you."

"Maybe not. It can't hurt to kick it around a little before we make up our minds."

"But my mind *is* made up. I am determined to fulfill my mission. I had hoped we might work together, but since that is not to be, then I'll proceed on my own. I only hope you don't get caught in the middle."

"Captain, I've been in the middle all my life. It's nothing new."

"Then what have we to discuss?"

"Do you know where Griffith's camp is located?"

"Yes."

"Does he have someone with him, an assistant maybe, or a lieutenant?"

"He has several, as one would expect. His organization is large and rather well structured. He must have been an admirable officer at one time. Why do you ask?"

"Come back, please. I want the others to hear this."

Bolan walked back to the clearing, Captain Nho trailing behind him. When Rogers spotted the Vietnamese, he flinched. Bolan thought for a minute he was going to reach for his rifle but, for some reason not immediately apparent, thought better of it. Instead, the big man leaned over to whisper something to Margot. Captain Nho looked on, his face a mask of impassivity.

"Jimmy, listen to me," Bolan said, dropping to one knee in front of the tall man. "Captain Nho has offered his help. I've decided to accept it."

"What's wrong with you, man? You gonna listen to a goddamn slope? You gonna trust him?"

"Why not?"

"It's crazy, man. You don't even know the guy. And he's a gook besides. Why should he help us? I was humping through the boonies a lifetime ago, blowing creeps like this guy away. They *paid* me for it, man."

"If I'd work with scum like Garth to get Griffith, I'd work with anybody. And I want Griffith. To get him, I'll work with the devil, if I have to."

Rogers didn't move. Bolan stared at him a minute, and when the man showed no sign of responding, Bolan understood his dilemma. It wasn't easy to make a full 180-degree turn on a dime. Finally, like a defiant teenager, the Irishman snarled, "This is your last chance, man. It's me or them. Choose..."

"No contest."

"And you really think this'll work?"

"I hope to God it does. I just don't know...."

"I'm in."

Rogers glared at the Vietnamese, whose features remained as quiescent as they had been since his arrival. An impenetrable silence descended, as if someone had lowered a curtain. Something radical had changed, something had happened, and none of them was quite sure what it was.

Finally Margot broke the silence. "This should be interesting. But anything is preferable to working with a man like Garth." Her voice was husky, almost a whisper, as if afraid Garth might still be able to hear her.

"We don't have to worry about that now."

"I'm not so sure, Mr. Bolan," Captain Nho said.

"What do you mean?" Margot asked.

"A man like that has a price. If there is anyone within a thousand miles of here who can afford to pay it, it is Colonel Griffith."

"You assume Griffith would trust him."

"No, I don't. Griffith trusts no one but himself. But he knows how much a soul costs. Your Mr. Garth wears a price tag on his sleeve."

"But Griffith doesn't need him."

"As you wish. I hope you are right."

"What difference does it make? Garth is no more a threat to us than Griffith himself."

"That is true, if you assume he has not been working for Griffith all along."

"Do you think he was?" Bolan demanded.

"I have no way of knowing. I merely suggest it because I think it strange he would prefer the jungle with only two barbarians, to the relative security of a much larger, better-equipped company."

"Barbarians?" Bolan was nonplussed.

"Forgive me, Mr. Bolan. I can't expect you to understand. Out here, ethnic considerations die hard. Even Marxism is no match for two thousand years of history."

Bolan smiled. "You have no monopoly on racism."

Captain Nho nodded, whether in agreement or satisfaction, Bolan wasn't sure. "I think we should move on. If Garth is inclined to cooperate with Griffith, the sooner we reach our objective the better."

"How far to Griffith's stronghold?"

"It is about ten miles, high in the mountains. If we move quickly, we should be within sight of the camp by tomorrow afternoon."

"Why so long?"

"The terrain gets rougher. Our maps are only approximate, but I have been here before, more than once. The jungle alone is a serious obstacle. If we assume Griffith is a prudent man, and I think we must, the jungle will be the least of our worries."

"You want to take the point, Captain?"

"The point?"

A familiar voice fired off fluent Vietnamese, explaining to the captain that he should lead the way. Nho and Bolan both stared at Margot.

"I didn't know you spoke Vietnamese so well, Margot," Bolan said.

"There's a great deal about me you still don't know," she said dryly, arching an eyebrow suggestively.

She stood, and Bolan admired the long curve of her thigh as she bent to retrieve her pack and rifle. Even here, in what had to be among the lushest spots on Earth, she seemed to radiate an animal magnetism more powerful than nature at its most rampant. Like a ripe fruit, she dangled before his eyes, and it was all he could do to keep from reaching out to pluck her free.

25

Their number swollen to nine now, the little crusade began hacking its way through a slowly changing tangle of undergrowth. The ground had begun to slope upward, and the character of the foliage changed gradually, as the altitude increased. The jungle was a little thinner, but the gradual slope ate away whatever additional freedom they had gained.

Bolan and Nho were dual point men, alternating the lead every couple of hundred yards. Neither man spoke, conserving their energy for their physical labor. At the third switch, Bolan concentrated his attention on the smaller man. His stamina was amazing, and Bolan admired the economical motion with which the captain swung his machete. Not a stroke was wasted. Nho seemed to know precisely where to land each swipe of the blade to clear the maximum amount of jungle growth.

It was, Bolan realized, the product of years of fighting against the world's greatest military power in some of the least hospitable terrain on the planet. Survival, as Bolan knew perhaps better than most, gave one instincts crucial to its maintenance. In the kind of war Nho had fought most of his life, if you couldn't cut it, you didn't have long to wait before another kind of harvest gathered you in and ground you to hamburger.

They had covered two miles, and it had taken nearly four hours. Like Bolan, Nho was convinced the trails, such as they were, should be avoided at all cost. The heavy going was taking its toll on all of them. In a small clearing at the base of a particularly steep incline, Bolan consulted with Nho.

"Everybody needs a rest."

Nho, on point at the moment, turned with a faint smile just noticeable on his grimly compressed lips. The rest of his features were as immobile as a stone carving. "I thought you'd never suggest it, Mr. Bolan."

"I don't think we have much choice. If we wear ourselves out, we'll be useless for a day or so. Better to take it at a reasonable clip and have a little something left in case we run into trouble before we're ready."

Nho made no answer. He shouted an order over Bolan's shoulder, and the five members of his team dropped to the ground, their gear rattling in the general collapse.

Margot approached Bolan and whispered in his ear.

"Don't go far into the bush, Margot. Just far enough to give you a sense of privacy."

"Be back in a couple of minutes. Don't you peek." She stepped through the green curtain, and Bolan listened to the soft rustle of the leaves. He felt better about her presence, now that they had reinforcements. It was strange how circumstances could forge bonds between enemies and, thinking of Garth, realized that the reverse was no less true. The mutability of human relations was one of the great mysteries. Bolan doubted he would ever fully understand it.

Rogers moved in and dropped heavily to the ground. The big Irishman rubbed his calves and groaned. "Haven't walked this much in a long time, boyo."

"Can you hang in there a little longer, Jimbo?"

"What choice do I have? If you think I'm going to hang around here by myself, you got another think coming. I just wish we could have flown all the way in."

"There are easier ways to commit suicide, Jimbo."

"Yeah, but they're not as comfortable." He stopped working on his weary calves and turned his ministering hands to his left knee. "Remember Khe Sanh?"

"How could I forget?"

"This old knee hasn't been the same since. The damn thing is, I broke it falling out of a chopper. A thousand rounds a minute flying all over the goddamned place, and I fall on my keester and break a kneecap. The luck of the Irish, I guess."

Bolan patted him on the shoulder. "I'm glad you're here, guy."

Rogers smiled that melancholy smile that seemed the single universal Irish attribute. No one did it as well, and, on reflection, Bolan conceded no group had a better right to it. "You know, Mack, I feel bad about what I said back there, when we first hooked up with the Viets. I don't know what got into me."

"Forget it. I'm sure Captain Nho didn't expect anything different."

"Maybe so, but I feel like I owe him an apology, anyhow."

"So tell him."

The Irishman shook his head sadly. "Can't. The harm has already been done. I can't expect him to forget something like that. I have to *earn* his forgiveness."

"I got a feeling you'll have more than one opportunity for that before this mission is finished." He looked up as Captain Nho left his men and crawled toward him.

"The woman has been gone long enough, Mr. Bolan, don't you think?"

"I guess you're right. I'll get her."

Bolan got wearily to his feet and pushed through the small opening in the greenery through which Margot had gone. He listened for a moment, half expecting to hear her struggling back to the clearing. Instead, he became aware of a silence deeper than anything he could have imagined. His mind leaped back to the centuries he'd spent wrapped in such silence, hiding in the rain forest as the birds grew quiet, his ears straining for the snap of a twig, the squeak of a branch pushed a little too far.

Ambush after ambush, search and destroy missions, and just plain sitting and waiting—the forest was then, as it was now, a vast early-warning system as every living thing seemed to hold its breath, waiting for the first whining shell, the soft click of a mine trigger or the distant, hollow thumping of a chopper. And every fiber in his being screamed that something was terribly wrong.

He lost control, crashing through the undergrowth, calling aloud for Margot. His voice seemed to echo from every broad leaf, a thousand Bolans yelling back, the desperation in his voice transformed to mockery. Behind him, he heard the others charge after him, and the jungle came alive as a huge flock of brightly hued parrots rose as one, a feathered cloud featuring every color of the spectrum. Their collective screech was ear-splitting.

There was no sign of Margot. Bolan clawed through a tangle of vines, and came to a stop not five feet in front of Margot's gear. He scrambled forward, reaching the small mound of equipment just as Nho burst into the open behind him.

He grabbed the canteen and small pack, shouted her name again. It echoed just as hollowly in the dark recesses of the forest, seeming to lose itself in the shadows. He stared at the sky and saw its blue hue deepening even as he watched. The sun was approaching the horizon, and in little more than an hour, night would swallow them all.

Nho walked past him, bending low to see the earth more clearly. He seemed to have spotted something and bent to touch the ground. He scrutinized his fingertips closely, then muttered something barely audible. For some reason, he had chosen French.

"What is it?"

"Blood, Mr. Bolan."

Bolan turned then, and headed into the trees and stumbled headlong through the tangle onto the trail. Nho and the others rushed after him, and Bolan, spurred on by rage, found hidden reserves of energy he hadn't suspected. It was all the others could do to keep him in sight.

A thousand possibilities, none of them good, flashed through the warrior's mind, flipping past like a computer screen gone mad. Each came and was dismissed almost immediately, only to be replaced by another still more unthinkable. Bolan had gone more than a mile before Nho began to close the gap. A sudden steep incline slowed them both, and suddenly Bolan broke into a clearing.

A vague motion caught his eye, and he dived to the ground. A thud to his left caused him to turn, and he spotted Nho lying beside him.

"What is it?" the Vietnamese whispered.

"I don't know. Over there, across the clearing, near the tall tree to the left of the trail."

"I see it."

Bolan hauled his carbine around, and Nho released the safety on his Kalashnikov. A slow, steady movement, too regular, too rhythmic to be the random movement of leaves in the slight wind, seemed to be slowing down. A dark clump of shadow, barely visible against the dark green of the forest, seemed slowly to be winding down, as if spiraling to a halt on the end of a limitless line.

Bolan drew a bead on the movement, but even with the forced focus, he was unable to make out more than the dimmest of outlines.

"What is it?" Nho hissed.

"I can't tell," Bolan whispered. "But there's one way to find out." He climbed to his knees, then into a crouch, and began to inch forward. Nho turned to his squad and held up a hand for silence. Bolan glanced back over his shoulder and saw the small group of Vietnamese clustered where the trail widened into the clearing. Like the centerpiece of a macabre tableau, Jimmy Rogers towered above the Orientals. The six figures were frozen in the opening, banded with reddish light slanting through the trees.

Rushing forward, Bolan gradually left the crouch as it dawned on him that whatever it was wasn't sensible of his presence. Nho was right behind him. Two-thirds of the way across the clearing, Bolan stopped in his tracks. He lowered his carbine and walked the rest of the way fully erect, certain now that the swinging shadow posed no threat to him. He didn't quite believe his eyes, but as the gap narrowed, it was no longer possible to doubt the evidence of his senses.

Even in the shadows, Bolan knew something terrible awaited him. He stopped to listen, and the silence again washed over him, as the jungle waited for his reaction. He could hear a soft splash, something dripping irregularly, as if each drop were reluctant to fall or as if the fluid were thick, viscous enough to fall only occasionally when the pull of gravity overcame its natural cohesiveness. Two naked bodies swung at the end of a long rope, their combined weight slowly compressing the spiral through which they spun.

As Bolan drew still closer, he nearly gagged. Even in the semidarkness, he could see the yawning cavities. He stepped closer, nearly slipped and fell, catching himself with one hand on the ground. He didn't need *Gray's Anatomy* to tell him the nature of the slippery goo oozing through his fingers as he fought to maintain his balance. Both bodies had been eviscerated.

And when he finally realized that neither corpse was Margot's, he closed his eyes to mutter a silent prayer of thanks to whatever deity it was that had been merciful enough to spare her and savage enough to permit the ghastly vision slowly twirling to a stop before his eyes.

Nho stood at his shoulder, but said nothing.

And then he heard it. A voice, calling as if from a great distance. The sound was hollow, as if the caller were at the bottom of a deep well or isolated high on the mountaintop, his voice given resonance by the forest and the darkness slowly enveloping them all. Bolan pricked his ears and canted his head to one side, to get an aural fix.

"This way, Mr. Bolan," Nho whispered urgently. Without waiting for a reply, the wiry little man stepped onto the trail and began to run. Bolan plunged after him. They ran for several hundred yards, neither man stopping for breath. Ahead, in another deep clump of shadow, a bright glob of fire seemed to grow brighter and hotter as they approached.

At the heart of another clearing, a blazing stack of deadwood gradually grew in intensity, bathing the surrounding trees in its light, slowly changing from orange to yellowish white as the flames grew hotter. A deep trench had been cut around its perimeter, to keep the fire under control.

Roland Garth was propped against a tree across the clearing, as naked as his two dead companions, his skeletal frame laced with several coils of dark rope.

"Bolan, thank God you're here," he whimpered, as the big man stepped carefully around the still-growing conflagration.

"Where's Margot?" Bolan demanded.

"Griffith's got her."

"How do you know that?"

"Because he paid me to kidnap her, then took her from me. Get me out of here, will you? You can't leave me here!"

"Give me one good reason why not."

"I can help you. I know where the camp is. I can help get her back. Cut me loose, *please*!"

"I ought to cut your throat."

"But you need me."

"The hell I do. I have all the help I need. And she wouldn't be there if you hadn't taken her in the first place."

"I only wanted to cut a deal with you, that's all. I—"

Bolan waved him off, stepping forward with his combat knife in hand. As much as he despised the man, he couldn't leave him there. As he reached out to cut the line, Nho grabbed his shoulder. "Don't."

"I can't leave him, Nho."

"You have no choice."

"Why not?"

"Watch. Just stand back..."

Nho took several steps backward, finally slipping behind a tree. He motioned vigorously for Bolan to do the same. The big guy followed Nho's orders and stepped behind a huge clump of thick bamboo. Slowly and steadily, the Vietnamese raised his rifle, taking careful aim for several seconds. He fired once, then again, the second shot parting the rope coiled around Garth's lower limbs as the bullet slammed into the tree just to the man's left. Garth struggled to free himself from the remaining coils, but he never got the chance.

The deafening roar nearly shattered their eardrums as Garth vanished in a cloud of smoke. When it cleared, his shattered body, now legless and one-armed, lay face-down several yards from the tree.

"Booby trap," Nho said, almost as an afterthought.

"How did you know?" Bolan demanded.

"We used it against you many times during the war. Apparently your Colonel Griffith has learned at least one thing since he went native."

"Yeah," Bolan grunted. "But I got another lesson for him. And this one won't help him a bit."

26

Mack Bolan felt the change in himself, the rage burning deep inside, white-hot, hotter than the molten core at the center of the Earth. The anger energized every nerve, and he felt as if a powerful electric current were flowing through every fiber.

That Garth would have been willing, even under duress, to abduct Margot made him, as far as the Executioner was concerned, a prime candidate for maggot food. And now, even as parts of the charred corpse still smoldered, the onslaught began, insects beginning to swarm around the nearly limbless torso. Garth had landed on his back, eyes open, and ants had already begun to cover the sightless orbs, going first, as always, for the softest tissue.

Bolan turned away from the remains, cursing Garth for his part in this debacle, angry at Griffith, the prime mover in this latest waking nightmare. Captain Nho placed a hand on his shoulder and squeezed gently, trying to give a reassurance he seemed to know was impossible.

"We'll find her, Mr. Bolan. We'll find her or die trying."

Yeah, Bolan thought. We'll find her, all right. But will it be in time?

The whole jigsaw puzzle lay jumbled at his feet, as meaningless as the ground beef that once had been a man. Griffith seemed to have tentacles everywhere. Few times in his career had Bolan encountered a more elusive and more malevolent force than this renegade colonel. It was as if Griffith were some huge invisible cosmic force, a neutron star or black hole, whose existence could be measured only by its effect on everything else in the universe, but which itself could not be seen. Never had he wanted anyone more than he wanted Griffith.

And never had the odds against success seemed longer than at that moment.

"We better get rolling, Captain."

"It's too dark. It's lunacy to try to advance in the jungle at night. We can't use lights without being seen, and we can't see without them."

"Then I'll see you in the morning, if you catch up with me." Bolan stepped over the broken body, strangely more substantial now that the spindly legs were gone. The torso seemed now like that of a normal, robust man rather than a figment of Washington Irving's imagination. Bolan moved out of the clearing without a backward glance, keeping to the trail to maximize his mobility. And behind him, shaking his head at the passionate futility so alien to his own cold, logical approach to friend and foe alike, Captain Nho stepped onto the trail behind him, the forward motion of his hand already little more than a dim shadow to the five men who followed him.

Bolan heard the rustle of leaves at his back, but he was still too angry to be grateful. As he half walked and half ran, he grew increasingly conscious of the risk, the foolishness of his anger, but there was no turning back. Somewhere deep inside him was the belief, not susceptible to any logic he could articulate, that he was not fated to die yet, that although Griffith might kill him, it would not be by accident, nor would it be a nameless, faceless confrontation. He knew, as surely as he knew Garth would never draw another breath, that he was destined to look Griffith in the face.

Nho, too, seemed to sense this. He wondered what drove the man ahead of him, little more than a pair of broad shoulders bulling through the deepening darkness of the twilight jungle. He had seen this kind of commitment before, but never in an American.

As the Vietnam War had dragged on, the single thing that had kept Nho and his compatriots going was the belief that they were right and that the Americans, because they were uncertain, were destined to lose. Nho wondered what might have happened if all the Americans had been like this unusual man leading him on a fool's errand into the heart of a darkness much deeper, much darker than the simple absence of light.

Nho tried again to slow Bolan down, for the angry man's own good. Increasing his pace enough to close the gap, he drew up behind the man, having to settle for following closely in Bolan's footsteps because the trail was too narrow to permit them to move abreast. "There is a small clearing ahead," he whispered in a hoarse voice. "Let's at least take a break and wait for the moon to rise."

Bolan, beginning to rein in the furies driving him, consented with a nod. He broke into the clearing and threw himself to the earth with an uncharacteristic recklessness. Gasping for breath, he rolled onto his back, sat up and reached into his pack for some insect repellent.

The clatter of equipment filled the shadows ahead of him. He turned just in time to see Jimbo fall to the ground, surrounded by Nho's men, who seemed to have attached themselves to the big Irishman like he was a giant pet they collectively owned and for which they felt responsible.

Still breathing heavily, Bolan smeared some of the repulsive oil on the exposed skin of his neck and face, then rolled up his sleeves and applied more of the smelly stuff to his wrists and forearms. The alcohol in the repellent stung him in a hundred places, both where he had already been bitten and where the thorns had dug and scraped him. He started to cap the lotion then stopped and wordlessly extended the plastic bottle to Nho, who stood directly over him, hands on hips to help catch his own breath.

"Thank you, no," the diminutive captain replied. "I'm afraid I might come to depend on it, and once you are gone, there will be no more. Then what would I do?"

Leaning back on his pack, Bolan continued to try to pierce the impenetrable veil of darkness and of stoicism in which Nho had been wrapped or, more likely, had chosen to wrap himself. "You understand, don't you, that I don't expect you to follow me?" Bolan said.

"You flatter yourself, Mr. Bolan. It simply happens that my friends and I have the same destination and the same purpose as you. There is no question of following. Just as they do not follow me, but accompany me, I do not follow you. I journey and you journey. Like two lines, we happen for the moment to be congruent. Neither you nor I know how long that will be so."

"Sounds like Zen, to me. You a student?"

"Is the moon?"

"Then you are."

"As you wish. But actually, I have a doctorate in mathematics. From the Sorbonne."

"Then what are you doing in the army? What are you doing out here?"

"I was in Israel once, on vacation, when I was studying in Paris. I met a woman. I was . . . fond . . . of her. I wanted her to come back to Paris with me."

"I don't understand."

"She was in the army."

"Ah. . . ."

"That is how it is in my country, too. Perhaps, someday . . . things will be . . . different." As Nho continued to speak, his voice lost the tonelessness that had made him sound so much like an automaton. Feelings, Bolan could only guess how long suppressed, had begun to seep through the carefully cultivated demeanor. At the same time, Nho's face began to glow, first emerging only faintly from the shadow, then to radiate a pale silver light. It took Bolan a moment before he realized it was simply the light of the rising moon beginning to filter down through the canopy. Paradoxically, as Nho had come to seem more vulnerable, more human, he had, for the briefest of moments, come to seem more like a creature from another world.

"Did you ever see her again?" Bolan asked quietly.

Nho didn't answer. He turned his back to Bolan, then, in a hoarse whisper, said, "It's time to move on." The ambiguity of the reply was not lost on Bolan. Nor was the implicit message in Nho's resumed stoicism. If they failed to find Margot, it would be time for Bolan, too, to move on.

Grudgingly the big guy got to his feet. As he rose, he eclipsed the glow suffusing Nho's face, momentarily overshadowing the captain until the smaller man stepped to one side. Together, they walked silently toward the trail. The small detachment of Vietnamese volunteers followed without any overt sign from Nho, as if they were iron particles drawn to a powerful magnet.

Bolan glanced over his shoulder and felt himself, too, drawn to the smaller man. He thought how odd it was that simply allowing yourself to be open to another could change your perspective on him. In having made himself more vulnerable, more human, Nho had become easier to trust, harder to hate. The long years of the war had taken their toll on both men, and this shared abrasion, the slow but steady grinding away of the spirit was something they had in common. That, too, had made it more difficult to overlook the essential humanity at the core of each man, a likeness so much greater than the petty distinctions used to differentiate, to isolate and to ostracize. Ultimately, Bolan realized, he and Nho were not that different, less different than they were alike. The alikeness created a bond, provided a fertile soil in which respect, if left alone, would naturally grow. It didn't have to be tended, it simply had to be given a chance and sufficient time.

They were getting closer, now, to the foothills of the mountains. Away to the left, Bolan heard the mutter of running water, too soft to be a river, but lively enough to suggest a decent-sized tributary. He was about to check the hand-drawn map tucked in his pocket when something caught his eye. Uphill and to the left, something glittering, but motionless. He grabbed Nho by the shoulder and pointed.

Nho squinted, then grabbed a pair of binoculars from his pack. He trained them on the spot Bolan had indicated. He seemed to take a long time, fiddling with the focus and sweeping the glasses back and forth in a tight arc.

"What is it?" Bolan hissed.

"I think you should see for yourself," Nho said. Bolan reached for the glasses, but Nho refused to hand them over. "Up close. You should see it up close." His voice was hard-edged, with a chilly stiffness Bolan had thought banished permanently.

Bolan felt a little of that chill trickle down his spine. He approached an opening in the undergrowth, and the silvery puzzle vanished. He moved slowly, trying not to lose his bearings. Behind him Nho waited on the trail and Rogers pushed through the jungle while the Vietnamese whispered among themselves. The ground sloped abruptly upward, and the sound of moving water grew louder. Whatever it was, was for Bolan and Rogers, the Americans, to see.

And then, as the foliage grew thinner still and the ground fell away to the left, Bolan found himself walking a ridge sloping away on either side toward the top of a hill. High up, about a hundred yards above him, three trees stood on the crest. He recognized them as the background against which he had seen the silver vision. Their trunks were lighted by the nearly full moon, but the bark appeared gray, much darker than the glittering outline he had seen only with his naked eye.

Forty yards from his goal, Bolan tripped and fell, his foot echoing hollowly against something he immediately recognized as metal. He got to his knees and felt around in the shadows, but whatever it was eluded him, perhaps sent skittering down the side of the hill by the contact with his boot. Another twenty-five yards, and the undergrowth was all but gone, reduced to tall grass and an occasional shrub. Bolan began to run, heading toward the foot of the tallest tree. Rogers's heavy steps thumped along behind him, the older man's labored breathing raspy in the stillness.

And suddenly, like a hallucination or a mirage, there it was. As he moved closer, slowing his speed in awe, or reverence, or perhaps both, the moonlight seemed to flicker like a hundred small flames. There on the hilltop, covering a small area nearly naked of vegetation, lay the remains of a Cobra gunship. Broken glass, which was scattered throughout the clearing, some fragments still held in place by the rubber mounting strips, reflected the moonlight in a thousand directions. What from a distance had seemed otherworldly and mysterious was now reduced to something all too deeply rooted in this world.

Bolan stepped closer, bits of rusted metal crunching under his feet. The paint had long ago peeled away, and large parts of the ship's outer skin had crumbled, leaving the ribs and struts exposed like the skeleton of a prehistoric beast. But this beast was all too modern.

"Jaysus, Mack, would you look at that," Rogers whispered. Bolan, overawed by the discovery, had forgotten he was not alone, and his friend's voice had startled him. Like a man suddenly released from a trance, Bolan stepped forward, his right hand extended, palm out flat. Almost reverentially, he caressed the ruined metal, feeling the roughness of its rust crumble beneath his fingers. He stepped toward the tail of the chopper and leaned toward it, trying to make out its number, but the paint had flaked away, taking with it any chance of identifying the chopper from the outside.

He stepped toward the cockpit and leaned in. It was shadowy inside, light banding the shade where the ship's skin had rusted away. The dark bulk of a minigun loomed above him. He yanked a light from his belt and clicked it on, shining it first toward the tail section then back toward the front. The shadows seemed to dare him to explore more deeply, and he climbed up onto the rusted lip of the ruined helicopter.

Bolan broke out in a cold sweat. He'd dropped the light inside, and its beam angled up, glinting off the bleached white bone of the pilot's skull, still wearing his helmet, the headset askew, but still dangling before the grinning jaws.

"We have to mark this spot and get this guy out of here," he said.

"Guys," Rogers returned. "The gunner and at least one other man are inside, too. Come on, Mack, let's go. Nho can plot the location for us. There's nothing else we can do now."

Bolan nodded, backing slowly away from the ruins like a man in a trance. "So this is what it all comes to," he whispered. "Rust and bones...why do we even bother?"

And before the question had died away, he knew the answer.

They bothered because the alternative was worse.

27

Like a half dozen silver statues, the motionless Vietnamese stood in a semicircle around the two Americans. Nho looked intently at Bolan trying to find some trace of emotion on the big American's face, some evidence that things had changed, that Bolan was no longer a man to be trusted.

Instead, he found a profound sadness that had nothing to do with war or enmity. It was a feeling Nho, too, had come to understand. Confronted often enough with evidence of man's inhumanity, and the inevitable end waiting for good and evil men alike, there comes a time when all one can do is shake his head. You can lie down and die, or you can push on, trying to get past the overwhelming sense of futility. Bolan, as usual had chosen the latter course.

Nho would have expected no less.

Bolan said nothing about what he had seen. There would be time to talk about it later.

"I have plotted the location as best I can, Mr. Bolan," Nho said. Bolan, appreciating the simplicity of the declaration, nodded his head.

"Let's go," he said. His voice sounded hollow in his own throat, as if coming from someplace deep inside him.

Bolan led the way, moving with a detached grace, as if he had relearned something forgotten in his rage to free Margot. They had only two miles to go, now, and Bolan settled into a regular pace, moving swiftly but unhurriedly, without a trace of the frenzy that had marked his earlier progress. Nho noticed the difference with approval.

THOMAS GRIFFITH SAT in his hut, one small light burning in a corner of the room. He wondered whether he had made the right decision. He fiddled with a book, marked the page and closed it with a thud. He wasn't used to second-guessing himself, and the feeling made him restless.

It would have been easy to ambush the small team now so close to his camp. He had done it before more than once. Everyone from a Vietnamese army unit to a marauding band of Cambodians, remnants of Pol Pot's army, had tried to get to him and failed.

It was easy, still so easy, but every time it happened he wondered about the next time. Griffith was no fool, and he understood the law of averages. For a long time, he'd had the sense of some unnameable thing closing in on him, drawing ever closer, its approach impossible to chart and even less possible to describe. But in the night, lying awake on his cot, with nothing but the night sounds of the jungle to keep him company, he could sense its presence. For want of a better word, he'd begun to call it fate.

He knew too much about himself, and about the world, to believe the stories the Meo told about him, about his invincibility and his courage. He knew he was a brave man. But he'd been too well educated in the history of war to believe for a minute that he was unconquerable. He was arrogant to a fault, but in knowing it he blunted its effect.

That, perhaps, was what had preserved him for so long. But in the end, he understood only too well that it could not last forever. Anxious to control events rather than become their victim, sitting back passively while the world worked its way with him, he had decided to let his defenses, which at best could only postpone the inevitable, permit Bolan to come to him.

He knew as much about Mack Bolan as Bolan knew little of him. Both men were cloaked in mystery and in half-digested stories about their prowess thick enough to be called myth, but at the core of Bolan's myth was an iron will that could be understood, plotted, tracked, comprehended. If you had sources enough, and resources to match, you could get at the essence of Bolan.

Griffith, on the other hand, was more elusive than that. There was no way to get a handle on him. He was too remote, too far out of the mainstream. He recognized his own incomprehensibility and revelled in it. There had been times when he had done something simply because it was inexplicable and illogical. It enhanced his reputation, even as it made him still more elusive, still further removed from the normal patterns of human behavior.

Bolan might get to him, but he would never understand him. The idiots who worked for him believed he was motivated by money. And it was certainly true that his labors had been richly rewarded. He didn't even know how much money he had, because it didn't matter to him. It made no difference whatsoever. When you came right down to it, he took the money for only one reason: failure to do so would have earned him another reputation—that of a fool. It would be more trouble than it was worth to disabuse those anxious to prey on him.

Griffith moved slightly, shifting his chair, and he watched his shadow lengthen and dance on the crude, thatched walls of his hut. He contemplated the shadow as if it were that of a stranger. Detached from his own reality, he recognized nothing about himself, the distortion wrought by the light disguising his essential characteristics. And that distortion freed him, enabled him to invest the shadow with his own attributes and contemplate them with a certain disinterest.

The military life had appealed to him because it permitted him to manipulate, to use others with impunity, unfeelingly dispatching them the way a bored chess player would throw away his pawns, mindlessly, carelessly, respecting neither himself, his opponent, or the final outcome of the contest. Nothing mattered to him, and the more successful he became, the less things mattered. Until, finally, the only challenge that had any meaning at all was challenging the very source of his own authority.

And, so, he had turned his back on the military, walking away without so much as a by-your-leave. As a tactician, he had been a master, as a leader of men he had been aloof, too remote to be inspiring and too dispassionate to inspire either fear or loyalty. Even the Meo he had gathered around him had little feeling for him. They had coalesced around him as in some natural process, like water vapor collecting around a particle of dust to become a drop of rain, and the more followers he had the more he got.

He had no feeling for them, nor they for him. Each stayed because it was easier than not staying. It was not comfortable, but it was not uncomfortable. And when he had discovered they were willing to do what he told them, it had been as easy to establish the smuggling network as not to do it. Taking over some existing supply lines, things and people drawn to him with that same gravitic inevitability, he gradually became lost in the welter of followers, the constant activity swirling around him.

He leaned back in the chair, staring almost through a map of the world tacked to the wall. He shifted in his seat, and his shadow danced wildly as the flickering light of the small lamp fluttered in a stiff breeze. Slowly, like a man walking in his sleep, he lifted his hands before him, slowly interlacing the fingers and interposing them between the wall and the flame. The tangled shadow, like a spiderweb of silken ropes, spread slowly across the map, until it mirrored his influence and the reach of his tentacles. He smiled like a man about to have his dreams come true.

In a way, it was inertia that motivated him. His unwillingness to move had led him to make others do so. The immovable object he had become seemed capable of resisting any force. Bolan seemed like the ultimate test of his power. There was no point in postponing a confrontation that was destined to happen. His fate was rapidly approaching, in the shape of The Executioner.

He was ready.

As ready as he would ever be.

THE MOON RODE HIGH in the sky, nearly full, like a silver stain on a dark satin sheet. Its light was so bright that it washed out the stars all the way to the horizon in every direction. On the hill nearly three thousand feet above Bolan stood a ragged line of huts surrounded by a rough stone wall that was topped with razor-sharp wire. Starkly outlined against the dark sky, the compound seemed like the boundary line between heaven and Earth.

Somewhere up there, behind that wall, was Colonel Thomas Griffith. Against all odds, they had reached the den of the beast. Bolan understood men like Griffith too well to think it was simple good luck. There was no such thing for men like him.

Or for men like Griffith.

Bolan was convinced the renegade knew he was there. He hadn't seen a soul, no one had attempted to stop them, the silence had been total and undisturbed. That could only mean one thing.

Griffith was expecting him.

The enigmatic man at the top of the hill was willing to take him head on, winner take all. Whoever came out alive would be king of the mountain. For Griffith, it would mean some respite until the next challenger came along, the next pretender to his throne. And for Bolan, it would mean justice in its most bloody incarnation. Justice for Aloysius Mackenzie, justice for Ambassador Tranh, justice for the thousands who slowly poisoned themselves with Griffith's deadly commodity.

And somewhere up there Margot waited for him. He didn't realize until that moment how much that mattered and how much she mattered to him. Griffith must have known, or he wouldn't have gone to all the trouble to take her prisoner. And Griffith wanted something from him, that was for certain. If not, it would have been a simple matter to fall on them as they struggled through the jungle, picking their small band to pieces, one by one blowing them away until nothing was left but food for scavengers. He could have done that. His engineering of Margot's abduction was all the proof anyone could need. And the more subtle, more impersonal defenses, mines and punji stakes, pitfalls and deadfalls, were strangely absent. That one mine he'd seen and managed to skirt couldn't have been the only one. That there were no further incidents meant only that Griffith had wanted him to make it this far.

It was all he could do to keep himself from charging the last three thousand feet. Nho, of course, would have tried to stop him, and Jimbo would have used all his Irish charm to talk him out of it, but neither man had to do a thing. This business was best done in the bright light of day, not because darkness gave Griffith an advantage, but because darkness was where he lived. Bolan wanted the clear, pure, antiseptic light of the sun to bathe him, to disinfect arena and combatants alike. This was it, the last stand, and whoever won was more than the victor. He was the sole survivor.

And Bolan was determined to see another sunset.

Nho stood silently beside him and offered the field glasses without a word. Bolan took them and scanned the perimeter of the camp, end to end and back, sweeping the glasses in a slow surveillance. Then, satisfied that the time had not yet come, he sat to wait for sunrise.

28

Bolan sat up all night, staring at the dim outline of the mountain above him. Every nerve was alive, humming. He was wired, like a long-haul trucker on bennies. The moon slipped away, dropping off the edge of the world with a suddenness that would have surprised someone who'd never lived in the tropics.

For an hour it was pitch black, the stars staring down at him, winking seductively, trying to catch his eye. But the Executioner had eyes only for the stone wall, and his mind was concerned only with things ensconced beyond it.

And then the morning came.

The sun rose, its huge redness exploding over the Ailan Shan. The small, tight corner where Laos, Vietnam and China meet, but don't truly come together, seemed like the center of the universe. The brilliant red light bathed everything, leaving the ten-thousand-foot peaks all around Bolan stained with a deep ruby color that he'd swear would never fade. Like a small thing trapped in the bloody jaws of a predator, Bolan could almost feel the earth move beneath him, like a tongue preparing for another swallow.

And then he would be gone.

Bolan shook his head, trying to clear it from the sensory overload, to dislodge the chaotic storm of contrasting images.

Rogers was sitting to his left, sharing the long vigil. They whispered from time to time, trying to devise a plan that seemed workable, but the constant variations kept running into snags. Only one approach seemed to make sense. "I guess that's it, then, Jimbo," Bolan said.

The matter-of-fact tone might have been taken for resignation by anyone unfamiliar with Mack Bolan. Jimmy Rogers knew better. He slapped his friend on the shoulder. "By God, it's a beautiful morning, isn't it, boyo?" He stood and stretched, with a groan nearly drowned out by the crack of stiffened joints.

Bolan got to his feet. He took one last look at the sun, which floated above the horizon as if balanced on the point of a far-off mountain. He hoped his own position was less precarious. But the time to worry about such things had been exhausted.

It was time to do something about cutting the odds.

He nodded to the Vietnamese on sentry, then woke Nho. "It's time to go, Captain."

Nho shook his head, then stretched. "I suppose you are right, Mr. Bolan."

"You and I are going right up the front of this mountain."

"Alone?"

"Yeah. We'll make better time. Bring as many grenades and as much ammo as you can reasonably carry. I'll do the same."

"And the others?"

"They'll go around the other side and look for a way up. I'm betting Griffith wants us to come straight up this trail and it'll be clean. I'm not so sure about the rest of the routes."

"You'll pardon me if I observe that this is not much of a plan."

"You're right, but I don't want to try to outguess this guy. I want to let him think he's in command. If he makes a mistake, we'll be ready to jump on it. He can't be as smart as he thinks."

"But if he is?"

"We won't have to worry about it, will we?"

Nho drew a long breath and held it. Finally, when Bolan thought the man's lungs must be ready to burst, the breath exploded out of him, and Nho said, "No, we won't have to worry about it."

The captain quickly relayed the sketchy plan to his unit, then took several grenades from them, attaching them to his belt. He crammed ammo clips for the AK-47 and a .45-caliber automatic into his pockets, then stowed the rest of his gear in a hollow tree.

Bolan, busy making his own preparations, exchanged a few last words with Rogers then joined Nho. It was time to go.

Bolan led the way up the mountain, his heart thumping. This direct confrontation with Griffith was a calculated risk, but it seemed like the only way to tip the scales. Everything was on Griffith's side as it was. But if the colonel's confidence and self-assurance could be pushed a little, if he could be tempted just a bit, he might leave them an opening.

The unit pushed ahead, moving swiftly through the jungle, traveling cautiously along a well-worn footpath. Every so often they saw evidence of just how badly Griffith wanted to meet them: holes where mines had been dug up; the trip wires lying slack; a large pit full of stakes that had been uncovered, a small barrier erected before it.

It seemed as if Griffith had left no stone unturned in his effort to make certain they arrived safely. Their instincts warned them not to make the same kind of mistake they were hoping to see from Griffith. Just as every confessed sin frequently conceals two others more grievous, every trick and trap might be designed to hide something deadlier.

They were careful and fought to keep up their guard, but if they made a mistake, they were unaware of it when the jagged edge of the stone wall appeared over the edge of the slope, which was now only a hundred yards above them.

Bolan stepped into the undergrowth to the right of the trail, Nho to the left. Thinner than the jungle below, it was nevertheless an impediment to progress. They took turns crawling forward, one watching the wall while the other closed the gap.

The wall itself seemed even more imposing at close range. More than twelve feet high in some places, it was formidable...but not impregnable. Behind it, farther up the slope, the thatched roofs of primitive huts dotted the skyline. To the left, on a stone tower rising above the wall itself, was a satellite dish, its central struts pointed at some small speck in the sky, and Bolan turned involuntarily to look, as if it were a sign. But the sky was a flat, cloudless blue, already tinged with white where the bright sun seemed to bleach the color away.

ROGERS WAS BREATHING HARD. He and the detachment of Vietnamese had kept off the trails, and hacking through the thick undergrowth was taking its toll. He glanced at Thieu, who smiled and barked a command in

Vietnamese. As one, the six men collapsed to the ground, sprawled in near exhaustion. It was still early, barely seven-thirty, but the Irishman would have sworn he'd been walking for six hours. Lying on his back, he gazed disinterestedly out over the valley.

The mottled green stretched down and away, broken here and there by rolling hills in its gradual descent to the valley floor several miles away. Squinting against the sun, he scanned the immediate area, then worked his way down the slope. Something caught his eye, and he stopped. He couldn't put his finger on what it was, but something wasn't right.

He stared, but saw nothing. Starting again at a point just below him, he again swept his eyes back and forth across the slope, slowly working his gaze toward the valley floor, and again he was arrested by the same vague sensation that something was askew.

He borrowed Thieu's binoculars and repeated the sweep, again stopping involuntarily at the same point. But this time he knew why.

The greenery was artificial. He wasn't sure how, but he was convinced. He twiddled the focus wheel, sharpening the image in the field glasses a little, but the improvement neither confirmed nor contradicted the impression.

Thieu had been watching him closely, even before he borrowed the glasses. "What is it?" he whispered, not wanting to call the attention of the others to the discovery until he knew what it was. If it was bad news, there would be time enough for them to learn of it.

"Not sure, laddie. Have a look." Rogers thrust the glasses back into the man's hands.

"Where?"

"You look. See for yourself. If I tell you, you might see something that ain't there."

The Vietnamese corporal swept the field glasses slowly back and forth across the valley floor, choosing to work up from below instead of emulating the American. The big man watched carefully, holding his breath as the black binoculars combed the top of the canopy in a smooth, easy motion. Suddenly the glasses stopped moving.

"I see it," Thieu hissed.

"What is it?"

"I don't know. Something has disturbed the forest somehow. It looks like—"

"I know what it looks like," Rogers broke in. "The question is, *is* it what it looks like?"

He stood hurriedly and snatched his gear from the leaf mold beside him. "Let's go."

"Where?"

"We've got to get a closer look. We've got to make sure."

"But we are supposed to be going up to the camp," the corporal protested. "They will be expecting us."

"Thieu, old buddy, I got news for you. Me and Mack go back a long ways. Improvising is part of the game. If I'm right—and I'm willing to bet I am—it could make the difference in this here little contretemps. Now either you're coming with me or you're not. But either way, I'm going back down there. I've got to."

"You can't go alone. You are big, but not that big. And for somebody who claims he hates slopes, you are not so bad, either." Thieu barked a series of instructions to the other four Vietnamese, who jumped to their feet and grabbed their rifles. Khanh, a tall, thin young man, picked up Thieu's machete and began to move into the undergrowth. Without a word of protest, the others followed.

"No offense, but can you trust the lads to go on ahead without us?"

"Who won the war, Mr. Jimbo?"

"I got you." He slapped the smaller man smartly on the shoulder. "You're all right, boyo, you know that?"

BOLAN BURST OUT of the greenery and charged straight toward the wall. Nho swept the muzzle of his Kalashnikov back and forth across the parapet, but nothing moved. The wide strip of defoliated land was dry and dusty, one hundred feet of no-man's land. The small clouds kicked up by Bolan's feet seemed to hang a moment, then collapse in on themselves and disappear. Not a breath of air moved.

Then it was Nho's turn. Bolan, back pressed to the wall, watched as Nho raced against the small clearing. The soil, thin and slippery, more like powdered graphite than sand, made running difficult. But Nho moved efficiently, preferring to zigzag his way across.

The two men leaned back against the wall, listening. Not a sound came from behind it. It was as if they had stumbled on a ruined city, long ago abandoned by the inhabitants.

"It's too quiet," Bolan whispered.

"We may as well see what's behind this wall," Nho suggested.

"He has to be here."

The rough stone made for nearly effortless climbing. Bolan scrambled up, tossing one leg onto the rough platform at its top. Even here Griffith had made access easy; the razor-sharp wire had been removed. Bolan hauled his other leg up and turned to look toward the inside.

A low parapet wall, little more than two feet high, topped the inner edge of the main wall, and he could not see over it. Bolan rolled over to the foot of the shorter wall, and lay flat, waiting for Nho to join him.

When the Vietnamese captain had negotiated the short climb, he spun around then rolled over to a point just in front of Bolan. They lay face-to-face, both breathing heavily, each wondering what came next, neither sure just how much he could count on the man facing him.

The sound, when it came, ruptured the silence, destroyed their concentration. It boomed and echoed, accompanied by small bursts of static.

"Welcome home, Sergeant."

29

Bolan peered over the low wall into the center of the compound. For an instant, he thought his ears had deceived him. The place appeared deserted. He scanned the doorways of the dozen and a half thatched huts and came up empty. A different kind of structure stood by itself at the heart of the compound. Where the others were round or rectangular, closely modeled on the kind of huts found all over Southeast Asia, this building resembled a pyramid. It was taller than the others, and if it had an entrance, it was not visible from Bolan's vantage point.

The greeting had died away, and in its place, an eerie silence seemed to resonate, filling the air with a subliminal hum.

"Do you see anyone?" Nho asked.

"Not a soul. The place might as well be a ghost town."

For a moment, Bolan was tempted to call out, but he resisted. Starting this early to play Griffith's game could be a fatal mistake. Instead, he started to crawl along the wall, edging toward the far corner. Nho, catching on immediately, moved toward the opposite corner.

For the Executioner, so used to electronic warning systems, television surveillance and infrared photoelectric cells, Griffith's camp seemed like something out of time. It belonged more to the age of King Arthur than it did to the twentieth century. And as Bolan thought about that disjuncture, he began to understand, things began to shift, to come into focus.

Griffith was not about greed; he wasn't interested in money. Instead, what he wanted, craved, perhaps, in the same way a heroin addict needs a fix, was power. Griffith did what he wanted because it was the only way he felt alive. Conformity, recognition of authority, obedience, these were the attributes of a vassal, even of a slave. Griffith wanted to be the master, to decide who was conforming and who was not, to flout established authority by thumbing his nose at the law and at human decency. He could no more stop doing what he was doing than he could willfully stop breathing. It was a natural disorder that fueled him. Griffith was entropy personified.

And now that he understood that, all Bolan had to do was figure out what to use against him. All he had to do was stop him.

Yeah, a piece of cake.

Once he'd reached the far corner, Bolan poked his head above the low wall. A chip of granite flaked off, catching him in the cheek. He ducked his head quickly, banging his forehead on the edge of the wall. He heard the crack of the rifle a fraction of a second later, as he brought his bloody fingers away from the wound.

"Bo-laann..."

An eerie echo bounced through the deserted village like a tumbleweed. The voice was taunting, like that of a child in a park, daring him to come and play. Peeking over the wall again, he saw little swirls of dust, a ragged line of them, caught in suspension by a wayward gust of wind. Someone had run from one of the huts to the central building.

The warrior glanced down the length of the parapet and could no longer see Nho, who must have turned the corner and begun working his way along the far side of the wall. If anyone had run into the central building, it was doubtful that Nho would have seen him.

Turning back to the pyramidal structure, Bolan noticed a puff of smoke, followed shortly by a muffled crack. In slow motion, just barely overcoming their collective inertia, the walls of the pyramid had begun to mushroom outward, apparently propelled by the small explosion at its apex. Standing perpendicular to the earth, the walls, little more than thatched panels, seemed to shudder. They teetered precariously for several seconds, then continued their journey away from the center.

Bolan stared as if transfixed. That this odd spectacle had been arranged for his benefit was indisputable. But what it meant, what it was supposed to accomplish, was anything but apparent. Like a house of cards sundered by a firecracker, the pyramid now crumbled in virtually soundless collapse. Small dust devils were kicked up by the four panels as air rushed to escape from under them. The same powdery ash covering the arid moat around the base of the wall covered the entire interior of the compound.

And then Bolan knew why the walls had been removed. On a small stone platform rising three feet above the ground, stood a wooden pole about two feet in diameter. Arranged around the pole were three women, thick ropes binding their ankles and throats, their hands tied behind their backs.

It took Bolan a second to recognize Margot, who was the woman facing him. When he did, he half stood, straining forward over the parapet wall. Her clothes were in tatters, dangling from her shoulders and waist, as if some wild beast had tried to claw them from her body. The other two women were in profile, and he wasn't sure who they were. But Margot was enough to get his attention.

"Every game needs a prize, Bolan. Doesn't it?" the voice boomed. "How about it? The stakes high enough?" A burst of rifle fire punctuated the final question, shattering the stone to Bolan's right. He dived beyond the low wall, bruising his left shoulder.

"Kwan Lee is here, too. And her sister. They're counting on you. Don't let them down, now."

JIMMY ROGERS SKIDDED the last fifty yards downhill, coming to rest on the edge of a flat space carved into the hillside. Small patches of sunlight broke through the canopy overhead. From the underside, it looked just as artificial as it had from above. A thick rope netting, interlaced with recently cut fronds, stretched nearly a hundred feet across the square. The fronds had begun to dehydrate, betraying their artificiality by a flat, sheenless green. A few hours earlier, and he wouldn't have noticed it. A few hours later, and a blind man could see the difference.

Thieu stumbled and fell as he bounded down the hillside after Rogers, getting to his feet with an embarrassed grin. The Irishman whistled in admiration as he stepped toward the center of the square. Even in the canopied gloom, he was impressed.

"Pretty, ain't she?" he asked, reaching out to run a hand over the smooth skin. "Ever rode one like her?"

Thieu shook his head.

"Give me a hand with these ropes, will you, boyo?" Rogers yanked a survival knife from his hip and began to hack at the taut lines holding the canopy in place. "We ought to throw a little light on her, don't you think? They don't always look as pretty in the morning." He laughed a full-throated laugh, his sides shaking with delight. Thieu seemed baffled, but lent a willing hand.

"We get the cover off, then we got to cut her loose. Make sure you don't scratch her none."

Rogers stopped babbling, putting all his energy into sawing at the thick ropes. One by one, they parted, some of them just falling away, others, under greater tension, parting with a twang as the blade bit into the last few strands.

One side of the canopy suddenly gave way, falling to the ground. The two men grabbed the trailing edge of the lines at one corner and began to tug the canopy toward the far side, still anchored and tethered several feet above the ground. Despite their desiccation, the leaves were heavy, the rope netting no less so.

The men worked up a sweat before they finally got the free corner rolled into a thick tube. Then, hacking the former support poles off at ground level, they struggled to lift the cylinder of leaves and netting over the captive. When they had pulled the canopy clear, bright sunlight washed over the center of the square.

"Look at her. Just as pretty a little thing as I ever saw. What do you think, Thieu? A real beauty, ain't she?"

A SHRILL WHISTLE reverberated through the compound, then seemed to fracture into still-sharper-edged shards and bounce away. In a practiced unanimity that would have done the Rockettes proud, eighteen men appeared in eighteen doorways, sprinted toward the platform and arranged themselves in a circle, facing outward.

An instant later, a burly man in khaki leaped onto the stone platform, taking up a position directly in front of Margot. "I know all about you Bolan," the man hollered. It was the same voice that had been taunting him over the hidden speaker network. At long last, Colonel Griffith himself had taken center stage.

"You try to shoot me, your girlfriend here stops a slug or two. I'm as penetrable as the next man . . . or woman, eh? Something to think about, isn't it? Of course, she won't feel it. She's sort of sleeping. A little high grade can put you out of a lot of misery, you know? Especially if you're not used to it. Offhand, I'd say she was cherry. Never rode the dragon, Bolan. But now she knows. You coming down?"

"You're a bastard, Griffith. And a coward."

"Bolan, Bolan, Bolan," Griffith mumbled, shaking his head as if disappointed. "Come on, you can do better than that. What kind of a fool do you take me for? I'm supposed to get steamed, right? And make a mistake? Forget it. You want me, you'll have to work for it."

Bolan chanced a look over the wall. Griffith, strutting like the cock of the walk, paced in a small circle, looking like a showboating professional wrestler playing to the crowd.

"If you're so good, why do you need all the backup, Griffith?"

"Backup? Oh, no! You don't understand. Every contest needs an appreciative audience. Or else, where's the glory in victory? Savoring it yourself is only half the fun of winning. You ought to know that, Bolan. Hell, man, you were undefeated . . . until today."

"Now what?"

"Come on down, give it up. You can have the woman back and you can walk away."

"What's in it for you?"

"The thrill of victory . . . the laurel wreath . . . the World Series ring. Hell, man. If I take you down a peg, it's the MVP and Cy Young Award rolled into one. I will be *translated*, man. You read the Bible? You remember—He didn't die, He was translated. He became immortal. That's what I want. Immortality. But I don't want to live forever. I'm tired, Bolan. So tired maybe I've already lived forever. But I want that one last win. I want to be a legend. Undefeated and still champeen a' the woild, Bolan. Can you dig that?''

Bolan saw the opening, grabbed for it before Griffith could recover. "Big man. Legend. A myth? And you stand there threatening three defenseless hostages like a two-bit pimp. Some legend you'd make. How about it, big shot. You stand there gawking and take a fastball down the middle. That won't get you in the hall of fame, pal.''

Griffith stammered something unintelligible. He was caught with his guard down. Now, all Bolan had to do was push him over.

But how?

How do you know which way to push a lunatic? How do you know when he's off balance?

30

The roar of an engine erupted behind him, and Bolan turned sharply, but not before he noticed the look of shock on Griffith's face. Whatever it was, the colonel had no more idea than Bolan. The air seemed to fill with the noise, and then they all heard it—the *whup-whup-whup* of a chopper, and close by.

Bolan crawled back to the edge of the wall, and looked down the mountainside. Like the wings of a giant insect, the rotor blades came into view as the chopper seemed to leap off the jungle floor and rise straight into the air. It was an AH-1G Cobra, sister ship to the rusted hulk Bolan had found on the way in. But if Griffith was surprised, whose ship was it?

He heard an excited babble behind him and stood to look over the parapet wall. Griffith's closely drilled legion had scattered in every direction, their carefully polished, but never challenged discipline coming apart at the seams. The chopper was high in the air now, higher than the hilltop, slipping sidewise like a Frisbee then, spinning, it dipped its nose and dived straight toward the center of the encampment.

A minigun barked, its 7.62 mm rounds sending huge puffy clouds of dirt into the air as they ripped their way across the compound. The gunner was obviously a novice, but Bolan offered up a silent prayer of gratitude.

But there was work to be done. Griffith, seemingly oblivious to the gargantuan wasp hovering over the compound, raised his fist in the air and shook it at Bolan. Another burst from the minigun chopped into the earth near him, and he leaped from the stone platform and charged straight toward the Executioner, still waving his fist as if it were a weapon.

Griffith stopped in midcharge and wrestled an automatic from its holster. He fired round after round in the general direction of his nemesis, and, when the clip was empty, threw the gun in a great, shining arc. It flew end over end, striking the parapet wall butt first, then falling back into the compound below. By the time it landed, Griffith was racing in the other direction.

Certain now that the chopper was on his team, Bolan rushed to the center of the wall and looked for a stairway down. When he found none, he spun around, caught the parapet wall with both hands and flung himself out and down. When his boots slammed into the wall, he pushed out and <u>let</u> go with his hands, stumbling backward as he hit the earth, sending up a small cloud of dust.

He could no longer see Griffith, but the colonel's voice rang in the air as he tried to rally his troops. A few sporadic gunshots cracked from across the camp, but Bolan could see no one. Racing to the center of the compound, he jumped to the platform, knife already in hand. Quickly he cut the ropes binding the three women and dragged them free of the pole. Margot collapsed onto the stone without a sound. Kwan Lee seemed to be in the best shape, and she helped her sister, Chan, toward the edge of the platform. Bolan jumped down, taking the nearly unconscious woman in his arms.

"Take her to the wall. There has to be a gate somewhere."

"I know where it is."

Bolan climbed back to the platform and tugged Margot to her feet. She was deadweight, and a hell of a lot more of it than Kwan Chan. He slung her over his shoulder in a fireman's carry, then jumped onto the ground. The impact strained his knee joints, and he felt as if they would give way.

Rushing to one corner of the wall, he joined Kwan Lee and stopped to catch his breath. "Where is the gate?" he gasped.

"At the other end of the camp. Griffith has us cut off."

"If we can't go around him, we'll have to go over him," Bolan said grimly. Before Kwan Lee could argue, a steady crack of rifle fire broke out at the far end of the enclosure. Bolan hoped it was Rogers.

A moment later he knew that it wasn't.

With bloodcurdling howls, a half dozen men armed with AK-47s barreled from between two of the huts. They seemed momentarily disoriented, but spotting Bolan and the three women, they charged straight toward them. The Russian assault rifles spit fire in continuous waves, and Bolan pushed Kwan Lee to the ground, hauling Margot down as he fell.

Suddenly the chopper screamed across the compound, Bolan looking up in time to see it veering toward the charging men. A small figure dressed in black stood in the doorway, hanging on with one hand as the ship canted to a forty-five-degree angle. The figure lobbed three grenades in rapid succession, the explosion from the first missile halting the advancing troops in their tracks.

They flattened on the ground and turned their weapons on the climbing chopper as the second grenade went off. The third, planted with precision, exploded in the midst of the prostrate "soldiers," flinging their bodies about like straw men. A ball of smoke and ash mushroomed, engulfing the chopper for a moment, then, torn to rags by the whirling blades, drifted away in black tatters.

The warrior caught a fleeting glimpse of Nho, but the man vanished almost as quickly as he had appeared.

A figure materialized at the center of the compound and climbed onto the stone platform, and there was no mistaking that face. It was the triggerman who had killed Aloysius Mackenzie. He seemed disoriented, as if uncertain where to run...or where to look. And Bolan had no doubt that the man was looking for him.

The assassin's name exploded from his lungs in a roar. "Carlucci!" It echoed and swirled away in the churning winds. Bolan left the women huddled in the corner and charged straight toward the assassin.

Carlucci didn't see Bolan at first. Griffith had sent the high-priced assassin to kill the women.

Bolan swept up the M-16 and squeezed, but the gun jammed. Instead of the staccato hammering he'd expected, there was a single click, and then silence. He tossed the gun to the ground and continued his charge.

Carlucci had turned away, still looking for his assigned targets, when Bolan caught him in the ribs with a shoulder. Carlucci went down heavily, and Bolan pinned him. The surprised assassin tried to wriggle free, but the Executioner's weight was too much for him. His hand snaked to a pocket in his camou fatigues then reappeared with a flash. The knife nicked Bolan on the shoulder before a chop to Carlucci's wrist tore the weapon loose. It skittered away off the stone and dropped to the ground with a thud.

Desperate now, Carlucci began to heave, but Bolan was inexorable. He grabbed the assassin's throat in both hands and began to squeeze. Bolan saw it all in one panoramic view. The sinews of his hands bulged, his knuckles whitening. The assassin gasped, then tried to choke, but there wasn't enough air in his lungs. His face began to redden, then to grow purple, except for the ghostly white area around Bolan's clutching fingers. The rolling eyes began to go out of focus, to glaze. Then, as if let in on some cosmic joke, Carlucci grinned. The ghastly smile seemed fixed, frozen.

Bolan realized that the man was dead. He relaxed his grip, felt the blood flow back into his constricted fingers, which had cramped from the exertion.

A wave of concussion washed over him, and he turned to see a second hut disappear in a ball of fire. The chopper now seemed to be out of control, skittering across the sky, but the rain of shells was deadly accurate. Several huts took direct hits, smoke swirling outward and up, and enveloping the hail of debris. Bolan could hear the shattered poles and broken limbs clattering and hissing as they landed.

The Executioner got to his feet, grabbed Carlucci's Kalashnikov, which featured a pair of magazines taped back-to-back, and raced toward the corner, waving at the chopper to hold off until he got clear. Threading his way through the huts, he found himself flanking a handful of

Americans. They were firing on the run, obviously under pressure from the compound gate.

Bolan swung the AK-47 in a wide arc, and the surprised troops turned as his first magazine ran dry. Bolan yanked it out and flipped it over, jamming it home in a fluid motion. Only two of the original five men were still on their feet. The warrior dived to one side, just ahead of a tight curl of Kalashnikov fire, and took cover behind the ruins of a hut.

Three Vietnamese advanced out of the turbulent smoke beyond the Americans, their Soviet-made weapons speaking on the side of right. Caught between hammer and anvil, the two Americans threw their weapons to the ground and raised their hands above their heads. Bolan steeled himself for the inevitable, but it didn't happen. Instead of chopping the former GIs to pieces in a rage as old as the very mountains, the three Vietnamese simply shoved them back toward the gate.

The autofire had stopped, the only noise that of the chopper, hovering overhead. With a sound somewhere between a whistle and a tired sigh, the gunship dropped straight down, its engines cut all the way back. As it landed roughly, Bolan ran toward the ship, reaching the rear door just as it swung open. A green-faced, tight-lipped Thieu stepped out and staggered off to vomit. Jimmy Rogers, like a weekend sailor home from a jaunt, jumped to the ground, smiling from ear to ear.

"Margot?"

"I got her."

"She all right?"

"I think so."

Rogers's grin widened. "You get Griffith?"

"Not yet."

The smile faded. "Man, there's nothing left of this place. If you didn't get him, where the hell is he?"

"I'll get him. Don't worry about it. You got enough fuel in that thing to make it to your chopper?"

"Probably."

"How many can you carry?"

"Two, maybe three, if they're light."

"Three women."

"Three?"

"Tell you later. They're in the corner. Fly them out, then come back for me. They all need medical attention."

"You got it, chief. It'll take a few hours, though."

"Just do it."

Bolan pushed past his friend like a man in a dream. He could hear Rogers and Thieu escorting the women to the chopper. That part was over. Behind him.

Only Griffith lay ahead. The colonel was the center of Bolan's universe. He walked through the rubble that was the ruined compound. One by one, he checked each corpse.

Griffith had vanished.

The helicopter's familiar *whup-whup-whup* signaled it was ready to take off, and Bolan turned to watch it rise, clearing the smoke like a breaching whale then climbing straight up and veering off to the southwest. At least the women were safe. Nho called to him out of the smoke, and Bolan waved halfheartedly. The Vietnamese called again, more insistent, and Bolan turned.

Nho, like an apparition in the thick smoke, was pointing to the high stone tower that was crowned with the satellite dish. A dim outline danced an unearthly dance,

like an angel on the head of a pin. It had to be Griffith.
Everyone else was accounted for.

With the chopper gone, a great hush settled over the
compound, broken only by the soft crackle of burning
leaves. Bolan tossed the Kalashnikov aside and dashed
toward the tower. As he ran, the eerie voice of Griffith,
distorted and magnified by the parabolic dish behind
him, called to him again, just as it had that morning.

"Bo-laann. I'm over here!" And the laughter that
followed seemed to come from the bowels of the Earth.
It was deep, resonant. And maniacal.

Bolan reached the foot of the tower grabbing on to the
hand runners of an iron ladder set into the stone. He
started to climb, the voice echoing, gargantuan, taunting. And halfway up, he heard the ping.

Something clicked in his memory, another circuit
reactivated, and Bolan recognized the sound. A grenade
spring. He pushed out and down, falling backward,
tumbling and rolling in midair.

The blast took off the dish and the top of the tower.
Bolan landed flat on his back, arms outspread, the wind
knocked out of him by the fall. He rolled over and covered his head as hunks of rock and mortar showered
down around him, pelted his back and shoulders, one
huge slab landing three inches from his head.

Slowly the warrior hauled himself to his knees, turned
to face the ruined tower, raised one fist into the air and
cursed. His own voice seemed frail and weak after Griffith's magnified, monstrous bellow. He felt betrayed...
and cheated of sweet revenge.

But maybe it was better this way. He had wanted Griffith to pay for Al's death, had wanted to confront him

with it then kill him, up close and personal. Perhaps Bolan had been spared this day, spared the ignominy of sinking to the depths of the savages.

Available now!
SuperBolan #11

ANVIL OF HELL

Bolan tracks nuclear fuel across the stony wastes of the Sudanese Sahara to thwart the plans of a powerful consortium to attack the Middle East.

Available now at your favorite retail outlet, or reserve your copy for shipping by sending your name, address, zip or postal code along with a check or money order for $4.70 (includes 75¢ for postage and handling) payable to Gold Eagle to:

In the U.S.	In Canada
Gold Eagle Books	Gold Eagle Books
901 Fuhrmann Boulevard	P.O. Box 609
Box 1325	Fort Erie, Ontario
Buffalo, NY 14269-1325	L2A 5X3

Please specify book title with your order.

GOLD EAGLE ®

SB-11R

The Badlands Just Got Worse . . .

JAMES AXLER
DEATH LANDS®
Pony Soldiers

Ryan Cawdor and his band of postholocaust survivors make a
startling discovery when they come face-to-face with a spectre
from the past—either they have chron-jumped back to the
1800s or General Custer has been catapulted into the twenty-
second century. . . .

Available now at your favorite retail outlet, or reserve your copy for shipping by sending
your name, address, zip or postal code along with a check or money order for $4.70
(includes 75¢ for postage and handling) payable to Gold Eagle Books:

In the U.S.	In Canada
Gold Eagle Books	Gold Eagle Books
901 Fuhrmann Blvd.	P.O. Box 609
Box 1325	Fort Erie, Ontario
Buffalo, NY 14269-1325	L2A 5X3

DL-6AR

Please specify book title with your order.

**A secret arms deal
with Iran ignites a powder keg,
and a most daring mission is
about to begin.**

THE BARRABAS STRIKE

JACK HILD

**Nile Barrabas and his soldiers undertake a
hazardous assignment when a powerful top-
secret weapon disappears and shows up in
Iran.**

Available now at your favorite retail outlet, or reserve your copy for shipping by sending your
name, address, zip or postal code, along with a check or money order for $4.70 (includes
75¢ for postage and handling) payable to Gold Eagle to:

In the U.S.	In Canada
Gold Eagle Books	Gold Eagle Books
901 Fuhrmann Boulevard	P.O. Box 609
Box 1325	Fort Erie, Ontario
Buffalo, NY 14269-1325	L2A 5X3

SS-1R

Please specify book title with your order.

GOLD
EAGLE

You don't know what NONSTOP HIGH-VOLTAGE ACTION is until you've read your 4 FREE GOLD EAGLE NOVELS

LIMITED-TIME OFFER

Mail to **Gold Eagle Reader Service**®

In the U.S.
P.O. Box 1394
Buffalo, N.Y. 14240-1394

In Canada
P.O. Box 609
Fort Erie, Ont. L2A 5X3

YEAH! Rush me 4 free Gold Eagle novels and my free mystery bonus. Then send me 6 brand-new novels every other month as they come off the presses. Bill me at the low price of just $14.95 — an 11% saving off the retail price - plus 95¢ postage and handling per shipment. There is no minimum number of books I must buy. I can always return a shipment and cancel at any time. Even if I never buy another book from Gold Eagle, the 4 free novels and the mystery bonus are mine to keep forever.   166 BPM BP7F

Name   (PLEASE PRINT)

Address   Apt. No.

City   State/Prov.   Zip/Postal Code

Signature (If under 18, parent or guardian must sign)

This offer is limited to one order per household and not valid to present subscribers. Price is subject to change.

MYSTERY BONUS GIFT

HVSUB-1C

TAKE 'EM NOW

FOLDING SUNGLASSES FROM GOLD EAGLE

Mean up your act with these tough, street-smart shades. Practical, too, because they fold 3 times into a handy, zip-up polyurethane pouch that fits neatly into your pocket. Rugged metal frame. Scratch-resistant acrylic lenses. Best of all, they can be yours for only $6.99.

MAIL YOUR ORDER TODAY.

Send your name, address, and zip code, along with a check or money order for just $6.99 + .75¢ for postage and handling (for a total of $7.74) payable to Gold Eagle Reader Service. (New York and Iowa residents please add applicable sales tax.)

Remove from pouch...

unfold once...

unfold twice...

and they're ready to wear.

GOLD EAGLE

Gold Eagle Reader Service
901 Fuhrmann Blvd.
P.O. Box 1396
Buffalo, N.Y. 14240-1396

GES-1A

Offer not available in Canada.